A CROOKED MARK

A
CROOKED
MARK

LINDA KAO

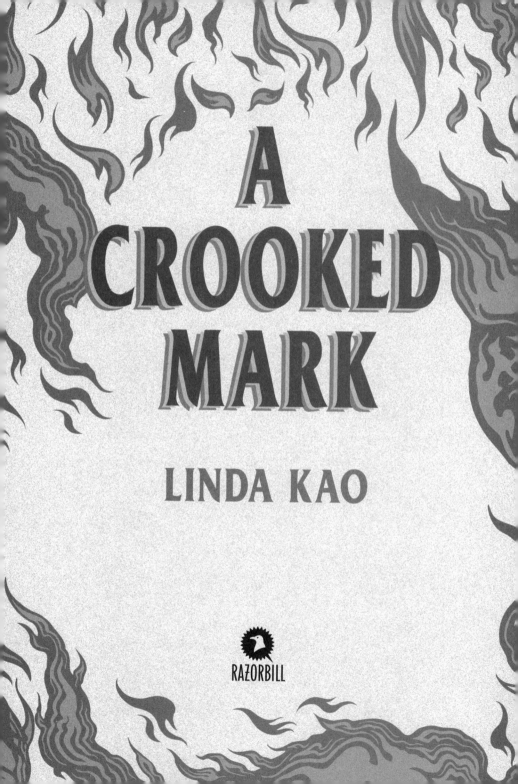

RAZORBILL

RAZORBILL

An imprint of Penguin Random House LLC, New York

LIBRARY OF CONGRESS CATALOGING-IN-PUBLICATION DATA
Names: Kao, Linda, author.
Title: A crooked mark / Linda Kao.
Description: New York : Razorbill, 2023. | Audience: Ages 14 years and up.
| Summary: Tasked with hunting down those whose soul the Devil has
marked, seventeen-year-old Matthew begins to question everything when
his first solo mission is sixteen-year-old Rae Winters, the girl he has fallen for.
Identifiers: LCCN 2022050885 (print) | LCCN 2022050886 (ebook) | ISBN
9780593527573 (hardcover) | ISBN 9780593527580 (epub)
Subjects: CYAC: Good and evil—Fiction. | Devil—Fiction. |
Interpersonal relations—Fiction. | LCGFT: Novels.
Classification: LCC PZ7.1.K313 Cr 2023 (print) | LCC PZ7.1.K313 (ebook) | DDC [Fic]—dc23
LC record available at https://lccn.loc.gov/2022050885
LC ebook record available at https://lccn.loc.gov/2022050886

ISBN 9780593527573

Printed in the United States of America

1 3 5 7 9 10 8 6 4 2

BVG

Design by Tony Sahara
Text set in Elysium Pro

Cover design by Vanessa Han

For Emmie and Andrew
With all my love

A CROOKED MARK

"The devil's finest trick is to persuade you that he does not exist."

—Charles Baudelaire, *Paris Spleen*

CHAPTER

1

I don't know how it feels when the Devil scratches a soul. My father says He must have the lightest touch, because no one ever notices His crooked claw leave a stain on something that should belong only to them. They smile their old smiles, crack the same jokes, eat and play and work and laugh just as they used to, but the Mark festers inside, growing and feeding like a parasite. By the time anyone notices something is wrong, it's too late. Lucifer has already won.

Not tonight, though.

I brace myself in the passenger seat as the car bounces down the moonlit road. Dad killed the headlights a mile back, and if we hadn't driven this way hundreds of times before, we would have run straight into a tree by now. Yet nine months of careful work have given us plenty of hours to prepare. By the time we finished documenting sweet Mrs. Polly's chilling descent from lucky survivor of a restaurant explosion to heartless killer Marked by Lucifer, Dad had it all planned out.

The matches sit in the console between us.

My mouth turns sour as my stomach gives another heave, and I clamp my teeth together, waiting for it to pass. Nine months of getting to know someone has a way of bleeding into an accidental friendship, making an already impossible job even harder. In the dim light, the determined line of Dad's jaw holds only cold certainty, but doubt shrieks at me like a knife on glass.

It's not easy to judge a soul.

I have to give Lucifer credit. There might not be any serpent in the tree or horned man with a pitchfork, but He's still banging on our door. He's just gotten a lot more creative. Clever bastard found a brand-new way to wreak havoc in the human world.

Accidents.

The semitruck bearing down on your car. The train you think you can beat across the tracks. The safety harness that snaps halfway up the mountain. One moment you're in this world, and then—

Bam!

Hello, afterlife.

There's a split second, however, when you aren't quite in either. You're right in the middle of the jump, eyes squeezed shut and both feet in the air, so you never see Lucifer extend a slender finger. It's a delicate scrape, the smallest Mark on your soul, and then He sends you back. You're alive, and everyone calls it a miracle, but God had nothing to do with it.

It's something much, much worse.

Of course, not everyone who survives an accident is Marked. Some people really do get lucky, but you can never tell the difference just by looking at them. The Marked appear as normal as you or me, and that jump from this world to the next makes anyone fair game. A life filled with kindness and charity offers no protection. No shield. If Lucifer feels like leaving His couch at the moment you ski into a tree, all bets are off, and no one knows whether luck or the Devil saved you in that second you nearly died.

I'm still not certain which saved Mrs. Polly. But Dad is.

The house comes into view—a modest cottage on the isolated road, the familiar porch swing motionless in the shadows. Blackness bleeds from sleeping windows, and the single light beside her door offers the only glow in the surrounding darkness. Dad turns off the engine, and silence falls like the thud of a gavel.

"Ready, Matthew?" he asks.

Not at all.

"Maybe we should give it more time." I brace against the frown growing on Dad's face. "Just to be sure. She volunteered at the animal shelter yesterday—"

"And the sign over the door fell and crushed Jessa Barney's skull twenty minutes after she yelled at Mrs. Polly for driving too fast in the parking lot," Dad finished. "If we had acted sooner, Jessa would still be alive."

"The chains holding that sign were old. One had already broken, remember?" My voice rises, and I fight to steady it. "Jessa's family plans to sue the shelter for not fixing it sooner."

"And it just happened to break the moment she stood under

it?" Dad shakes his head. "Matthew, we've been over this. You saw the changes."

The deaths and injuries that surrounded Mrs. Polly these last months had filled the pages of my notebook and made Dad's fingers tap faster each night. The accidents started small: Little George Winton fractured his arm after he left his skateboard lying out for Mrs. Polly to trip over, and Vicky Becerra slipped and fell off the stage as she went to collect her first-place ribbon for the blueberry pie that beat Mrs. Polly's in the annual fair. But then the brakes of Edward Fisher's car failed the day he insulted Mrs. Polly's new hairstyle, and Marian Wong choked to death on her steak as she laughed at Mrs. Polly for toppling a stack of dishes. A few more bodies dropped, and when a flowerpot finally fell off a balcony and killed Eileen Patterson minutes after she shorted Mrs. Polly at the cash register, Dad knew.

"Too much coincidence," he said, and I agreed. Verdict rendered.

But now . . .

I think of the afternoons spent in her kitchen, trying new recipes and sharing apple pie, and force my mouth open once more. "What if we missed something? A few more days, just to be sure—"

Dad interrupts. "I liked Elisabeth Polly too. But waiting will only make this harder." He picks up the matches. "Time to go."

My fingers dig into the seat, every part of me begging to turn the car around and drive home. But that's not the job. The lessons that began almost a decade ago ring through my head, and the rule by which Dad lives—by which he taught me to live as well—incinerates any last objections.

When Lucifer Marks a soul and returns it to this world, all we can do is light the fire and make it burn.

We open the doors and climb out.

CHAPTER

2

I lean against the car, every breath a jagged inhale, but Dad doesn't seem to notice. He opens the trunk and takes out the bag he prepared for tonight.

"Play the clip if anyone comes," he instructs, referring to the coyote howl I recorded on my phone last week. Packs of them prowl the area, and the noise won't strike anyone as unusual. He steps away in silence, and time slows to a trickle.

I could call someone. The police. The fire department. They would come, sirens blaring, and I could get Dad away in time to save Mrs. Polly. The disturbance might raise alarms, making our work harder, but the alternative creeping closer with each passing second feels worse.

Surely another week of watching can't hurt. My fingers are clumsy, the humming in my head deafening, but I dial: 9-1—

And then it's too late.

An orange glow blooms behind the cottage windows, and my chest squeezes so tightly I can't breathe. The charred air hits me, churning my stomach and clogging my throat. Wood snaps in the rising heat, and growing flames lick the night as smoke seeps through cracks in the walls.

The screams begin.

I want to cover my ears, but I force myself to listen, straining to hear the smallest hint of what lurked under her skin. The voice might come from Mrs. Polly, but the woman I knew is already gone. All that burns tonight is the human husk Lucifer's Mark left after rotting another person from the inside out.

I listen so hard my ears throb, and all I hear is her.

Bile creeps up my throat, and every shriek sends an ice bath over my bones. Behind those singed stucco walls, Dad's smoldering cigarette must have ignited the couch, and those burning cushions torched the rug and curtains. The photographs of her grown son Mrs. Polly once showed me are now cinders, and her cozy kitchen table is nothing more than kindling. Trapped in her bedroom, the door wedged shut by the stopper Dad jammed beneath it, Mrs. Polly doesn't stand a chance. Her windows won't save her.

The glue I used to seal them shut had three days to dry.

A shadow moves, and Dad runs toward me. "All clear?" he pants.

It takes two tries before my jaw unclenches. "Clear."

We drive away with our headlights off, and I catch the sound of a distant siren cutting through the fire's roar. The neighbor must have called, though he won't come speeding over the ridge to check on Mrs. Polly anytime soon. A faulty spark plug has made certain of that. By the time the fire truck completes the eight-minute drive over the winding highway, Dad and I will be long gone.

I rest my forehead against the window and listen for Mrs. Polly, but the screams have stopped.

They always do.

CHAPTER

3

Streetlights flicker over the motel parking lot as I slip out the door for my morning run, leaving Dad snoring in bed. Pockets of darkness litter the road, and headlights from passing cars throw shadows across the pavement. Every step I take carries me a little further from the thoughts I can't shake, of smoke and fire and screams, though a quiet week has passed since the burning. We said goodbye to our neighbors and moved out of our apartment a few days ago, and not a police car was in sight as we crossed the town limits and kept going.

Nobody will ever miss us.

News outlets covered the tragedy briefly, always ending with a warning that smokers fully extinguish their cigarettes, and even Mrs. Polly's son who lived a few states away sadly acknowledged his mother could be forgetful. He was right, since I often helped her hunt for her misplaced glasses, but Mrs. Polly was actually quite good about her cigarettes.

"Don't want to leave these burning!" she told me a few months ago, cheerfully stubbing one out in the ashtray she kept on her counter.

It was how we got the idea in the first place.

The memory brings a whiff of smoke, so I push my legs faster until I'm flying over the sidewalk, lungs burning and brain bouncing with no room for thoughts or questions. I run until the sky lightens and my legs ache, and my mind finally clears.

When I return to the motel, I find Dad sitting at the desk, staring at his laptop and sipping coffee from a paper cup. Despite the fact we both pulled clothes from suitcases this morning, his outfit is crisp and pressed, while my T-shirt and shorts were a wrinkled mess even before my run. Mrs. Polly once joked I'm a younger, messier version of him, though he's blue-eyed and fair while I inherited half my genes from my Chinese mother. My eyes are brown, and I stand an inch taller than his skinny five-ten frame, which is crowned by a head of meticulously groomed gray hair. I've got a dark brown mop that refuses to stay in place.

"Not your looks," Mrs. Polly said, when I pointed all this out. "There's just something about the two of you. The professor and his apprentice, keeping secrets from the rest of us."

I laughed along as she placed a bowl of chicken and dumplings in front of me. She didn't mean it in a bad way, but I didn't know how to feel about it.

I still don't.

Dad's slight smile rises in greeting as he looks up at me. "How was the run, Matthew?"

"Fine." I fill a cup with water and gulp it down. "Feels good to get outside."

He nods. "The room's pretty cramped, but we won't be here much longer."

His words send a jolt through me, since any move out of this motel will take us to our next project.

"No rush." I shrug as casually as I can. "It's not that bad."

He adjusts his wire-rimmed glasses, examining my face though he tries not to be obvious. "You sleep okay?"

"Yes," I lie. Mrs. Polly's screams haunted those dark hours, but sharing my nightmares will only invite more questions. Besides, from the way he eyes the elephant I started carving from a bar of soap around three this morning, he already knows. "What are you working on?"

"The final report for Elisabeth Polly." He picks up a black device lying beside the laptop, and I recognize the transmitter I fastened under Mrs. Polly's bed the month before we made our decision. The electronic bug hadn't yielded much—just that she suffered from insomnia—but restless sleep can be a sign of Lucifer. Though I suppose if that's all it takes, Dad would find me Marked as well.

Not him, though. He sleeps as well as always.

He slips the bug into his suitcase. "Almost done."

I stretch out on the mattress and reach for my knife. Dad gave me the blade years ago when I needed something to keep my hands busy during long stretches of surveillance, and my whittling soon graduated from sharpening sticks to shaping animals, complete with tusks and tails. My half-carved elephant leans against the framed photo that always sits at Dad's bedside—him, Mom, and me as a baby in her arms—and I finish its trunk as he offers me the laptop.

"Want to see?" he asks.

No hangs on the tip of my tongue. After all, I know how the story ends, and it's not the way I wanted. Instead, I nod, and approval flits across Dad's face. My stomach clenches as I begin to read, but I scroll through months of careful work that inched us closer to the project until she called us friends.

I suppose I called her that too.

As usual, Dad's documentation is thorough. Her baseline behaviors. The slow but terrible changes.

The burning.

Each neat bullet point showcases the descent that began nine months ago when Mrs. Polly walked away from a devastating oven explosion with hardly a burn. Her encounter with Lucifer would have been so fleeting she wouldn't remember it, and since nothing suggests He stays to see the wreckage of His work, Lucifer likely continued along His merry way, leaving Mrs. Polly with a Mark on her soul and a new set of abilities. She couldn't influence the living, but as the Mark within her grew, the objects in the physical world became her toys.

And Mrs. Polly played.

A brake cable, a piece of steak, a flowerpot—all it took was a simple thought to transform the ordinary into a weapon, and no one ever suspected the smiling woman in the corner.

That's where we come in.

The Second Sweep hunts those who survive the accidents that should have killed them. Our leaders find the stories, uncover the names, and search out the addresses. Then they send people like Dad and me. We find an opening and settle into their town. We learn their habits, their quirks, their schedules. We gain their trust.

And if they change—if that Mark consumes everything that's good in them and lets evil fester in its place—we bring the flames to destroy them. The Marked can be incredibly resilient to injuries from knives or bullets, so unless you have a match ready, all you're doing is drawing their attention and making yourself an easy target. Those who escape the Sweep's notice live on with that stain on their souls until old age finally sends them to their graves years too late, leaving behind paths of death and destruction. The sooner we find and stop them, the less damage they can do.

Mrs. Polly left quite a path.

I take my time reading Dad's report. He included photographs as well, and something inside me flinches as Mrs. Polly's cheerful face fills the screen. Dad cropped the other half of the picture so I'm nowhere in sight. I posed with her the first week we "accidentally" met at the ice cream shop, and the smiling image perfectly blends Dad's real work as a professional photographer with our other job.

Her smile makes my heart pinch.

We didn't know for certain, not right away. The shift between an ordinary life and one tainted by the Mark is always blurred. Souls don't surrender easily, and things like coincidence and bad luck throw even more confusion into the mix. Within a year, however, we usually have enough evidence to render a judgment. If all we've seen can be attributed to normal living, we declare the project's soul clean and move on, though we come back once a year to ensure they haven't changed.

They rarely do. It's those first twelve months that really matter.

Mrs. Polly lasted nine.

The accidents around her progressed from bruises to broken bones to bodies, and Dad's final hesitation vanished with that flowerpot smashing into Eileen Patterson. Everyone else was running to the body crumpled on the sidewalk, but Mrs. Polly just stood watching, her smile bright and her gaze dark as she finally lifted the sunglasses she always wore near the end. Dad saved the photograph he snapped in that moment for the report's last page, and the chill it sends over me feels as if Lucifer Himself reached out and tickled my soul.

Above her grin, Mrs. Polly's pupils bleed black, the weeping midnight tendrils swallowing her blue irises like spilled ink. Ever hear the saying "The eyes are windows to the soul"? It's true. When the soul dies, the window closes.

We made our decision on the way home.

My eyes twitch as I stare at the screen, waiting for the proof to overcome my last lingering doubts. Instead I see a trick of light, a shadow, a speck of dust on Dad's camera lens. There's even a medical condition called aniridia, where people are born without irises or with them only partially developed, so it appears as if their eyes are black. I looked it up. It usually manifests in newborns, though couldn't eye problems develop later, especially if someone's in, say, a kitchen explosion?

Doubt pulses at my temples, and a headache looms. "Looks good" is all I say, and hand back the laptop.

Dad nods, satisfied. He'll print it out and mail it to a PO Box registered to a Mr. James Trainer, who doesn't exist. Someone will pick it up and whisk it away to wherever the heads of the Sweep reside, their file cabinets filled with reports of the Marked. No email, no electronic trace. The only technology the Sweep uses is the emergency phone number Dad made me memorize, reserved strictly as a last resort for when sirens are screaming. We've never called it, and I hope this never changes. All that's left now is to burn our notebooks, wipe our hard drive, and move on to the next project.

"Your notes were very helpful," Dad says, scanning his report once more. "You did a good job."

He means it as praise, but his words only sharpen the ache snaking through me. Hope dies hard. Mrs. Polly lasted five months longer than Mr. Whittmeier, the first burning I did with Dad, and I had begun to think she might be like Ms. Rivera, who lasted the entire year. There had been a few worrisome incidents in the beginning of that project as well—dropped ice cream cones by children trespassing through her garden, a bike accident involving an especially harsh critic of her paintings—but these soon stopped, which is why it's so important not to jump to conclusions at the first sign of trouble. Our year ended with friendly conversations and regular surveillance that showed no sign of the Mark, and relief poured through me when Dad pronounced the verdict. Ms. Rivera had been outside the day we drove away, painting on her porch, and I wished every project could end like that.

But they don't.

Dad reaches over and picks up my elephant, smoothing his thumb over it as the silence stretches. Then: "Do you know what day it is?"

Eight days since we burned Mrs. Polly. "Saturday?"

"It's September twentieth. Your birthday."

Seventeen years old, and I couldn't care less right now. "I don't really feel like celebrating."

"I know. But I have something for you." He picks up a long white envelope and drops it into my lap. "Open it."

I turn it over, and the emblem of a torch stamped in the red wax seal sends a wave of dread through me.

The symbol of the Second Sweep.

My heart skips as I slice my knife through the seal. A single page sits inside. The paper crackles as I unfold it, revealing a printout of a news article.

FATAL CAR CRASH LEAVES SOLE SURVIVOR
Sixteen-year-old Rachel Winter walked away from a crash that left two dead, including her father, Timothy Winter. They were driving home Wednesday afternoon when, according to eye-witnesses, their car approached the quiet inter-section of Haims and Drifter. They stopped at

the crosswalk and had just pulled forward when thirty-year-old Malcolm Harrison collided with them. Mr. Harrison, whose blood alcohol was later found to be over twice the legal limit, died immediately. Mr. Winter was taken to Mills Creek Community Hospital, where he passed away an hour later.

Rachel, who had been sitting beside her father, escaped with only bruises. "It's a miracle she survived," said Captain Veronica Walsh, the first officer to arrive . . .

"This one's different." The paper trembles in my hand. "The project's only sixteen."

"I know." Dad's lips stretch in a grim line. "But Lucifer wouldn't care. If she's Marked, someone needs to stop her."

"It says she was wearing her seat belt." I hold the article up like evidence. "The police think the other driver hit exactly the right spot so she didn't get hurt."

"And what are the odds of that?"

I don't say anything. I don't need to. The answer is printed right in front of me: *one in a million.*

My stomach curdles, and I rub an old scar on my leg, its raised line smooth and reassuring. The stupid part of me hopes this will be another Ms. Rivera, with a quiet year of watching and waiting that ends with the matches still in our bag. The rest of me is already gearing up for a repeat of Mrs.

Polly. Either way, someone has to do the work.

And maybe this time, I'll finally see the Mark as clearly as Dad does.

The red torch pulses. "So she's our next project?"

"Not quite." He pauses. "The Sweep would like to offer this to you."

My breath stills. "By myself?"

Dad nods. "The project is yours if you want it. From start"—his jaw twitches—"to finish."

If I hadn't already been sitting, the thought of that burning match in my own hand would have dropped me to the floor, where I'm pretty sure my stomach just landed. My first solo project.

A sixteen-year-old girl.

Looks like the Sweep decided to take the training wheels off. It's a compliment, I suppose—the chance to observe Rachel Winter on my own, without Dad steering me toward the final verdict. The decision would be mine, and if I judge her Marked, it would be up to me to strike the match.

This is everything I've worked toward.

My throat tightens, blood pounding through my head like a tidal wave, but I lift my chin and hold his gaze. "I'll take it."

Dad hesitates, worry deepening the wrinkles on his brow. "Are you absolutely certain? You need to understand, Matthew: This solo project is a test. There won't be a second chance. Accept it, and it's yours until the end—whatever that brings."

The concern etched on his face almost makes the *No* pushing against my teeth jump out, but I swallow it down.

"I can do it," I tell him, and those four words might haunt me more than Mrs. Polly's screams.

Dad's head dips, hiding his face. When he finally looks up, his expression is impossible to decipher.

"I'll let them know." He hands me a file containing everything the Sweep prepared on Rachel Winter's accident: articles, maps, pictures.

This is the worst birthday present ever.

CHAPTER

4

Mills Creek lies an hour east of San Francisco, though the small suburb feels about twenty years behind the big city. I drive past the welcome sign and ease up on the gas pedal to match the lazy crawl of cars around me. Thick trees rise on either side, their branches heavy with leaves, and beneath them slope the streets: cracked sidewalks lined with houses, small shops, and a six-screen movie theater that—like the rest of this place—could use a fresh coat of paint.

In the rearview mirror, the afternoon sun bounces off the windshield of Dad's silver SUV, which he picked up at a used car lot yesterday. That's one perk of this solo project: Our old sedan is now mine. He trails me down the main boulevard and onto a shady side street. A few more turns, and the road ends in front of a rickety two-story house.

The weathered wood lost its shine long ago, and dusty windows break the lines of dingy brown planks. With a bent weather vane poking out of the roof and weeds sprouting from an overgrown front lawn, the place looks more like a haunted house than the creatively named "vintage home" described in the rental ad. At least we won't be staying inside, though the "comfortable and cozy" guesthouse we rented in back probably won't be much better. I park at the curb, and Dad pulls in behind me.

"Mr. Garrett said the key would be under the mat," I remind him as he climbs out. I grab my backpack and lead the way around the side of the house. A leaning gate blocks the path, and I try not to knock it over as I undo the latch and push it open.

No grass grows behind the house, but a giant oak tree towers in the middle of the barren yard, its branches stretching in all directions. A tired wooden fence provides an ugly but effective barrier from any curious neighbors, and the ivy creeping over it might have been pretty except for its promise of rats and spiders. A small, peeling guesthouse sits in one corner, wedged against the steep slope sweeping up the rear of the yard.

"Beautiful," Dad says. "And private. You'll be safe here."

Something in his voice stops me. "Aren't you going to be here too?"

He shakes his head. "This is your project, remember? I'll get you settled, but the Sweep asked that I do some work of my own."

I wait for the relief his words should bring, since no one will be around to criticize me or second-guess my choices. Instead, it feels like Mr. Garrett's backyard just tilted sideways. Dad has been beside me since Mom died fifteen years ago, and while I didn't expect his help, I was counting on him sticking around and being—well, my dad. Instead, he'll leave me to decide Rachel Winter's fate on my own.

He gives my shoulder a squeeze. "I'll visit whenever I can. The Sweep understands that even though I won't interfere with your project, I need to be seen around here so my absence doesn't draw attention. But you can do this, Matthew."

"I know." Maybe if I say it enough, we'll both believe it. "I'll be fine."

Mr. Garrett's "mat" is a piece of cardboard lying in the dirt in front of the guesthouse. At least the key works, though opening the door brings a stale, charred smell that reminds me of Mrs. Polly, and I nearly gag. Stepping inside, I find the culprit—a fireplace filled with ash—along with a lumpy mattress in one corner and a plastic table and chair in another. I open the lone window to let in fresh air before following the chipped tile floor past a bathroom in need of a shower curtain and into a small kitchen. The rusty stove makes me wonder when it was last used, and a mini fridge and stained sink complete the furnishings of my new home.

"Good enough," Dad says. "Let's get you settled."

Before I can unzip my bag, the back door of the big house slams, and a wiry man with wrinkled brown skin strides across the yard. His black hair is sprinkled with white, and the sour expression on his face would make a lemon feel inferior. Despite a slight limp, he carries himself with a rigid posture that screams of a past in the military.

"Allen Garrett?" Dad asks, and the man grunts. "Jonathan Watts. Thanks again for renting to us."

Mr. Garrett ignores his outstretched hand. "Found the key?

Good. No pets, and no smoking. Rent's due the first of each month. Just leave it in my mailbox."

"This should cover the first few months." Dad slips his unshaken hand into his pocket and takes out an envelope. "I travel a bit for work, but Matthew here can take care of himself. You've got my number in case you need anything."

Mr. Garrett eyes me like I'm a skunk about to spray. "No parties either."

He's safe there. "Don't worry," I assure him. "No parties."

He grunts again. Taking the envelope, he gives me a final scowl and stomps back inside.

At least I won't have to worry about an overly involved landlord. Mr. Garrett seems perfectly content to ignore us the rest of the day, and we keep our distance as well. Dad takes me shopping to purchase groceries, a printer, and supplies for school, and our landlord never appears as we carry everything inside. Still, that doesn't help the loneliness poking me the next afternoon when Dad heaves his suitcase into his car.

"I'll only be three hours away," he says through the open car window, though his expression tells me the tornado hammering my stomach also twists in his. On the seat beside him lies his own letter from the Sweep, with the address of a man who survived when a tree crashed down and somehow spared him, leaving him standing amidst its fallen branches. Luck or something else? Dad will find out.

He goes on. "Remember, Matthew: This is your test. Once you pass, everything will change."

For a moment, he looks as if he might say more, but then just pats my arm and starts the engine. I step back, hoping he doesn't notice how my teeth grind so hard my jaw hurts. Even the air feels empty as his car vanishes around the corner. When I finally turn to trudge back to the shack—"guesthouse" seems far too grand for it—curtains ruffle in Mr. Garrett's window.

Nosy old man.

It doesn't matter. I'll take a few minutes to check my notes, and then I'll go for a drive.

I've got some watching of my own to do.

CHAPTER

5

The Winters' home sits on a quiet street with worn curbs and lopsided fences. No one is outside when I drive by, though a bicycle leans against the house. White shutters border windows that flank a small front porch, and age and sun have lightened the blue paint on its walls. Leaves trace the lines of the slanted roof, and neatly cut grass covers the lawn except for a single patch of dirt, which lies scuffed beneath the swing dangling from a stout tree.

I wonder if Rachel's dad hung that swing. Does she think of him when she sits in it, or has the Mark already made her stop caring?

I don't know. But I will soon.

The Sweep's file on Rachel contained little beyond news of the accident, and I couldn't find much about her on the internet. A couple high school track competitions list her name in their results, but her social media sites offer little. Either she's too busy to update them, or she doesn't share much. The most useful post is her photo, which shows a pretty girl with light brown hair and striking hazel eyes.

The articles about the accident painted a horrific scene,

complete with pictures of the demolished cars and clusters of EMTs crouched around them. Workers had to cut through metal to reach the drunk driver, but Mr. Winter had been carted off in an ambulance within moments of its arrival. Mrs. Winter had come screeching up in her own car a few minutes later since someone recognized her daughter and called, leaving Rachel's thirteen-year-old sister with a neighbor to spare her the trauma of the crash site. One article had gone for the emotional jugular with a family photo of the Winters, and Rachel's wide smile looked exactly like her dad's. The joy in that picture had been impossible to miss.

I turn my car toward the intersection where Malcolm Harrison ran his drunk ass right through that joy. The corner is silent when I arrive, the shattered debris and ruined vehicles long since carted away. I park, step outside, and replay the tragedy that brought me here.

Mr. Winter behind the wheel, Rachel in the passenger seat. Maybe they were talking about her day or what they would do when they got home. Maybe they were just listening to music. They stopped at the crosswalk. Waited.

Pulled forward.

Did they see it coming? Harrison hit Mr. Winter's side without ever slowing, so they never heard brakes squeal. The impact must have spun both cars around before they slid to rest, their mangled metal shells wrapped around two broken bodies.

And Rachel, who walked away unscathed.

In a town as small as Mills Creek, most people must have

known Mr. Winter, and the funeral pictures the Sweep provided showed a well-attended ceremony. Casseroles likely appeared on his family's doorstep, and a neighbor might have stopped by with a lawn mower to take care of the grass. Even now, people probably watch over them more than usual.

I'll have to be careful.

Fortunately, the new-kid angle works. I start school tomorrow, which will hopefully make me look more normal than a random teenager living in Mr. Garrett's backyard. Classes actually began a few weeks ago, but the school still had openings. Dad showed them a copy of our rental agreement and explained I had been homeschooled since second grade, which is actually the truth, and that did it. A new ID card is already nestled in my wallet, declaring me a proud student of Mills Creek High School.

Rachel's school. We'll both be juniors, which means overlapping classes. Shared lunch periods.

A way to get close.

Something along the opposite curb catches my eye. Its edges are too distinct to be a simple tire scuff, and closer examination reveals an infinity symbol carefully drawn in dark blue paint. A cross stands on the middle of the curved lines, right at their point of intersection. The drawing can't be more than a few inches tall, but a chill of recognition shivers down my back.

The Leviathan Cross. An old alchemical symbol for sulfur, and a sign of Lucifer.

But it can't be intended for me. I look more closely, and

relief descends as I realize I'm wrong. It needs another horizontal line to form the symbol's double cross. No, this is something else, though its presence here feels too intentional to be coincidence. Maybe someone left it as a sign of grief, of the horror brought about by Malcolm Harrison's choices that day. Maybe it's just some kid messing around. I stare at it a minute longer, but the design offers no clues, either about its meaning or the person who put it there.

Hopefully, my next stop will bring more answers. I pull out my phone and snap a photo of the drawing before climbing back into my car. With a final glance at the curb, I check the road twice before rolling through the intersection.

Bet I'm not the only one who does that now.

The quiet streets that pass for Mills Creek's downtown are only ten minutes away, and I park in front of a little bakery sandwiched between a vacuum repair shop and a used piano store. Wavy letters spell CHARON'S LAST STOP on the clean window, and a black bench carved in the shape of a boat sits beside the entrance. I open the door, and the sweet smell of freshly baked cake wafts out.

The silver-haired man at the register is busy with another customer, which gives me a chance to examine the large display case. Mrs. Polly would have loved this place, and part of me crumples since it's my fault she'll never see it. Now isn't time for regret, however, especially when it will come at night, like always. I lean over to study a pomegranate cake labeled "Persephone's Revenge," and a girl's voice stops me.

"Can I help you?"

I look up, and any thought of dessert evaporates. An article mentioned the part-time job, but I hadn't been certain she would be here today, especially with the accident still fresh. Maybe she needed something to occupy her, a distraction from the grief that clings to her despite the smile she's attempting. Her hair has grown longer than in the photo and her face wears a new sadness, but those are definitely Rachel Winter's eyes watching me from behind the counter. I glance at the name tag pinned to her shirt: Rae.

Time to work.

"I hope so." I offer a sheepish grin and gesture toward the case. "I want everything."

She nods, her smile unchanged, though it looks as if it's taking every bit of effort to keep it there. "It's all really good. The 'Damned If You Don't' cake is our bestseller, but my favorite is 'Night in Tartarus.' Brownies are popular too."

The answer sounds mechanical, as if she's repeated it countless times, and she probably has. Shadows pool under her eyes, but she waits patiently as I examine the Night in Tartarus cake. Its layers of chocolate would have been my first choice anyway, but it doesn't matter now if it had been frosted with broccoli. That's her favorite, so it's mine too.

"Sold," I tell her. "It looks delicious."

"Good choice." She slides the cake from the case. "Would you like to eat it here?"

"I'll take it with me. Thanks." Several tables line the front of the shop, but this first contact with a project should be brief. Casual. I just need to spark a connection I can build upon later.

"I'm new in town. This place is my best find so far. Is the high school around here?"

I already know the answer, but it's an easy start to a conversation.

"Mills Creek High?" she asks, and I nod. "It's only fifteen minutes away. I go there too. I'm Rae." She gestures to her name tag. "But you probably figured that out."

I did, but not the way she thinks. "I'm Matthew. Is it going to be awful? I've been homeschooled until now, so I'm kind of terrified."

Her smile turns genuine, flashing a glimpse of the humor she must have worn closer to the surface before grief smothered it. "MCHS isn't bad. The teachers are okay, as long as you don't have Mr. McNally for math." She catches the look on my face. "You've got McNally."

"Second period."

"Well, at least we can suffer through it together. I'm in there too." She cuts a thick slice of cake and slides it into a white box. "What else do you have?"

I rattle off my schedule, which isn't hard since I memorized it minutes after the smiling woman in the front office handed me the list. "First period is Spanish with Torres. Then McNally, English with O'Brien, and fourth period's biology with Doherty. After lunch is history with Timmult, and then study hall since they figured I'll need it to catch up." I wince. "They're probably right."

Rae blinks. "Wow. I don't think I knew my classes that well until the second week of school."

"I'm a little nervous." I give an embarrassed shrug, and the flutter in my stomach tells me I'm not completely acting right now. "I'm fairly certain I'll get lost and end up in the wrong classroom."

"You'll be fine." She seals the box with a sticker of a black boat identical to the bench outside and hands it to me. "I don't know Timmult since she's new, but Torres is nice. O'Brien's hard, but she's good. I'm in that one too. And you got lucky with Coach Doherty."

"Coach?"

"Cross country. You run?"

"A little." Five miles or more each morning, but I keep that to myself. The surprise can come in handy if things go wrong. "I'm not fast or anything."

"That's okay. No one gets cut. You should come out." Rae glances over my shoulder to where a line is forming, and her shoulders sag a fraction before she pulls them straight, her smile back in place. "Mr. Yamamoto can ring you up. See you tomorrow?"

"Sure. See you." I move to the register, and Rae greets the woman behind me. They chat while I pay, the woman clearly a regular as she asks about Rae's family. Rae's polite answers—we're fine, doing better, everything is all right—make me want to shake the woman, because clearly it's not all right and nothing is fine.

Rae just smiles and cuts another slice of cake.

She's tough. I'll give her that.

The bright sunlight stings my eyes as I step outside, cake

in hand and the clock ticking. If I'm lucky, I'll spend the next year in Mills Creek watching Rae Winter do nothing out of the ordinary. At least I'm off to a good start, since from our brief encounter, she certainly doesn't *seem* Marked.

Then again, neither did Mrs. Polly. Not in the beginning.

A gentle breeze cools the heat pounding through me, and I check my watch, noting the time and surroundings for the entry in my project notebook. A mother perches on the bench, feeding a cookie to a toddler, and a man leans against a nearby tree, munching a brownie. His gaze meets mine, and a new thought nearly makes me drop my cake.

Dad called this project a test. How will the Sweep know I'm passing if they don't watch me?

They won't. Which means I'm not the only Sweeper in town.

Everyone around me is a stranger, but it's not like the Sweep hands out the company directory when you sign up. Existing members identify new recruits, and if the leadership approves, an old-fashioned apprenticeship begins. There's no secret school, no hidden camp, no annual company picnic. The Sweep is essentially a network of isolated dots, which makes sense since anyone who doesn't know about Lucifer's Mark will think we're just going around setting people on fire. Secrecy is critical. Dad and his mentor are the only members I've ever met, which means I wouldn't recognize another Sweeper if he or she were standing right in front of me.

Maybe one is.

Suddenly, the sidewalk holds too many eyes: the man

eating the brownie, an elderly couple out for a walk, a teenager sauntering past with headphones blaring into his ears. Even the line in Charon's is no longer filled with customers trying to satisfy a sweet tooth but people who observed my entire interaction with the project.

As casually as I can, I head toward my car. A quick glance back shows the door to Charon's opening again, and the woman who had been speaking with Rae appears, box in hand. She makes it only halfway through the exit before the door swings closed, smacking her from behind with enough force that she stumbles forward and drops her cake. My feet freeze midstep.

Maybe Rae didn't like her questions after all.

The next moments reveal nothing more. Someone retrieves the box and hands it to the woman, who lifts the lid to peer inside. She must make a joke, because the people around her laugh, and she carries her cake away as another customer leaves Charon's, the door closing smoothly behind him.

It could mean nothing.

Or, I can almost hear Dad saying, *it could mean quite a lot.*

The bustle of the sidewalk returns, and I climb into my car and drive away. No one stares after me, but it doesn't matter either way. Any Sweeper watching would call my morning a success. Not only did I connect with the project and see a possible hint of a Mark, but I even laid the foundation for our next meeting.

After all, we're going to be classmates.

CHAPTER

6

Mills Creek High School is built like a fortress. Four beige buildings surround an inner quad, and a metal gate encircles the entire campus. I almost relax as I pull into the parking lot in back, since the Sweep can't watch me inside these walls.

Unless they're already here.

New students, teachers, custodians . . . any one of them could be a Sweeper. I scan each face as I head for my first class, but the gymnastics routine my stomach launches into when I enter the room has nothing to do with the Sweep or even the project. I hadn't lied when I told Rae school terrified me. It's one thing to read about crammed hallways, banging lockers, and rowdy cafeterias, and another entirely when it explodes around me: too much noise, too many people, too little space to maneuver without hitting someone with my backpack.

Dad might have trained me to handle the Mark, but he sure didn't prepare me for high school.

It doesn't help that sleep still fogs my brain since I stayed up late last night, writing the first project entry in my new red notebook. I asked Dad once why we didn't write the notes on our laptops like we do our reports, especially since those can be protected by passwords so no one can just flip one open and start reading. He pointed out that it's not hard to keep a notebook safe, and computers are difficult to use during surveillance. A notebook is far easier to carry, and you can jot a quick observation without having to sit and type. Also, paper doesn't cast a glow on your face when you're trying to scribble something in the dark, which can draw unwanted attention when you're right outside a project's window. We usually take our messy notes and refine them for our typed reports to the Sweep, paring everything down to the essential details.

This time is different, however.

"Keep your notebook neat," Dad had ordered. "Date it, and be thorough. Someone from the Sweep may want to look at it."

His warning kept me at that old plastic table in Mr. Garrett's shack until midnight, detailing both my conversation with Rae and the customer's unfortunate encounter with the door. I couldn't help adding a line about how the woman simply might not have opened it wide enough, and every sentence took twice as long as it should have since my mind kept wandering to the sorrow on Rae's face and the moment I made her smile turn real.

Conversations with other projects—other people—aren't new, but they've rarely been with anyone my age. Dad and I don't keep in touch with neighbors when we leave, and we move so often I haven't made many friends.

No friends at all, in fact.

Mills Creek won't change that—I'm here for the Mark, not

my social life—but getting to know Rae Winter might be fun. It could make the ending harder, but I don't need to worry about that.

Not yet.

I muddle through Spanish class, understanding Señora Torres's cheerful "¡Hola, Mateo!" and nothing else, and the hard chair beneath me offers little comfort as McNally marches through another torturous math problem. Rae sits two seats over, her head bent low as she takes notes, and I do my best to pay attention. When the clock's creeping hands finally signal release, I grab my backpack and follow her out the door.

"Hi." I fall into step beside her. "Is math always like that?"

"Yup. Welcome to MCHS." She weaves through the cramped hallway and I bump along after her, though it's like swimming upstream in an overcrowded creek. "Look on the bright side," she says over her shoulder. "You survived your first class with McNally."

"True. Nice guy." The short, balding man had basically flung a textbook in my direction and then ignored me, barking numbers and formulas as he paced the aisles with a sharpened pencil behind his ear. "Had no idea what he was talking about, though."

"Functions?"

"Yeah." Dad taught them to me last year, but I add a frantic edge to my voice. "Please tell me he was joking about a test."

She shakes her head as we stop at her locker, and I realize I'm not actually supposed to haul all my books around the entire day.

"Next week." She pulls out the English book I've been carrying for the last two hours. "It's not that hard. McNally has office hours in the morning if you want to go."

I grimace. "Yes, because I'm crazy like that. I'll figure it out."

Her smile feels like a victory.

"I can help if you want," she says.

"Really?" Perfect. "That would be awesome."

We cross the grassy courtyard to English, which ends with half of Toni Morrison's *Beloved* to read before the weekend since I'm behind the rest of the class. Rae has art next, but she hands me off to a tall, lanky boy named Moose so I don't get lost on my way to biology. His freckles and reddish-orange hair remind me more of a carrot than an antlered animal, but an easy smile lights his face.

"Mills Creek scores another!" he says cheerfully as Rae disappears in the opposite direction. "What made you move here?"

I almost feel bad lying to him. "Dad got tired of the big city. This is his chance to give me the small-town life he never had."

"That's pretty high hopes for this place." Moose points me toward the science building. "What'd your mom say?"

His question catches me off guard, but the truth works. "My mom's dead."

"Oh." He flushes. "I'm sorry."

"That's okay. Happened a long time ago." I change the subject. "What's Mills Creek like?"

"It's all right." He steers me down another crowded hall. "The movie theater gives discounts with your student ID. Pit Stop has the best burgers, and the Wallflower's good for coffee.

Let's see . . . most teachers are okay, but watch out for McNally. He's Dean of Students, and he's always patrolling for victims. Steer clear."

"He's my math teacher."

Moose pats my back. "My condolences. You'd think he'd be busy enough with all the dean stuff, but he decided he missed teaching so they gave him a class too. Lucky for you."

Room 104 is unlike any classroom I've seen. Big foam cubes form a large circle in its center, and tables covered with bright mounds of clay line the perimeter. A tall, thin man claps his hands, and the few of us still standing scuttle for empty cubes.

"That's Coach Doherty," Moose whispers as we sink into the foam. "He doesn't believe in 'traditional' classrooms. Still likes homework, though."

"All right, people! We've added someone new to our ranks." Coach gestures at me like I'm a celebrity. "Do you go by Matthew or Matt?"

Dad used to call me Mattie, but that was long ago. I've been Matthew since I was seven. Yet my name sticks in my mouth as all eyes turn my way, and "Matt" pops out, as if my tongue made the decision on its own. It's a good one, though, because Matt Watts sounds like a fun guy—someone who makes friends and cracks jokes and fits in without drawing a second glance.

Someone just right for this project.

We spend the hour shaping clay models of cells, though Moose seems more interested in building a superhero army than mitochondria. Still, the work provides an opportunity to talk, and between his chatter about movies and comics, he tells me I'm one of four new students in the junior class. I don't know how many people my age are part of the Sweep, but it's worth checking out.

"Matt, here's everything we've read so far," Coach says, interrupting Moose's recap of the latest zombie movie to stack several packets on the table beside me. "Come ask if you've got any questions. I'm here in the morning and at lunch, but I coach after school. Any chance you're a runner?"

"Say no," Moose whispers, but I'm already nodding.

"Great!" Coach beams as the bell rings. "Meet us at the track after your last class today. Let's see what you can do."

It won't be much—no need to call attention to myself—but the hours with Rae will make the workouts worthwhile. "Sure. Thanks."

"Sucker!" Moose crows as I follow him to the cafeteria, where one look at the turkey casserole tells me I'll be bringing my own food from now on. Bodies and voices pack the big room, but we get our meals and head outside to find Rae sitting under a shady tree. Beside her, a girl wearing a black tunic and leggings peels a tangerine, her purple nails expertly winding the rind in a single long strip. Judging from the way she and Rae talk, their heads close as Rae writes something on the back of the girl's brown hand, their friendship stretches far back.

"This is Sahana," Rae says, and the girl nods at me as a stocky boy wanders over and dumps a heavy backpack beside her. "And that's Juan."

"Geez." Moose wrinkles his nose at Juan's backpack, which

is heavier than mine since I finally dropped off half my books. "They give us lockers, you know."

"I came from the library." Juan flops down on the grass, though his hair holds enough gel that it doesn't move. "Avery assigned another history report. I can't believe you haven't even had to write one."

"That's because you're in *honors*." Moose smirks. "Who's smarter now?"

Juan rolls his eyes as Rae chuckles. "How about you, Matt?" she asks. "Bio go okay?"

I nod. "And Coach said I can join cross country. I'm coming to practice."

"Today?" Juan gives me a pitying look. "Monday is Coach's speed day. Gonna be painful."

"I tried to warn him." Moose shrugs. "He didn't listen."

Sahana snorts. "Have fun. I'll probably be sitting on my couch. Eating chips."

Rae taps her hand, where blue ink is visible, and Sahana groans. "And doing page 29 in the French workbook."

"Nope." Juan shakes his head knowingly. "You'll be at the Wallflower, making some weird new coffee drink."

"I'm thinking peanut butter latte, and it will be delicious," she shoots back. "It will definitely beat running."

He lets out a heavy sigh. "True."

Too late to back out now, though whatever Coach has planned can't be worse than my long run this morning. Lunch passes quickly, with the others pointing out the best shortcuts around campus and McNally's favorite corridors to patrol, and history with Ms. Timmult provides an excellent nap as she drones on about the effects of the Civil War. She's new to MCHS as well, though if she is a Sweeper, they really could have found a more engaging instructor. No need to ruin an entire class on my behalf. Study hall gives me the opportunity to start my mountain of homework, and I work until the final bell rings and I head to practice. About thirty runners trickle over, including Rae, and Moose's loud "Hey, team! Meet Matt!" brings a chorus of greetings. We spread out to stretch at one end of the field encircled by a track, and Moose grins at the football players warming up on the other side.

"Speed workouts are the worst," he says. "But at least the view is good."

Juan leans over. "See that guy?" He nods at a tall boy with dark brown skin and an easy stride jogging across the field. Another player throws the ball his way, and he catches it with one hand, pulling it to his chest with ease. "That's Tyson Walsh. Someday, Moose is going to work up the courage to ask him out instead of just gawking at him from a distance."

"Never." Moose shakes his head. "He's a senior, and his mom is a police captain. She's super nice, but the whole thing is kind of terrifying, you know?"

I do, but not for the reasons he's thinking. Going to school with the son of a police officer means I need to keep my head down and my eyes open. The last thing I want is to catch her attention. At least Tyson and the rest of the football players ignore us, and Coach soon jogs up, clipboard in hand and whistle around his neck.

"What are we doing?" Juan asks hopefully as we gather around him. "A walk to the park? Maybe a picnic?"

Coach laughs. "Nice try, Esparza. We're sprinting today, everyone. Eight laps." A collective groan rises, and he shushes us. "Attitude, people! Varsity boys, you're up first."

Moose and several others take off at Coach's whistle. I wish I could keep pace with the leaders as they surge around the track, but Mills Creek Matt can't run that fast. I'll be a slow plodder on Junior Varsity, as well as average in class and always in dress code.

Completely nonthreatening and quite forgettable.

Varsity girls go next. Rae flies around the first turn, right on the heels of the girl in front, and I shoot Juan a look. "She's good."

"Yup," he says proudly. "Might qualify for state this year."

Even as he speaks, Rae sprints ahead on the backstretch, and a gap opens between her and the others. She reaches the final turn, arms pumping and ponytail streaming, and crosses the finish line a full six seconds ahead of Coach's target time.

Not what I expected.

Coach calls the JV boys next, and I line up between Juan and a skinny boy with glasses and shaggy black hair named Toshi, who turns out to be the other new boy at MCHS. He arrived only a week before me, and by the first turn, it's clear the three of us will be bringing up the rear. The look on Juan's face— somewhere between "this hurts" and "kill me now"—makes an excellent model, and I borrow a similar expression as I hobble around the track. The workout feels miles away from my solitary runs, with people yelling encouragement and offering high fives each time I stagger across the line, but I do my best to join in. After our last lap, I even slap palms with Toshi, who seems too exhausted to pay me any attention.

Though I might not be the only one pretending.

"This is good for us, right?" Juan gasps, collapsing to the ground. "Exercise and all that . . ."

"And you love it!" Moose chirps, crouching to pat Juan's perfect hair. "Well, you hope Stanford will love it. Valedictorian *and* athlete. But c'mon—isn't this kind of fun?"

"If by 'fun' you mean 'terrible,' then yes." Juan closes his eyes. "This is fun."

"But you made it!" Rae pokes him with her toe, and the sadness that haunted her even at lunch seems to have faded, brushed away by the workout. "Hey, Matt, at least you're still standing. What do you think? Going to stick with us?"

I let out a groan, though of course I'll be back tomorrow. Cross country means more time with Rae. Greater familiarity. Easy surveillance.

And maybe there's a tiny—*very* tiny—part of me that almost enjoyed those intervals.

"Bring it on," I tell her, and Moose gives me a high five.

"All right, people!" Coach calls, gathering the team. "Good job today. Remember, we've got a meet next Friday, so let's keep working hard. Take a lap to cool down."

We straggle back onto the track, and I shuffle along between Juan and Moose, slowing my pace even more to let Toshi plod past. If he is a Sweeper, having him breathing down my neck is the last thing I want. Rae jogs ahead with a few other girls, and though the shadows are making their way back to her face, her ponytail swings jauntily with each step. She's pretty. Graceful.

Fast.

If I ever have to run, she just might catch me.

CHAPTER

7

The unforgiving bells of MCHS bring a new routine, starting with a morning run that shows me the sunrise. Few people are outside in these early hours, though that doesn't stop me from scanning the streets for possible Sweepers. We're supposed to blend in, so I'm looking for mistakes—a peculiar alertness, too many coincidental meetings, a furtive glance I wasn't meant to see. Besides Toshi and Ms. Timmult, my list includes:

A neighbor who sets out on her daily walk around the same time I finish my run.

A street cleaner whose path always seems to cross mine.

A driver who tosses a rolled-up newspaper onto Mr. Garrett's stoop each morning.

All are friendly, offering quick nods or a brief smile, and then we're past each other. Each just looks like a regular person beginning his or her day.

But so do I.

My runs help me get to know the little neighborhood, and the distinct stores and shops say Mills Creek is a town forgotten by brand-name companies. I've also seen that little blue symbol—the almost–Leviathan Cross—in a few more places: the planter outside an ice cream store, the bottom corner of the Pit Stop's facade, a bench in the park. Each is small and carefully drawn, with no hint as to the person who put it there.

Looks like Mills Creek has a tagger.

My run ends with a shower and a bowl of cereal, and I arrive at school early enough to go to my locker before my real work begins. Mrs. Winter usually rolls up to the high school around 7:45, and Rae hops out of the car as a girl with the same light brown hair slides from the back seat to take her place in front—her younger sister, Cady, according to the Sweep's file. The middle school drop-off must be next. I've walked past their car twice this week, waving to Rae both times, and I once managed to pass her locker just as she arrived. We chatted until the warning bell rang, about classes and running and how weekends should really be three days instead of two, and I arrived at Spanish in my best mood all week.

It's part of the job. Nothing more.

When I'm not watching Rae, I throw myself into the colorful fabric of MCHS, which is turning out to be not quite as scary as that first day. Of the two new junior girls, one has lived in town for years and simply transferred schools, and the other rarely appears anywhere near me, shrinking the odds that either is a Sweeper. Even Toshi raises no alarms. He remains friendly during practice, but he hasn't forced a friendship or stalked me through the halls. I trail him home one day to find he lives nearby with his parents, though I suppose that doesn't tell me much.

Until this project, I lived with Dad.

I spend my lunch periods with the little group of Moose, Juan, Sahana, and Rae, and though others occasionally join us, the closeness between those four shines. Rae tells me she and Sahana met in first grade, when a boy stole Rae's book and Sahana, armed with a bouncy ball in one hand and a jump rope in the other, hunted down the culprit. They've been best friends ever since. Moose began tagging at their heels in third grade, and Juan moved here freshman year, though he's spent enough time with them running, studying, and drinking milkshakes to make up for his late arrival. Sometimes—when Rae and Sahana exchange a look and burst into giggles, when Moose is pelting Juan's hair with pretzels, when Rae's face wears more sorrow than usual and the others cluster around with hugs and jokes and offerings of junk food—it's as if I'm watching through a window, sitting beside them but still separate. Maybe this is what it's like when friendships have history, built upon shared moments and experiences.

I can't help wondering how that would feel.

"It's a good start," Dad says when he calls on Thursday. It's his fifth call in as many days, every night at eight o'clock as if he expects me to be in the shack waiting to deliver my daily report. The fact that I have been since I have nowhere else to go is starting to grate. "But remember, it's not enough to see her at school. You need to get closer. Does she have a boyfriend?"

"Dad! Stop it." The answer is no, at least as far as I've seen, but the fact he even raised the idea makes me squirm—first because it just seems wrong, and second because if I tried that strategy, I'd have to learn how to be a boyfriend. "I'll figure it out, okay?"

"All right, but keep me posted," he says. "You know how important this is."

Of course I do, since he reminds me every time we talk. Irritation rubs at me, and I change the subject. "How's your project going?"

"Good, I think." His voice turns thoughtful. "Got another show later tonight."

His project is a musician who spends days composing and nights performing, which makes access simple. Dad has already been to two shows, clicking away on his camera and spawning whispers of a professional photo essayist who could bring fame and recognition to unknown artists. His project will probably reach out to *him*. It's brilliant, and if he stopped aggravating me with his constant advice, I would tell him so.

Dad clears his throat. "By the way, I talked with Kendrick this afternoon. He said he's going to come by and see you."

"Really? That's great!" At least I don't have to fake my enthusiasm right now. I haven't seen Dad's mentor in the Sweep for almost a year, but Big Bobby Kendrick has taught me so much he's basically co-mentored me as well. Dad met him soon after Mom died, and their friendship pulled my father out of that pit of suddenly finding himself a widower with a two-year-old toddling after him. It didn't take long for

Kendrick to read Dad's grief and recognize a good soldier in need of a cause, and he sent word to the heads of the Sweep that he had found a new recruit. I always thought he was family until they let me in on the truth at the ripe old age of eight.

Well, most of it. They didn't talk about the burnings until I turned thirteen.

"Be careful, Matthew." The warning in Dad's voice scrapes at me. Too many instructions, too little trust. "Kendrick isn't just coming for a visit. He's evaluating your work, so check your notes. Everything must be in order."

"Dad, stop worrying." I don't point out that my notes on Mrs. Polly were just as good as his, and afternoons usually found me, not him, in her kitchen. "I know what I'm doing, okay?"

His voice softens. "I know. It's just strange not being there with you. But you're right. You're doing fine."

"Thanks. I gotta go, okay?"

We say our goodbyes, and I toss the phone onto my mattress. At least I'm done with that for tonight. Picking up the red notebook, I skim my entries once more, scratching out Rae's name and replacing it with "the project." As Dad would remind me, this is a job, not a friendship.

And Mrs. Polly taught me to never get confused again.

8

On Friday, Coach takes pity on us with a three-mile loop. The previous days brought nothing shorter than five, and everyone cheers when he announces the route. We make it back to campus earlier than usual, and it's finally the weekend.

"Get a run in tomorrow!" Coach calls as we scatter.

"No chance of that," Juan whispers, but we nod along with everyone else. Moose cuts in front of him at the water fountain, and their shoving match ends with Moose in a headlock as Juan takes a long drink.

"Go ahead, ladies." Juan sweeps his free hand grandly toward the fountain as the girls' team approaches. "Take your time."

Rae bends for a drink as Moose wrestles free. "Unlike you," he informs Juan, "I was going to let them go first anyway. *I* am a gentleman."

"*You*," Juan says cheerfully, "are thirsty."

Rae shakes her head, though the corners of her mouth twitch in a smile. "Matt, do you still want help with math? We can meet at the Wallflower tomorrow. Sahana's working."

"That would be great!" A weekend tutoring session brings

our relationship to a new level, and I know Dad will be pleased. "Are you sure you don't mind?"

"Of course not. Nine o'clock?"

My morning suddenly looks brighter. "Okay. Thanks again."

"Hmm." Moose raises an eyebrow as Rae heads for the front of school, where her mom will be waiting. "This sounds . . . interesting."

"It's just math," I say, though alarm flickers through me. "McNally's not exactly slowing down while I catch up."

"Tutoring?" Juan grins. "Is that what we're going to call it?"

Moose snorts, and understanding brings a rush of heat to my cheeks. I punch his shoulder. "It's *math*."

"I bet." His smile fades. "Hey, just so you know . . . Rae's dad . . ." Juan rubs his neck, all humor gone. "Did you hear about the accident?"

"What accident?" I wrinkle my brow, squashing a ripple of guilt, and they tell me about the car crash. It's the same story I already know, but their version brings life to Mr. Winter in a way my folder of facts never did. The Sweep is concerned with survivors, not victims. The only details included about the father who died that day were that he had been forty-six and worked as a software engineer.

"He used to come to all Rae's meets, pick her up each day, that sort of thing." Sadness creases Moose's freckled face. "They were really close."

Grief hangs between them, creeping over until it brushes me as well. "That's terrible. Rae wasn't hurt?"

"No. She got really lucky." Moose sighs. "But it's rough right now. You know how quiet she is sometimes, and she hardly ever laughs. She didn't used to be like that. And she has her driving permit, but she won't even get behind the wheel anymore."

"So you have to be careful." Juan's worried eyes meet mine. "We're not telling you what to do, but just—don't do anything stupid, all right? It's hard enough for her already."

The frown stays on his face until I nod, and Moose exhales with a grin.

"Good," he says. "Because if you mess up with Rae, Sahana will totally kill you. For real."

I laugh along with them, but their words stay with me long after we say goodbye, Juan hurrying to meet his dad and Moose heading for the bus stop half a mile away. Changes in Rae's behavior should be expected; after all, she survived a horrific accident that killed her father and shattered the life she knew. But changes could also be signs of the Mark, small deviations that escalate over time.

If they do, it's going to be Mrs. Polly all over again.

Still, Juan and Moose are right about one thing: I need to be careful. Marked or not, Rae doesn't deserve more pain if I can avoid it.

Besides, I think I just made a promise.

Saturday should bring a lazy morning, especially after staying up late last night to finish my first weekly report for the

Sweep. It took hours to summarize the week in Mills Creek and my observations about Rae, though the idea of strangers analyzing her actions makes something inside me squirm. Maybe that's why my eyes pop open hours before I'm supposed to meet her at the Wallflower, and any hope of sleep escapes through cracks in the shack's walls.

I head out on a run.

The cold air slaps me awake, though silence rules the streets at this early hour. My feet choose the direction, and buildings glide past until the Winters' house lies just ahead, the swing hanging from its tree. Rae and Cady must be fast asleep, and Mrs. Winter too, with an empty space beside her where her husband once slept. I speed up, my gaze locked straight ahead, and a soft *clink* stops me.

I whirl around, but no one appears. Instead, the noise comes from a homemade wind chime hanging beneath the eaves of the house. Heavy string connects four clay pieces to an upside-down flowerpot whose paint has faded from time and weather. Still, a faint "R" decorates its center. I tiptoe up the neighbor's driveway for a better look, and sure enough, there's the rest of Rae's name in little-kid letters. More names decorate each shape: Cady's diamond is pink, and Rae gave herself a green circle. "Mommy" is written on a purple triangle, but that's not the one that makes me slip a little inside. The "Daddy" painted on a blue square does that.

I retreat to the sidewalk before anyone notices me, and my feet find their pace as I leave the Winters' house behind. Each step feels a bit harder, however, and a new heaviness weighs me down.

That home holds so much pain.

Mr. Winter's blue square will forever swing from that wind chime, and every clink, every glimpse of it, now serves as a memorial. Other reminders of him must crowd their house— the sofa where he used to sit, the photographs with his smile, the beds and bookcases he built for his daughters. Walking through that space must feel so different than it once did, and finances can't be easy either. A lost parent means a lost income, and child support doesn't rain down from above.

That family is already hurting. But if Lucifer chose Rae in that awful moment, if He reached for her as cars collided and metal screamed, their grief is far from over.

"Something chasing you?" Mr. Garrett frowns as I come tearing down the sidewalk, my lungs on fire as if I'm trying to outrun Lucifer Himself. My landlord wears a ratty gray bathrobe over his pajamas, and a folded newspaper sticks out from under one arm. I think he's retired, but I'm not sure what he does all day besides glare at people, especially me.

"Just running," I gasp.

"Stop kicking so high. It wastes energy. And you look absurd. Do it like that guy over there."

He jerks his head, and I turn to see Toshi crossing the street, his morning jog far slower than mine. If he really is a Sweeper here to monitor my test, he's doing a much better job maintaining his cover as the tortoise of the cross-country team.

Any hope he didn't notice me crumbles when he waves at us before plodding on his way.

Mr. Garrett's narrowed eyes rake over me. "How'd you get that?"

My mind is so stuck on Toshi—Did he see me outside Rae's house? Would he report me as being too reckless on my morning runs?—that it takes a moment to realize Mr. Garrett's finger points at my scar. The thin white line starts below my left knee and traces a jagged path halfway to my ankle, and it's been with me so long I usually forget about it. Except, of course, when some grouchy old man points it out.

"I was playing in the park when I was little," I tell him. "Dad says I slipped and fell off a rock."

That's the truth, but Mr. Garrett's lips purse knowingly. No doubt the image of tiny Matthew terrorizing the neighborhood is running through his withered brain. Just another detail to stash away as he hides behind his windows, watching me every chance he gets.

A sudden thought turns the sweat on the back of my neck cold. The Sweep doesn't provide housing—Dad found Mr. Garrett's rental ad on his own—but if someone knew the details of my project, it wouldn't have been hard to make the shack seem like the optimal choice.

Forget Toshi. Having a Sweeper as my landlord would make it even easier for the organization to monitor my progress.

I edge toward the backyard. "I'll see you later—"

"Your dad still gone?" Mr. Garrett snaps.

Surely we're not this desperate for members. "Yes. Do you need something?"

"Not me. There's some guy here to see you. He's waiting in the yard."

No wonder the dented blue truck in front of the neighbor's house looked familiar. The worries haunting me slip away, and I call a quick "Thanks!" before hurrying through the gate.

Bobby Kendrick sits on the shack's cardboard mat, his back resting against the door and his cowboy hat tipped forward like he's asleep. His black polo shirt, neatly embroidered with the logo of his home security firm, stretches across his broad chest, and its sleeves cling to biceps that make me momentarily consider going to a gym. When I was little, he could toss me in the air so high it felt like I was flying. Those days are long past, but I still feel lighter as I tiptoe toward him.

Kendrick's head jerks up. "Matthew!" He jumps to his feet, grabs my hand, and pumps it with enthusiasm. "Good grief, you've grown. How've you been?"

"Great." His calloused hand dwarfs mine, and it's like a patch of warm sunshine suddenly appeared in Mr. Garrett's yard. "Come on in."

I lead the way inside, Kendrick ducking under the door-frame, and the shack shrinks as he enters. The scratches on the floor that never mattered before seem dark and ugly now, and the mattress looks even sadder than usual. I smooth the blanket, as if that might make it better.

"Don't worry about it." Kendrick settles in the lone chair. "I've stayed in worse."

He probably has, since he'll do whatever it takes to get a project done. Dad told me Lucifer messed with the wrong man when one of the Marked killed Kendrick's new wife years ago. The Sweeper who acted too late to save her told the grieving husband the truth, and the Sweep gained its best recruit. Kendrick and his new mentor tracked down a woman who had survived a deadly roller coaster derailment seven months prior and who happened to be near the construction site when a nail gun misfired, shooting Elaine Kendrick through the heart.

He did his first burning that night, and he hasn't stopped since.

"Do you want to see my notebook?" I take it from under my mattress, every entry dated and double-checked. "I see the project almost every day. I can tell you about her."

Kendrick's laugh rumbles. "Relax, Matthew. I was just passing through. Heard you were out here and figured I'd drop by. Though I did promise Jonathan I'd let him know how you were doing."

He looks me over, eyes twinkling, and Dad's warning suddenly feels silly. Kendrick might be here to inspect my work, but he's also been a friend for as long as I can remember. No project can change that.

"Well?" I turn in a slow circle. "Do I pass?"

Kendrick gives a satisfied nod. "I shall report you haven't wasted away from eating nothing but cereal, and you don't seem to have spent the night partying at some delinquent location."

"Thanks. Good thing you can't see my tattoos."

He laughs, and then his face sobers. "First solo project, right? That's a big step."

I tell him about the assignment, and he listens quietly, stroking his chin every so often. The project slides into focus as I speak, and it's a comfortable return to the old days spent learning and listening beside him. When I finish, he reads my notebook and the weekly report, and the smile on his face as he finishes makes up for the time I spent laboring over each word.

"You're doing good work, Matthew," Kendrick says. "You talk to your father lately?"

I nod. "Last night. He said you'd come by."

"How's he doing? You're out here by yourself, he's got his own project . . . things are pretty different."

"Yeah. I think he's worried." I leave out the part where Dad warned me about him, though it would probably give his old mentor a good laugh. "He calls a lot."

"Well, he's your dad. It's his job to worry about you." Kendrick scratches his shoulder, and his shirt lifts enough for the gun holstered inside his waistband to peek out. A bullet won't stop the Marked—only fire can do that—but it can incapacitate long enough to strike a flame. Kendrick's been in a tight spot often enough for him to stay prepared, even if it means occasionally ignoring a state's laws on concealed weapons, and his choice of a silver lighter over Dad's more ceremonial matches reveals a preference for single-handed efficiency.

He goes on. "Did your father mention anything special about this project?"

"Dad called it a test. The Sweep wants to see if I can work alone." I nearly ask if other Sweepers are watching me, but that feels like cheating. Instead, I raise the other question keeping me up at night. "Uncle Kendrick, how come my project's so young? It's fine, I just didn't think . . . I mean, Dad and I never had one my age before. Have you?"

Kendrick nods, his mouth tightening. "The younger ones are harder, that's for sure. But their age doesn't make the Mark any less dangerous. That's probably why the Sweep gave her to you. You need to prove yourself, Matthew. I'd say once that worry starts tickling, reach for those matches. The worst mistake you can make would be to wait too long."

"How will I know for sure it's the Mark?" The questions that haunted my morning run come rushing back. "Accidents happen all on their own. I could just be missing something."

"One accident perhaps. Maybe two. But then . . ." Kendrick's blue eyes turn cloudy. "You'll know it, Matthew. You've seen it before."

"What happens if I don't? If I fail?" My voice falters, and I cover my worry with a cough. "Would I go back to working with Dad?"

"Well, once you accept the solo project, that ship's kind of sailed." He scratches his chin. "The goal is to build more Sweepers, not keep the ones who aren't cut out for the job. And it's not like we could let you go wandering off to talk about us, right?" His eyes take me in as I wait for him to laugh, to tell me he's teasing.

He doesn't.

Instead, Kendrick shrugs. "Don't worry, Matthew. You're doing great. Besides, if your father didn't think you would pass, he wouldn't have let you take the project in the first place." He rises. "How about grabbing breakfast?"

If I ate any food right now, my stomach would probably heave it right back up. Dad hadn't told me what would happen if I failed, though I suppose he did warn me I wouldn't get a second chance. Still, he could have made the consequences clearer. Might have made me think a bit more before saying yes.

"Breakfast?" Kendrick prods.

I shake my head. "I'm meeting the project soon. How about dinner?" Maybe by then, I'll be able to keep my food down.

"Wish I could, but I can't stay. Got a training to run. We're opening a new center nearby, and I've just hired a crew." Kendrick's security firm beats even Dad's photography as the best job for a Sweeper. No one can get into houses as easily as the person who installed the system to keep others out. He eyes my door. "Why don't I put on a new lock for you? That one seems like an invitation for robbery."

I manage a laugh. "Thanks, but I've got nothing worth stealing."

"You sure?"

His gaze slides to my notebook, and Dad's warning comes screeching back. "Maybe a new lock is a good idea."

"Smart boy. I'll bring it next time I'm here." He pulls me into a bear hug, and I inhale the scent of his peppermint aftershave. I gave him a bottle for Christmas last year, and he swears it's the best he's found. "Don't worry, Matthew. When you see the signs, you'll know what to do."

When. Not *if.*

I don't correct him. "Thanks. And thanks for coming by."

He leaves with a quick wave, and his long strides carry him out of the yard before I notice the shirt he left on the table. The cheerful My Friend Went to Cancún and All I Got Was This Lousy T-Shirt makes me smile, and the old certainty washes over me, calming the queasiness that rises whenever I look at my red notebook. This might be a solo test, but Dad and Kendrick have been preparing me for more than half my life. If they think I can pass, I will.

I'd better, because the alternative doesn't sound good.

CHAPTER

9

I take a quick shower and drive to the Wallflower, pausing a minute after I park for my usual scan of the streets. Mills Creek is small enough that faces are already turning familiar, and I recognize a woman lingering in the shade. Her eyes dart my way, and I'm almost certain I've uncovered the Sweeper watching me when she waves to a man pushing a stroller. He greets her with a kiss, and they disappear into a café without a backward glance.

This project is making me paranoid.

I send Dad a text: **Saw Kendrick. All good. Meeting project now.**

Gritting my teeth, I wait. Sure enough, a flurry of texts pops up, each bursting with unwanted advice.

Good job with Kendrick. Stay careful.

Maybe keep project as tutor? Need to get closer.

Take notes on everything. And mail weekly report.

I'll call tonight.

That last one sounds like a threat. Nothing he wrote deserves a response, but if I ignore him, his messages will keep coming. I suppose this project is partly his test as well, since he's my mentor, but he's starting to drive me crazy.

OK, I punch in, and shove the phone into my pocket.

The Wallflower already buzzes with activity when I enter. Sahana stands at the register helping Ms. Timmult, who nearly smacks her forehead on the glass as she scrunches her face against the display case.

"Is that cranberry?" she asks.

"Yes," Sahana says politely, rolling her eyes at me. Her neon green nails flash against her black outfit as she plays with the tongs. "And the scones next to those are blueberry."

"Hmm. And you said those were apple?"

Sahana nods.

Ms. Timmult taps her fingers against her chin the way she does in class when she's thinking. "I'll take . . . maple."

"Great choice!" Sahana drops the scone in a bag so fast, Ms. Timmult doesn't have time to change her mind if she wanted. "That'll be two dollars."

"What kinds of teas do you have?" Ms. Timmult asks, and Sahana practically wilts.

I can't hide my grin. The thought of Ms. Timmult being a Sweeper is still on my mind, but if she is, I'm fairly certain I can handle her. At last, she collects her drink and scone, giving me a surprised "Oh, hello, Matt!" as she leaves.

Sahana collapses across the counter with a groan.

"So," I say as I approach, "what kinds of scones do you have?"

She points the tongs at me. "Don't even start."

I laugh. "I need coffee. What'll wake me up for math?"

"I'll surprise you." Her eyes brighten. "Hey, Rae!"

I turn to see Rae hurrying toward us. Her red T-shirt fits

perfectly over dark jeans, and even the bike helmet dangling from her hand looks great. She reaches up to cover a yawn as she nears.

"Let me guess," Sahana says. "Double mocha for you?"

Rae nods. "With extra whipped cream, please. I need it."

Sahana's brow wrinkles. "Everything okay?"

"Couldn't sleep." Rae lifts one shoulder in a tired shrug. "And Cady's having another rough morning. She won't even get out of bed. I went to see her, and she just kept crying—" Her voice breaks off, and Sahana reaches over to squeeze her hand.

"It'll get better," she says softly. "She just needs time. You both do."

Rae nods, her lips pressed together, and I touch her elbow gently. "Juan and Moose told me. I'm really sorry."

She ducks her head, and Sahana holds out the canister of whipped cream. "You can just take the whole thing," she offers, and Rae's lips curve in the smallest grin.

"Go sit down." Sahana gives her a final squeeze as I pay for our coffees. "I'll bring the drinks when they're ready."

We head for an empty table, and Rae slips into the chair across from me. She rubs her cheeks with both palms, her expression bleak, and digs out her math book without a word.

"You missed Timmult," I tell her and replay the morning, doing my best imitation of our teacher's indecisiveness and Sahana's fracturing patience. The smallest sparkle lights Rae's eyes as I finish, and something inside me glows.

"Wish I could have seen that." Rae glances at where her friend hovers over the bottles of flavored syrups like a witch concocting a brew. "Sahana loves making the drinks, but if she could get rid of the customers, I think she would."

"I believe that." After a week with our little lunch group, it's clear patience isn't one of Sahana's strengths. Protectiveness, however, ranks high on her list, and her appraising stare whenever I sit beside Rae lets me know I need to work harder to gain approval. "Thanks again for meeting me. I'm pretty sure I'm going to fail McNally's test."

"It's not that bad," Rae assures me. "You just need to remember the steps. I'll show you."

She dives in, carefully explaining each problem and checking to see if I understand before moving to the next. Sahana delivers our drinks, and the ridiculously tall mound of whipped cream on Rae's mocha makes both of us laugh.

"What is this?" I sip the drink Sahana puts in front of me. It's sweet, spicy, and definitely strong enough to keep me awake. "It's really good."

"I'm calling it 'Shark Bite.'" She grins. "Two shots of espresso with vanilla, raspberry, and jalapeño. Guaranteed to improve any homework. You're welcome."

She heads back to the counter, and Rae resumes my lesson. I nod along as she talks, asking some questions and deliberately making a few errors she patiently corrects. Her tutoring certainly would have helped if I hadn't already understood the concept.

Still, this wouldn't be a bad way to pass the year in Mills Creek. Rae leans across the table, head tilted as she watches me struggle through a problem, and math suddenly becomes far more interesting than it had been in the hours spent at the kitchen table with Dad. Her hair hangs loose to her shoulders, and a slight curl ripples through it. Pink eye shadow is her only makeup, though her cheeks turn pink as well when she looks up from my work and catches me staring.

Judging from the heat in my face, we probably match.

"Sorry." I tap my paper. "I'm stuck."

"Oh!" Her gaze flies to my scribbled numbers. "Check this part."

We finish reviewing the notes and start our homework, since McNally is one of those teachers who enjoys destroying weekends with extra assignments. Halfway through, Rae's phone buzzes. She glances at it, and a smile plays over her face.

"It's my mom." Rae shows me the screen, where **Have a good day!** is written beneath a squirrel attacking a cake. "She's always sending pictures and stuff."

Mrs. Winter's text definitely beats the ones Dad sent this morning. "That's sweet. Does this mean your sister is feeling better?"

"I hope so." Rae sends a quick text back—**u too!**—and glances at the time. "Think you can finish the rest on your own? I need to get to Charon's."

"I think so. It makes more sense now," I tell her. "Thank you."

"No problem." She calls goodbye to Sahana, who looks up from a steaming metal mug to flash a smile. "Going to stay and keep working?"

"I'll walk you over." Charon's is only two blocks away. "It helps me procrastinate."

She laughs. "I thought you said it made sense."

"It does." I finish the last of my coffee and wave to Sahana. "But it's still math."

Rae tells me about her job as we walk, how she's learning to mix cakes and decorate sugar cookies and how frosting can fix almost anything, and I offer to eat all mistakes deemed beyond saving. She grins.

"Careful. Mr. Yamamoto's always trying weird flavor combinations in his monthly specials. Think bacon and raisins. Some turn out pretty good, but others—"

Her voice cuts off suddenly, eyes narrowing on an old gray sedan waiting at the corner light. An older woman hunches over the steering wheel.

My pulse quickens. "What is it?"

Rae scowls. "That's Cady's piano teacher, Mrs. Archer. She comes to the house every week, and last time, she actually told Mom she should stop being so sad because she's pretty and will find someone new soon." Her voice rises, anger bubbling in each word. "I mean, seriously? Like we can just replace Dad like that?"

I wince. "I'm sorry. That's terrible."

The light turns green, and Rae glares at the sedan as it passes. We make it only a few more steps before a loud *pop!* comes from behind us, and I turn to see the car skidding out of its lane. It plows onto the curb, swerves around a pedestrian, and crashes into a tree. The impact crumples the fender like an accordion, sending dust and glass flying.

Mrs. Archer remains upright in her seat, eyes wide as she clutches the steering wheel. People run toward her, and steam hisses from under her hood. She won't be driving anywhere soon.

"Did you see that?" Rae cranes her neck, stretching up on her toes to peer over the cars braking to avoid the wreckage. "I think she just popped a tire. Karma's kind of awesome, isn't it?"

I can't answer. The timing of it all—Rae noticing Mrs. Archer, her anger at the woman's thoughtlessness, the exploding tire—feels too perfect to be coincidence.

My heart sinks a bit.

We continue the walk to Charon's, and I manage a stumbling conversation despite the dread snaking through me. Rae invites me inside, her cheerful mood restored, and I do my best to act normal as I choose a "Styx and Stones" cupcake featuring pretzels and popping candy.

"Thanks for helping me with math," I say.

"Anytime. And I mean that, okay?" She adds a few more candies to my cupcake before handing it over. "Unless you'd rather talk to McNally."

I force a smile. "I think you're stuck with me."

She laughs, and I say goodbye and walk back toward my car, slowing as I approach Mrs. Archer. The woman sits on the curb, her face pale and hands gripped together as she speaks with the police officers now on the scene. She doesn't appear injured, but I can't say the same for either her car or the tree, which leans at a precarious angle.

"—just veered that way on its own!" she says as I pass.

The officer nods. "Blowing out a tire will do that. Looks like you ran over something sharp."

The street seems clear of debris, though the store behind Mrs. Archer is undergoing some type of renovation. Remnants of construction work could have skittered onto the asphalt, where a piece of metal would make short work of a tire, especially one worn thin like those on Mrs. Archer's car.

I think of Ms. Rivera, Dad's project whom he judged free of the Mark. There had been moments when similar questions rose—when accidents happened near her and the possibility of a different judgment reared its head. Unfortunate events happen to everyone, however, and a Sweeper's job is to determine whether a project bears responsibility. A single accident, or even several, isn't proof someone is Marked. It's the progression and frequency we watch for, trying to separate coincidence from something more.

I hope what I just saw was coincidence.

The morning gives me a strange entry for the red notebook—a description of Rae's patience as we worked together, her anger at Mrs. Archer, the popped tire and resulting accident. Then again, maybe it makes perfect sense. Rae could be nice enough to help a classmate but enraged by those hurtful words, and her fury at Mrs. Archer aimed the Mark's dark power at a deserving victim.

Or maybe the woman just ran over a nail.

"Very good, Matthew," Dad says when I tell him about it that night. "It sounds like you're making excellent progress."

"It could have just been coincidence," I point out.

He brushes that aside. "Not if it keeps happening."

A heavy silence falls, and goodbye becomes the safest thing to say. I hang up, his parting "Keep watching, Matthew" still coming through the line, and the difference in the wait stretching before us feels like a chasm. Dad is so sure of the Mark he won't even entertain an alternate explanation, while I'm still wondering exactly what I saw this morning. It's the same way I felt each time an accident happened near Mrs. Polly, and I know how that project ended.

The only difference is this time, I'll be the one holding the match.

CHAPTER

10

Sleep stays distant all weekend. When I do manage to drift off, nightmares descend, bringing a strange mash-up of Rae and Mrs. Polly walking around that little cottage, now burned to cinders, or moving through a silent version of Mills Creek. I trail behind, and no matter where the dream takes us, the ending stays the same.

Someone screams. Someone burns.

I can't tell who.

Still, Rae looks worse than I do when we arrive at school Monday morning. She wears her usual ponytail and jeans, but shadows darken her eyes, and she trips over an untied shoelace as we push through the double doors.

I catch her elbow to steady her. "You okay?"

"Yesterday was my parents' anniversary." She fumbles her locker open and dumps in a pile of books, and her breath hitches in the smallest whimper. Her face wilts, and she pauses as if gathering herself back together, sheer force of will refusing to let tears fall in the high school hallway. "Eighteen years. Mom's eyes were red all day. I got off early from Charon's to be with her, but it was just hard."

Her voice breaks, and a lump hardens in my throat. It's a strange and sad reshuffling that happens when someone dies. Most of the time, the survivors somehow patch the remaining bits of their lives together, though perhaps the pieces don't fit quite as well as before.

Sometimes they just stay jumbled.

We walk to her French class in silence, and her downturned mouth makes me hesitate at the door. I should step away, let her go inside to where Sahana might already be waiting, but something causes me to reach out and touch her shoulder. She looks at me, tears filling her eyes, and my arms wrap around her before my brain can stop them. She leans into me, bringing warmth and the scent of coconut shampoo, and I wish I had shown up at MCHS for any reason but the truth.

"Thanks." She straightens. "Better run, or you'll be late."

"See you in math," I tell her, and she disappears inside the classroom.

I turn to go, and my feet stumble over each other at the sight of Toshi standing across the hall, his books tucked under one arm and his stare aimed at me. I manage a stuttering "Hey" before edging past, but I can feel his eyes boring into my back as I hurry away. I had almost dismissed him as a Sweeper since he didn't pay me much attention, but the intensity of his expression scorches my mind as I sprint to Spanish.

If he is part of the Sweep, what will he think of my hug with Rae? Surely he would have only seen me doing my job.

Because that's all it was.

The idea of Toshi evaluating my work strikes me as odd,

however, because it feels like the Sweep would send someone older and more experienced. Unless he joined when he was in diapers, high school would be the right time for Toshi's first solo project too.

The timing of his arrival fits. And when I think about it, he's popped up around Rae enough to make me wonder.

Maybe he ignores me because I'm not the one he's here to watch.

Maybe the Sweep sent him to judge Rae, just like they sent me.

The possibility hits like an ice bath, and I yank open the classroom door and sink into my seat as my legs turn to jelly. Señora Torres hands me today's worksheet, but the words make even less sense than usual. My brain replays every encounter I've seen between Rae and Toshi, and the signs become so clear they might as well be written in spotlights: Toshi weaving past her in the hall, daily walks near our lunch group, his continued presence at cross country though he ends each workout gasping for air at the back of the pack.

We have the same test.

It's a brilliant move by the Sweep. Give Toshi and me the same project, and if Rae is Marked, only one of us will strike the flame and pass. The organization gains the stronger soldier.

And disposes of the weaker one.

Señora Torres's voice fades to a hum as my brain chugs through the implications of this new information. Each project can take up to a year, but that usually only happens if signs of the Mark don't manifest. These are the projects judged lucky and left to live, like Ms. Rivera. If a Sweeper gathers enough evidence to determine someone is Marked before that twelve-month deadline, the burning can take place immediately. Dad judged Mrs. Polly after nine months, but Mr. Whittmeier took only four. The Sweep doesn't question the outcome as long as our reports support our decision. Kendrick's had a few he dispatched within weeks.

Which means Toshi could burn Rae any day.

By the time class ends, I've nearly crawled out of my skin trying to sit still. I bolt out of my chair, scanning for Toshi as I cross campus, and make it to math class at the same time as Rae.

"After you." She waves me inside the empty room. "First victim."

I try to smile back, but as the room fills and McNally prepares to torture us once again, I remember Toshi arrived at MCHS a week before me. I'm already seven days behind. The knowledge brings another hot cascade of frustration, and I almost pull out my phone right in the middle of class to text Dad and ask what the hell the Sweep is doing. At least McNally is so preoccupied with checking homework he doesn't notice I'm having a meltdown in his front row, and it helps that the kid in back—Doug something, I'm not sure—doesn't have his work again.

"—really don't know why you keep wasting my time. You're an absolute disgrace, and if your parents would bother to show up for a conference—"

McNally's face is turning purple, spittle flying, and he's so into his rant that he jerks his head and the pencil behind his ear slips free. He grabs for it and misses, knocking a stack of papers to the ground, and the pencil arcs gracefully toward his coffee cup. It lands inside the mug with a clatter, and a spattering of brown liquid splashes across his white shirt.

An abrupt silence falls. McNally stares unbelieving at the stain, and the rest of us are too shocked to move. Then Doug snickers, and the room explodes with laughter.

Even I can't stop the grin sliding across my face. Beside me, Rae presses her hand to her mouth. A giggle slips free, and the odds of the pencil landing just where it did wipe my smile away.

She leans back in her chair, lips curved with satisfaction as McNally hollers at us to clear our desks for a pop quiz. I'm fairly certain I fail, because I can't concentrate on the problems. All I can think is that even if Rae did send that pencil falling to save Doug, perhaps it wouldn't be the worst thing in the world.

Maybe if the Mark is used to help someone, it doesn't count as evil.

"Well, that was awesome." Rae chuckles, her shoulder bumping mine as class ends and everyone flees our still-glowering teacher. "I needed that today."

Around us, whispers and giggles fill the hall. McNally's story spreads, smiles and smirks trailing in its wake, and suddenly Toshi's wide grin appears among the sea of faces. His gaze skips over me to land on Rae, and he catches her eye.

"Hey," he says. "Were you just in McNally's?"

She nods. "Best class ever."

He laughs, and then he's gone, one more interaction with the project under his belt and a new entry for his notebook.

Worry hovers over me like a thundercloud all day, and seeing Toshi's eyes linger on Rae during practice almost makes me run him over on the track. I walk her to the front of school when we finish, chatting until Mrs. Winter's car pulls up, but there's little I can do about the hours between now and tomorrow morning.

If he heads to her house, I won't be there to stop him.

By the time I drive home, I've nearly chewed a hole through my cheek. It doesn't help that the MC tagger, as I've started calling the person leaving the almost–Leviathan Crosses around town, has drawn another blue symbol on the wall outside the movie theater. It's positioned in the corner but stands almost a foot tall, which means whoever left it is getting bolder. My mood slips even more when I park, since Mr. Garrett glares at me over his newspaper from the porch, but I give a brief wave and retreat to the safety of the backyard.

A gleaming new lock on the shack's door catches me by surprise. I'm debating whether I need to hold an actual conversation with my landlord when I check my phone and find a text from Kendrick.

Sorry I missed you. Key is under the cardboard. I'll give your dad a copy.

He didn't waste any time following through on his promise. The shack even smells like his peppermint aftershave, and the familiar scent calms me, sliding the project back into focus.

I can do this. Competition or not, I know my job. If the Sweep wants to throw me a curveball and pit me against Toshi, I can handle that too.

Though I'm not sure what it means to win.

CHAPTER

11

Jansford Park isn't much of a park. It has no playground, no picnic area, and no grass, unless you count patches of dry weeds covering the acres of dirt. But it does have a starting line, dusty trails, and a finish chute.

And hills.

Compared to the rolling fields I envisioned for my first cross-country meet, the course looks like a small mountain range. From my place at the starting line, I can't even see the bottom of the path ahead, which dips in a steep decline before curving through some withered shrubs. Somewhere in the prickly branches, it turns and climbs all the way back up.

And that's only the first mile.

"Isn't this great?" Moose punches my shoulder. He has the last of four races today—the Junior Varsity girls just finished; Juan, Toshi, and I run next with the JV boys; and Rae's and Moose's Varsity races will follow—which probably explains why he still looks so cheerful. "You'll be awesome."

I groan. "I should have joined chess club."

"Me too." Juan grimaces at the hill. "No college is worth this."

Rae pats his back. "Think of the application you'll be able to write: Determination! Teamwork! Perseverance! They'll love it."

I can't help laughing, and even Juan's lips twitch as Coach joins us, fist-bumping everyone with an exuberance that practically rolls off him. Here's a man who loves his job.

"Let's see some PRs, people!" He points at me. "That's Personal Record, Matt. You'll definitely do it, since it's your first race. Make it a good one!"

He steps back. Someone yells, "Runners, take your mark!" and a gun goes off. Everyone sprints like crazy off the line, including me, though I'm really just trying not to get trampled. I lose Juan somewhere in the pack as we stampede down the hill, but a blue-and-white uniform identical to mine surges past, and I recognize the back of Toshi's head. Picking up my pace, I settle into a smooth stride half a step behind him, so close the back of his shirt brushes my knuckles.

Here's one way to keep an eye on him.

I asked Dad last night if I had competition on this project, and though he didn't think so, he didn't know for certain. The Sweep doesn't share much about its procedures. He asked plenty of questions, though—parent questions about my schoolwork and today's meet, and project questions about Rae. I didn't want to mention McNally's pencil incident, but I slipped in a question about whether anyone could manipulate the Mark to help others. Could Lucifer's cruel gift somehow be used for good?

Dad hadn't hesitated. "No."

"But what if—"

"Matthew." His voice deepened to that old lecturing tone from our lessons, stealing any space for argument. "In a war between Lucifer and a human, who would win?"

"Lucifer." I could almost see him nodding approval. "But what if she's got others to support her? You always say the Mark works differently in different people. Maybe family or friends can help someone fight Him off, or even make the Mark something better."

"And what happens when families fight and friends leave? Would you really rely on factors so far out of your control?"

His tone clearly implied the answer. Before I could say anything, he went on. "Why do you ask? What happened?"

Lying to everyone else might come easily, but lying to Dad is new. My mind spun in a frantic scramble, and the "Matthew?" that came through the phone made me spill the whole story.

When I finished, his silence blared volumes.

"It starts small," he finally said, his voice gentle. "But it is a start."

The memory of that phone call turns my feet faster now, and I almost crash into Toshi as we plod around the curve and begin the climb up the hill. A good kick would serve him right. I caught him staring at Rae again on the bus ride over, and I'm about to stomp on his heel when a voice breaks through.

"Come on, MC! Go, Matt!" Rae shouts.

"You can do it!" Moose yells. "Juan, move it!"

They wait at the top of the hill, looking right at me, jumping and yelling and clapping. I keep my face contorted in pain, my panting exaggerated, but the corners of my mouth creep up as I plod past them.

Nobody has ever cheered for me like that.

I hold my sluggish pace through the next two miles, slowing even more as I climb the Monster, a short but steep rise Juan gloomily pointed out during our warm-up. Toshi races ahead to finish seconds before me, and my overall time is about eight minutes slower than what I could have run. Moose jogs over as I hobble through the finish chute, and I clutch my stomach and double over.

"Hey," I wheeze. "That was terrible."

"You did great!" Moose grips my elbow and pulls me upright. Rae has vanished, probably warming up with the other Varsity girls. "Keep walking."

He steers me toward our team's area, and I collapse onto the dusty ground. Toshi sprawls nearby, and Juan and a few others straggle over. We congratulate each other between gulps of water, and no one even attempts to stand again until Moose points out the next race is about to start. Juan and Toshi drag themselves to their feet to follow him, and I jump up as a familiar figure catches my eye.

Mrs. Winter strides through the opening in the chain-link fence separating the course from the parking lot, and Cady's sneakers drag lines in the dirt behind her. Her hands are shoved deep in the pockets of her blue sweatshirt, and she rubs her sleeve across her eyes. She looks so much like Rae, standing nearly as tall with that same light brown hair, but Cady wears her emotions far closer to the surface. Maybe being younger means she hasn't yet learned to hide them, and the pain that rolls off her in waves also churns behind Rae's careful smile.

I let them move ahead of me before following them to the starting line. The gun fires, and we cheer as the Varsity girls charge forward, raising a cloud of dust behind them. They spread out around the turn, and in far less time than it took me, the runners are around the bend and heading back up, with Rae near the front.

"Go!" I shout. "Keep it up! Good job!" I sound ridiculous, but her eyes flick my way, and I yell even louder. She climbs the hill in seconds and disappears down the trail.

"Wow." Toshi stares after her admiringly. "She made that look easy."

I agree, but that doesn't stop the annoyance spiking through me. He doesn't seem to have figured out my role with the Sweep, and I plan to keep it that way. No need to give him a reason to burn sooner. He tags after us as Juan and Moose hurry me toward the Monster, and we spread out along the steep rise to cheer on the team. Rae flies past, chasing a girl two steps ahead, and I do my best to drown out Toshi's cheers with my own.

"Come on," Juan calls from the top of the hill. "We've got to get to the end. Remember?"

We run across the course toward the last stretch, where Coach and the rest of our team have already gathered. Mrs.

Winter is there as well, one arm tucking Cady close to her side.

"What's going on?" I ask.

"Mr. Winter used to stand here." Moose cranes his neck, trying to see around the bend. "He'd cheer Rae on all the way through the end. Since he can't be here today, we're going to do it for him."

And we do. We spread out along both sides of the trail, and when Rae appears behind the first two runners, the roar that goes up rocks the ground. Her face, already red from exertion, crumples a bit. My yell sticks in my throat, and I have to clear it before I can shout for her again.

She picks up her pace, and the girl in front of her doesn't stand a chance. We scream and holler as Rae sprints down the straightaway, almost catching the blonde girl in a white uniform who finishes a step before her. Both stumble through the chute, and Mrs. Winter is there to fold her daughter into a hug.

Rae looks at us, eyes bright and voice torn as she whispers, "Thank you."

"We miss him too," Juan tells her, and several heads nod. "But we're here for you, okay?"

She manages a small smile. "I know."

Mrs. Winter lets her go, and Rae steps toward us before pausing, her gaze falling on her sister. Cady stands with her shoulders hunched, her body rigid as she blinks furiously at the ground. Rae touches her elbow.

"You okay?" she asks softly.

Cady shrugs without looking up, and then shakes her head.

"Me neither." Rae carefully wraps her arms around her

sister's stiff shoulders. "But I'm glad you're here."

For a long moment, Cady doesn't move. Then her body softens, and she returns the hug as Mrs. Winter watches, her face drawn and eyes wet. They let each other go at last, and I can't help thinking that Marked or not, this family would never survive another loss.

Rae tucks Cady's hair behind her ear. "There's just one more race. Varsity boys. You can yell at Moose to run faster."

This brings a tiny smile to Cady's lips, and she and Mrs. Winter decide to stay near the finish line to cheer him through the final sprint. Rae joins Juan, Toshi, and me as we head for the start, but her steps are slow, and it's clear Cady isn't the only one struggling today. Before I can say anything, Toshi moves beside her.

"What about you?" he asks. "How are you doing?"

"I'm okay. You guys really help," she tells him, and a smile spreads across his face.

A new feeling roars through me like fire as I watch him worm closer to her, and my hand curls to a fist. I slow, and Juan bumps into me from behind.

"Hurry up!" He prods my shoulder. "They're about to go."

I let him jostle me forward, my anger still seething, but Rae elbows me as we reach Moose.

"Wait for it," she whispers.

As if on cue, Juan launches into a barrage of last-minute instructions, and Moose listens attentively, giving each leg a final shake. For a guy who can't run fast, Juan actually has an excellent grasp of race strategy, even pointing out the fastest competitors. Knowing him, he's done research. We send Moose off with shouts and cheers, and the jealous part of me wonders how quickly I could run this course if I actually tried. I'll probably never know.

Though next time, maybe I could at least beat Toshi.

I glance at Rae, about to comment on Juan's enthusiasm for racing when he's not the one running, but the grin on her face morphs into a scowl that makes me pause. Her eyes narrow on a group of girls in white uniforms several yards away, and I recognize the runner who finished seconds ahead of her. My pulse picks up speed. Rae didn't strike me as a sore loser, but if she is, this would be a prime opportunity for the Mark to rear its head.

"What is it?" Juan asks Rae, and turns to see the girl. "Oh. It's all right. You'll beat Haley next time."

"Would have beaten her this time if she hadn't pushed me on the back trails." Rae jerks her head to where the dirt course winds out of sight, dipping behind taller shrubs and dry branches before reappearing near the Monster. "She went past and shoved me off the trail. That path was plenty wide for both of us."

Her words come hot and angry, and Haley's head whips around. Turning on her heel, she marches over to us.

"No." She stops a foot away from Rae. "*You* pushed *me*. The faster person gets to pass the slower one, you know. That's the point of a race."

"I pushed you *back*." Fury simmers in Rae's voice. "You had room."

Haley just smirks. "Second place sucks, doesn't it?" She lifts one shoulder in an innocent shrug. "I wouldn't know." With that, she stalks away, leaving Rae with her fists clenched and face red.

"Can't you report her?" Juan glares after Haley. "The race officials should be able to do something."

Rae shakes her head, jaw still tight. "She'll just say I'm complaining since she beat me. I'll handle it."

My breath catches, and I wait for a branch from a nearby shrub to snap loose and hit Haley, a dust cloud to rise up, even a water bottle to jump from the ground and smack her shin. Nothing happens. Haley reaches her friends and says something I can't hear, and they all turn to sneer at Rae.

"Ignore them." Juan nudges her. "Don't give her the pleasure."

"Has this happened before?" I whisper to him, as Rae glowers down the hill to where Moose and the others storm around the curve.

He shakes his head. "Not this. But Haley would totally do it. You know those shelves in the back of the Wallflower with gum and pencils and stuff? Sahana caught her stealing from them over the summer and got her banned from the coffee shop, so Haley posted a bunch of crap on social media. Called Sahana a terrorist and some other racist bullshit. Rae was furious. She confronted Haley and told her to take it all down, or she'd go to her principal with screenshots of everything. Would have gotten her suspended at the very least. She deleted it, so Rae let it go, but Haley's been out for blood ever since."

No wonder it feels like I'm watching a silent war. The air

between the two girls blisters, even as they pointedly ignore each other, but there's no sign of any Mark: no strange acci-dent, no unexplained injury.

Though I suppose the day's not over.

The thought hurts even more than my run up the Monster, and the chatter and cheering around me only make it worse. For just a few minutes, I'd like to stick the project into a drawer and lose myself in the regular life I'm finally learning about—hanging out with my friends, laughing at their jokes, and getting to know a girl who actually seems really nice.

MCHS Matt Watts might be slow, but his life is far better than mine. Letting him take over for a little while might just keep me sane.

Shoving away thoughts of the project, I take a deep breath and let my arm brush Rae's. Anger still reddens her cheeks, but she glances at me and flashes a quick smile. Beside us, Juan cups his hands like a bullhorn as the runners make their way back up the hill.

"Move it, Moose!" His voice booms. "My grandma goes faster!"

Rae shakes her head at him. "So encouraging."

"It's working," he says smugly.

Moose picks up his pace, red hair flopping as he climbs the hill, and we yell at him to hurry up as he passes us and sprints down the path. Juan glances at his watch.

"Not bad. Went out a bit slow, but he might make it up. We should head for the Monster."

"Aw, you really do care." Rae throws her arm around him. "That's so sweet."

Juan's indignant look makes me laugh out loud, and I sink into the relief of good old Matt Watts. Rae's eyes sparkle as they meet mine, and the tightness inside finally lets go.

A new voice, deep and familiar, cuts in. "Hello, Matthew. Hope I didn't miss your race."

Guilt shrivels my smile as the project bursts back into the open, wrapping around me like the bars of a cage. I turn and sure enough, there he is.

"Hi, Dad," I say.

CHAPTER

12

Dad beams at Juan, Toshi, and Rae. "You must be Matthew's friends."

The warmth in his voice stings like acid, but I slap on a smile. The project is watching.

"Hi, Dad." I gesture to the others. "This is Juan and Toshi." Neither my father nor Toshi show any hint of recognition as they shake hands, but it's not like the Sweep would have introduced them. My fingernails dig into my palms. "And this is Rae."

"Hi." She returns Dad's smile. "Matt already raced. He was fantastic."

"Really?" The pride in Dad's voice must sound real to the others, but I know better. "Good for you, Matthew!"

"Want to come with us?" Juan checks his watch. "They'll be coming up the Monster soon."

"You guys go ahead," I say. "We'll catch up."

They sprint off, and the sight of Toshi running beside Rae brings a fresh surge of annoyance. He's probably going faster than he did in his race, and thanks to Dad, all I can do is watch.

I wait until the others are out of earshot. "What are you doing here? Is everything okay?"

"It's fine. Just thought I'd surprise you." His eyebrows arch. "Is it all right I came?"

Not at all. His appearance changed everything, sucking the humor from my laughter and reminding me MCHS Matt is nothing more than a charade.

"Of course," I tell him. "But are you supposed to show up like this? Will the Sweep mind?"

"Kendrick said any visits are fine as long as I don't help with your test. I'm your father, after all. I'm supposed to put in an appearance every now and then." Dad rubs his chin, staring after the others. "Was that the project?"

"Yes." The word feels like a betrayal. "And Toshi's the one who might be a Sweeper."

"No one said anything about giving you competition." He frowns, and I can almost see the gears in his head shifting. "Let's get over there. You should keep her close."

I don't point out I would already be with her if he hadn't pulled me away, and we reach the finish line as she sprints over with Juan and Toshi. Everyone hollers at Moose, who comes tearing down the runway, and he crosses the line and stumbles through the chute, chest heaving and both hands on his head.

"Whoa there." I hurry over and steady him. "You okay?"

"Tired," he gasps.

"You did good," I say, and Juan runs up to pound him on the back.

"Nice finish!" he yells, nearly sending Moose pitching forward. "Whoops. Let's walk."

He takes one arm, and Rae slips onto Moose's other side. They steady him between them as they move away, Toshi trailing behind as Juan breaks down Moose's performance with suggestions for improvement. I don't realize I'm smiling until Dad clears his throat.

"Careful, Matthew," he warns softly. "Remember why you're here."

His words make me bristle. "I do."

We watch the rest of the race in silence. When the last runners cross the line, Coach gathers us together. "Well done, everyone!" If his grin gets any wider, his face will split in two. "I'm proud of each of you. Grab your gear and meet me on the bus. If you're going home with someone, be sure to let me know."

I catch his eye and point to my dad, and Coach gives a thumbs-up.

"Great running, Matt!" he calls, and Juan and Moose wave to me before jogging toward the exit. Toshi follows, his feet shuffling as if they're too heavy to lift.

Though he certainly didn't seem to mind keeping up with Rae.

She stops next to me, her mother and Cady a few steps behind. "Do you love cross country now?"

"Absolutely," I assure her. "Especially the Monster. Can't wait to do that again."

Rae grins, and we walk out to the parking lot as Dad

appears on her other side to ask how her race went. Her modest response of "Fine" almost makes me chime in to tell him about her second-place finish, but I keep my mouth shut.

The less Dad knows about Rae, the better.

Both he and Mrs. Winter left their cars on the far side of the lot, near clusters of weeds and a few abandoned shopping carts that have migrated over from the enormous all-in-one store across the street. We're almost there when I spot Haley ahead of us. Judging from the steam I can almost feel coming off Rae, she noticed the other girl as well.

"You'll beat her next time," I murmur.

"You bet I will," Rae shoots back, and Dad perks up to listen.

I cut her off before she can say more, chatting instead about Juan's encouragement tactics for Moose, and she cheerfully points out their effectiveness. We reach the Winters' car, and I'm about to steer Dad away when sudden movement near the back fence catches my attention.

One of the abandoned grocery carts begins to roll.

No one stands near it, but the wheels pick up speed as it hurtles across empty parking spaces. Haley doesn't see it, her back to the whizzing cart as she calls to a teammate.

"Look out!" the other girl yells.

Too late.

The cart plows into Haley, who pitches forward with a startled yelp. She tumbles to the ground, and I already know the cracked asphalt will draw blood.

Several people rush over to see if she's all right. Haley sits up, her face contorted with pain as she brushes gravel from her scraped knees. The cart rolls to a stop a few feet away. Calls of "What happened?" are met with blank expressions, everyone looking from the cart to each other, and the general exodus slowly resumes.

"You're smiling," Dad murmurs to Rae, his own lips quirking in a conspiratorial grin. "Not a friend of yours?"

"Let's just say it couldn't have happened to a better person," Rae whispers back.

Every part of me tingles with alarm. Dad's old teachings about Lucifer rise up, the evidence of Rae's Mark crashing over me, but a different cause—normal and completely natural—cuts through my panic. The hills of the cross-country course extend to the parking lot, leaving the ground so angled and uneven it basically invites such accidents. The cart might have been balanced precariously in the slanted lot, and given the number of people at the course today, someone could have easily bumped it as they passed. Haley just happened to be in its way.

Dad's tightened jaw says he's reached a different conclusion, but I'm not convinced. Ms. Rivera once strolled past a children's soccer game as the ball flew out and smacked a bystander in the head, and it took weeks with no other incidents for us to deem it a good old-fashioned accident. The memory anchors my mind even more in the realm of coincidence and questions, and I settle on the hope that time will make this fade to nothing but Haley's bad luck. We say goodbye to the Winters, and Dad waits until our car doors close behind us to speak.

"Did you see?" He watches in the rearview mirror as the

Winters drive away. "The project's control of the cart toward her target?"

A chill slides over me. "The ground tilts that way. It could have just been an accident."

"Shopping carts don't roll by themselves, Matthew." Dad's eyes gleam. "Given this and the other incidents, I'd say you're well on your way."

"On my way?" I sputter. Horror seeps into each word. "I've been here two weeks!"

"You said Toshi has been here for three," Dad reminds me, his face grim. "If you've got competition, your process needs to accelerate. I've been watching him since I arrived, and he's been shadowing her the entire time. He saw what happened just now, and you can bet he's not thinking about the tilt of the ground. Matthew, one of you is going to fail this test. You need to move first."

The urgency in his voice pierces like a blade. "It's too soon," I choke out, though my voice sounds strangled and my hands clutch my backpack. "Remember Ms. Rivera? Things can change. There's not enough evidence."

"Then find more," Dad says as he starts the car. "You're running out of time."

CHAPTER

13

Dad packed his suitcase with enough clothes to stay for the weekend, and though I greet the news with a loud "Great!", I don't mean it. I had been looking forward to two days without school, free to fill the hours with the project of course, but Moose and Juan had also suggested a tour of Mills Creek, with apple picking followed by milkshakes at the Pit Stop. No way will Dad allow any of that, not without Rae along, and she's working at Charon's both afternoons.

I text Moose and Juan that with Dad in town, I can't come.

Moose's text pops up: **No worries! Totally get it.**

Yup. Juan chimes in. **Another time.**

Somehow, I only feel worse.

Saturday morning doesn't help, especially when Dad wants to come to the Wallflower with me to meet Rae for tutoring. I try to remind him this is a solo project, but as always, he has an answer ready.

"I'll just get coffee and leave," he says. "The Sweep can't argue with that. Besides, don't you think it looks odd that you're here all alone? You want the project to view you as normal."

Normal doesn't describe me in the least, since another

education I'm getting at MCHS is about the quirks and habits of regular teenagers. No part of my life fits, and though that doesn't surprise me, I can't help wondering what I might be missing.

"I won't be normal if my dad keeps following me around," I tell him now. He grudgingly agrees, and I escape out the door alone.

I get my drink from Sahana, and the strong mint and coconut brew turns out to be surprisingly good. Listening to her imitate Ms. Timmult, who left minutes before I arrived, distracts me from the morning's annoyances, and I even let her talk me into buying one of the water bottles stamped with the Wallflower's signature daisy.

"Since you're a runner and all." She taps a bottle, her nails painted today in alternating pinks and purples, and throws me a knowing glance. "Besides, Rae has one. You two can match."

My cheeks warm, which makes Sahana smirk, and we talk about school until Rae walks in. She compliments my new bottle, and when Sahana winks at me, I can't help grinning.

"Are you sure?" Rae asks as I pay for her mocha. "I can get it."

"You save me from McNally, and I'll buy all the coffee you want," I tell her. Dad makes enough as a freelance photographer—he's actually quite good at his work—that we've never had to worry. The money he gave me for food easily covers my peanut butter sandwiches and cereal, leaving plenty for coffee, milkshakes, and movies.

Project costs, I would say if he asks.

"It was nice meeting your dad yesterday." Rae dumps her

textbook on the table. "How is it having him home?"

"It's all right." I don't mention how my shoulders ache from the tension that's been building in them since he arrived. "Have to clean up more."

She laughs, and we pore over the latest math lesson, making it through the examples and starting the weekend homework. Halfway through, Rae glances at her watch and groans.

"I need to get to work," she tells me, so we pack up and wave goodbye to Sahana. I walk Rae to the bakery, and she disappears through the door as a familiar SUV passes.

Dad sits behind the wheel.

He doesn't do anything without deliberation, which means it's no coincidence he's cruising down this street right now. Whatever victory I felt after convincing him to let me go to the Wallflower alone vanishes in a sharp burst. He never entered the shop while Rae and I were inside, but he must have been close.

I hurry to my own car and drive home, hot annoyance buzzing through me the entire way, and nearly run up the curb as I slam to a stop. At least Mr. Garrett isn't outside to criticize my driving. Dad hasn't returned, so I storm into the shack and begin to pace. An hour passes, and the only answer I get from the text I send is an infuriating **Be home soon.**

By the time he opens the door, I've nearly worn a path in the floor. "Where were you?" I demand even before he steps inside. "I saw you drive by the Wallflower. Were you watching me?"

He pauses in the doorway, surprise clear on his face. "I'm your mentor, Matthew. I won't interfere, but I can still check how you're doing. Besides, I'm supposed to live here, remember? I need to be seen around town." Dad's tone is even. Calm. "The project appears to trust you, which is excellent. Did you notice any changes today?"

"No!" At least he's not trying to hide the fact he was spying on me. "We just did math. That's all!"

"Yes, she seems very pleasant. Polite as well."

There's something in his tone, a glint in his eye, that makes me stop. "How would you—"

He steps inside, and my heart drops at the white bakery bag in his hand, a black boat stamped in its center. "Don't be fooled though, Matthew." He opens the bag and offers me a cookie. "Even the Marked can fake a pretty smile."

The rest of the day passes with strained conversation and stilted silence. Dad takes me to lunch at a barbecue place, where half the town can see us, and drives me home past the Winters' house. We go to dinner at the Pit Stop, and Dad pauses at the blue symbol the MC tagger left on its steps.

"Have you noticed these around town?" he asks.

"Someone's bored," I suggest. He frowns, taking in the drawing, but lets it go as the hostess motions us to our table. I wave to a few of my classmates who are dining with their families, and Dad nods approvingly.

"Good," he says quietly as we open our menus. "You're fitting in well."

His words kill my appetite, and the food that smelled so good when we first entered now turns my stomach sour. I order anyway, but I can't even finish my meal.

"What are you doing tomorrow?" I ask when we drive home at last. "I should probably focus on the project, so . . ."

"Your notebook mentioned her house was empty last Sunday morning." Dad drums his fingers on the steering wheel. "Where do you think they went?"

Any hope we could spend tomorrow separately fizzles. My surveillance last Sunday had passed without anything of interest, though their car had been missing from the driveway most of the morning. I arrived at their house too late to see them leave, but one guess makes most sense.

"Church?" I suggest, and Dad grunts in agreement.

Which means tomorrow, we're going as well.

CHAPTER

14

Sunday morning dawns bright and cheery, though the beginning of fall crisps the air. A church bell chimes through the shack's open window, its soft peal drifting over from a few blocks away. Service begins in fifteen minutes.

Dad and I pull on our jackets and start out on the short walk. I kick through the leaves of red and gold decorating the sidewalk, and the quiet of the street settles over me. Mills Creek may not be the most exciting place, but there's something special about the little neighborhood. It's like if someone loses a wallet here, everyone will do their best to get it back to the owner with the cash still inside.

I hope it still feels that way when I leave.

A block from the church, Mrs. Winter's white sedan passes. Rae sits in the passenger seat, and Cady's head bobs in back. The turn signal blinks, and the car swings into the parking lot beside the chapel.

Looks like we guessed right.

I slow my steps, dropping to one knee to fiddle with an already knotted shoelace, and Dad stops beside me to wait. Mrs. Winter and Cady rush around the corner and disappear through the ornate doors as the music begins.

Dad straightens his tie. "Where's the project?"

"I'm not sure." I can't see the parking lot from where we stand, but Rae must be close. "Why don't you go ahead, and I'll find her?"

He hesitates. "I'll come with you."

Either he's completely oblivious to the hints I keep dropping, or he just doesn't care.

"No, go inside. She's more likely to talk to me if you're not around anyway." Without waiting for an answer, I hurry toward the parking lot, leaving him to enter the church alone.

The lot is empty except for a young couple steering their toddler toward the church doors, and I crane my neck to see past windshields and bumpers. The white car sits near the back, empty. A wooden fence marks the end of the lot, and a gravelly path leads through its opening to rows of marble stones. Some lie flat while others stand, each carved with a name and date.

A graveyard.

The smell of recently cut grass lingers in the groomed plot, and newer slabs shine with a polished gleam. Most of the flowers brought by family and friends have begun to wilt, but a bouquet of red carnations stands tall. Rae huddles next to it, a ball of misery beside a rectangular patch of sod outlined by an inch of dirt. The grave is so fresh it doesn't even have a stone.

I shouldn't be here. Putting in an appearance at church is one thing, but invading this moment seems horribly wrong. I back away, right into the car behind me.

Its alarm blares, and Rae looks up.

Tears dampen her cheeks, though she hurries to wipe them away. I should leave and let her be alone with her grief, but the sorrow on her face catches me like quicksand. When she beckons, there's nothing to do but walk through the gate and join her.

"I'm sorry." At least I don't have to pretend right now. "I saw you drive by and when you didn't come inside . . . I didn't mean to interrupt. I'll leave—"

"It's fine, Matt." Her smile wobbles, but she pats the grass beside her. "I stay out here while Mom and Cady go to the service."

I lower myself carefully, trying not to think about Dad waiting inside. "How come?"

Her gaze drifts to the grave in front of her, where "Timothy Winter" is typed on stiff paper tucked inside the temporary plastic holder staked in the ground. "Because it feels wrong now. To believe in something that let Dad—" She swallows hard. "This is Mom's compromise. I have to come with them, but I can wait out here."

She stares at her father's name, her chin trembling, and a weight settles in my chest. Either I'm a better actor than I used to be, or something else is happening. My mind scrambles for a response, for something to say that might ease the grief pouring off her, but nothing comes. I'm not Sahana or Moose or Juan. I don't know how to chase away her sadness.

"I forgot this morning." Rae's voice cracks, and she hugs herself tightly. "I heard Mom moving around the kitchen and thought it was Dad making waffles like he used to. Then I remembered."

Each word cuts deeper, but all I can manage is a feeble "I'm sorry."

She sighs, rubbing her cheeks with both palms. "No, I am. You can go. You're missing the service."

The offer of escape looms, a chance to slip away and corral the feelings prickling through me. They're too genuine, too honest for a project. Dad would order me inside before they spill out, tumbling into the open for Rae to see. He would walk away right now and leave those tears trembling in her eyes.

But I can't.

"I'll stay," I tell her.

She adjusts the flowers beside her father's grave. "Can I ask you a question?"

It's my job to ask the questions. Then again, if I were really doing my job, I'd be watching her for signs of the Mark instead of noticing the light dusting of freckles across her cheeks. "Sure."

"You said you moved here with your dad." She tilts her head at me. "What about your mom?"

She's not the first person to wonder, and I give my usual response. "She died when I was two."

"What happened?" Rae asks softly.

Most people say, "I'm sorry" and change the subject quickly, since dead parents are apparently a taboo topic. When you're sitting in front of your own father's grave, however, I suppose nothing's off limits. There's a long silence as I try to figure out how to avoid answering. It's one thing to share little truths about myself, like my favorite color or that I hate tuna fish, but the stories that matter need to stay locked behind strong walls. This project is hard enough already.

Rae waits quietly, and my walls crack.

"We were camping in the mountains." Dad's memories sound strange coming out of my mouth, and I glance over my shoulder to make certain he's not striding toward me. "Mom went to collect firewood, and there was an earthquake. The rocks started coming down. Dad and I were okay by the tent, but she was right under them." I swallow hard. "It's stupid. I don't even remember her. It's just . . ."

How do you explain the gaping void left by a person you never really knew? I used to wonder what she would have been like, especially when other kids passed by with their mothers. Something about the closeness they shared—the smiles and hugs and silent exchanges—seemed almost magical, but Dad caught me watching once and the sadness on his face made me careful to never stare again. I learned pretty quickly not to talk about her, and since she didn't have any relatives Dad was close to, she simply faded away.

But I never stopped thinking about her.

Dad might claim her in memories and photos, but she lives in me. I see her in the parts of me that aren't him, in my brown hair that's halfway between his blond and her black, in my eyes and chin and even in the way I prefer the outdoors to being inside, since Dad once told me she dragged him on hikes and camping trips every weekend. Maybe she watched the clouds too, searching for funny shapes that shifted with the winds, or she might have agreed that horror stories were completely unnecessary since life itself could be scary enough. Certainly my life is, though that only changed after she died.

How different would it be if she had lived?

"It's not stupid." Rae's voice pulls me from the questions swirling through my head, the what-ifs and might-have-beens, and she slides her hand into mine like an anchor I didn't know I needed. "It doesn't matter if you remember. She's your mom."

Something in her voice says she really does understand, and that thorny ball of loss shrinks a little.

"Do you think it will ever stop?" She stares at her father's grave, eyes shiny with unshed tears. "All the hurting and crying and being sad? Sometimes I hope so, and then I hate myself for even thinking that. It would mean I don't care anymore. That it doesn't matter he's gone."

The misery in her voice drowns me, and no easy answer comes. Dad's teachings never prepared me for this, because any response to her question isn't something I can fake.

This needs to be real.

"I don't think it will mean you don't care. You'll always care." The words scrape out of a place that's supposed to be just for me. "It's like a really deep cut. Right now, it's new and bleeds every time you touch it. But even when it heals and doesn't hurt so much, the scar is still there. You love him. And he loved you. That will never change."

Tears slide down her cheeks, but she nods like something

I said made sense. "Sorry to unload on you. It's just everyone else is being so careful, like they're holding their breath until I go back to normal. You don't know what normal is. I can just be me. No pretending."

At least that makes one of us.

With a soft sigh, she scoots closer and rests her head on my shoulder. No girl has ever done that, and I'm caught between how much I like the feel of her against me and panic at the thought of Dad walking out and finding us like this. I glance toward the fence, and it's like diving into a bucket of ice as Dad disappears inside the church through an open side door.

How much did he hear?

My heart thuds, but Rae's soft hair brushes my cheek with a soothing touch. She fits against my side like she belongs there, and the sun breaks through the clouds with enough warmth that I can shrug out of my jacket before sliding an arm around her. A peaceful quiet settles, broken only by the calls of nearby birds and the low notes of the organ.

Maybe I'll tell Dad I saw an opportunity. He should appreciate that.

Neither of us moves until people begin streaming out the doors. Service is over, which means Dad is on his way. I drop my arm as Rae climbs to her feet, leaving an emptiness beside me.

"Thanks for listening," she says.

"Same to you," I tell her, and I mean it.

She straightens her father's flowers one last time, and I follow her to the parking lot. We reach the Winters' car as her mom and Cady approach from the opposite direction.

Dad trails a few feet behind.

"Hey, Mom." Rae gestures to me. "Remember Matt?"

"I do." Mrs. Winter's warm smile melts the sorrow that drifted out of the graveyard with us. "It's nice to see you again."

"You too." She still wears her wedding ring. "And you're Cady, right?"

Cady gives a short nod and murmurs hello before scrambling inside the car. Dad steps forward to take her place.

"There you are, Matthew," he says, and my shoulders automatically tense. I want to hustle Rae and her mother away, but it's too late.

"Hi, Mr. Watts," Rae says, and introduces her mother. "Sorry for making Matt miss the service. He was keeping me company."

"Then it was for a good reason," Dad tells her, and his gentle smile makes my insides curdle. We say goodbye, and I pretend not to notice how all their heads turn toward the graveyard before they drive away.

"You two seemed cozy sitting together, Matthew," Dad says as we start for home. "I assume this is all for the project?"

"Of course." I answer in the same reasonable tone, as if we were discussing what to have for dinner. "We're becoming friends. I mean, she sees me as a friend."

Dad eyes me. "It looked to me like you were more than friends."

"This was your idea in the beginning, remember?" I ignore the bitterness creeping up my throat. "It was a good one."

He nods slowly. "What did you talk about?"

"Just her dad." Hopefully, he hadn't been near enough to hear the conversation. "What he was like, how much she misses him. You saw her—she was really upset."

He asks a few more questions, searching for any trace of the Mark, but I have only normal and natural grief to share. It's not until the afternoon, when Dad insists on going for a drive, that I realize my mistake.

"We'll stop by the bakery," he says, opening the car door. "Since the project was so upset, it makes sense you wanted to check on her."

"No!" I shake my head hard. "I just saw her. It'll be too much."

"You need to move faster," Dad reminds me. "Having competition compresses your timeline. Get in."

I don't move. "I'm going to scare her off. And you're not supposed to interfere, remember?"

"Matthew, it's a bakery. People go there all the time."

"I don't," I snap. "It'll look weird, okay? Like I'm stalking her or something. It's my project, and I'm saying the pacing is wrong. We're not going."

We glare at each other over the hood, my gaze locked with his. For all our time together, through the projects and burnings and everyday life, we've never argued like this. Even when we disagreed, his words always won over mine without much effort.

This time, I don't back down.

"Hey, Matt!"

Toshi leans out of the driver's window of an old brown van pulling up behind us. I had been so focused on Dad I hadn't noticed him turn down our street, but the sight of him makes my already clenched jaw tighten even more.

Right on cue, Dad's smile slides into place.

"You forgot this." Toshi holds out the jacket I left at the graveyard. "I was going to give it to you at school, but I was driving by and saw you out here." He glances at Dad. "Hope I'm not interrupting."

My arm sticks to my side, but I force it up to take the jacket. "You're not. Thanks. How'd you know it was mine?"

He shrugs. "I was picking my mom up from church this morning. She doesn't like to drive."

I hadn't seen him in the lot, but then again, I didn't look. My skin prickles as Toshi flashes another smile. "I'd better go. See you tomorrow?"

I stutter an agreement. He pulls away and disappears around the corner, and Dad finally exhales.

"Matthew," he says, "you know what this means."

Has Toshi figured out we're both here for the same reason? "If he was watching us, he didn't see anything strange," I point out. "There wasn't any sign of the Mark."

"Not this time." Dad frowns. "Let's go to the bakery. I wouldn't be surprised if Toshi ends up there as well."

Of course he brought it back to this. "No! I'll see her tomorrow, okay? That's soon enough, and it's my call. Not yours."

An objection brews on Dad's face, but I cross my arms and step away from the car. At last, he sighs.

"Fine," he says. "Let's just drive. We won't go into the bakery, all right?"

I agree, and though he coasts down every street in Mills Creek, I think he's doing it more to pass time than to research the project. We drive by Charon's twice, but true to his word, he doesn't slow as we pass. We stop at the grocery store so Dad can load my fridge with food, and it's a relief when he says he needs to leave that afternoon.

"Should I visit you sometime?" I ask as he loads his suitcase into the car. "So your project can meet me?"

Dad pauses. "I haven't told him about you."

That makes sense, since explaining why he left his son three hours away in a stranger's backyard would raise more questions than we want. Still, the fact he edited me out stings. "Guess I won't then."

Dad studies me, eyes watchful, and I do my best to shrug it off. Finally, he starts the engine. "I'll be by next weekend, all right?"

A groan almost slips out, but I catch it in time.

"Sure," I say, and shove my hands into my pockets as he drives away.

His absence makes it easier to breathe in the little shack, and I rearrange the furniture back to the way I like it. Dad had pulled the table farther into the corner, which admittedly is only a foot from where I had it since the place is so small, but it feels satisfying to put everything exactly where I want. I go to adjust the blanket and see an envelope full of cash lying on the pillow.

For new running shoes, Dad's neat printing says. *And food that is not cereal.*

Of course he noticed, since he notices everything. Guilt nips at me for arguing with him, but it's quickly balanced out by the conviction I made the right call. I toss the envelope onto the table, and it flips, revealing the "P.S." written on the back.

It's okay to miss Mom. I do too. But be careful.

You know how this ends.

CHAPTER

15

The routine of school and running and homework brings a new rhythm to my days, punctuated by drives past the Winters' house, updates to the red notebook, and nightly texting with my lunch group. The banter that happens during school apparently goes on through all hours, and the fact they've included me eases the loneliness of the shack. It's the one time I know the Sweep can't watch me—at least I don't think they've hacked my phone—and I can join in with Juan teasing Moose about his crush on Tyson, Moose shooting retorts back, and Rae and Sahana offering tips on the best ways to win a man's heart.

It's all ridiculous, and I love it.

Even the nightly phone calls with Dad have become a habit, though I'm careful to edit out all the parts he doesn't absolutely need to know. My updates on Rae provide the shallowest review of her activities, and it helps that no sign of the Mark has appeared since that shopping cart struck Haley. I'm still not convinced that wasn't a random event, though Dad refuses to even listen to my argument. He's adamant I accelerate the timeline, but I tell him without more proof, there's nothing to judge.

"If I'm not seeing anything, neither is Toshi," I remind him each time, and he reluctantly lets it go.

I don't mention how I aced my presentation in biology, giving Moose's grade a much-needed boost since he was my partner, or that Ms. O'Brien's class discussions have made English my favorite subject. Even math with McNally isn't so bad, since something about suffering through class with other terrified teens makes my old homeschooling with Dad feel lonely.

I don't tell him that either.

Friday morning, I fall into step with Rae as she hurries to her locker. "You just get here?" My watch shows two minutes before first period.

"It took forever to get Cady out the door." Rae rushes through her combination. "She's always late getting up, and I can't even get mad. Her eyes are so red when she comes out I know she's been crying. Mornings are just tough."

"Why don't I pick you up?" It's a great move for the project, which is what I'll write in the notebook, but the real reason lies far away from Lucifer. Rae's presence makes room for laughter and lightness, letting me slide into the comfort of being Matt Watts. "Then your mom can just focus on Cady."

It's the perfect delivery, even phrased so a "yes" from Rae would help Mrs. Winter. There's really no reason my palms start sweating.

"Are you sure?" She chews her lip. "Mom would probably appreciate it, but I live over on Maple. Isn't that out of your way?"

If only she knew how often I drove past her house. "Just a few blocks. I don't mind."

Her face lights up. "Okay! I promise not to be late. And I'll help with gas."

A smile breaks over me. "Don't worry about gas. I have to drive here anyway. I can take you home too if you want."

Rae shakes her head. "Mom gets me on her way back from work, so it's easy. But thanks."

She tells me her address and I nod along, like it isn't already seared into my brain, and the rest of the morning passes quickly. I grab my sandwich from my locker and meet the others in the courtyard, where Moose is busy poking Sahana with Juan's ruler.

"You."

Poke.

"Are."

Poke.

"So."

Poke.

"*Bor—ing!*" he sings out.

Sahana snatches the ruler and whacks his arm. "I'm working! Not everything stops for a football game, okay?"

Moose sticks his nose in the air. "Rae's going. *She* took the time off."

"She only works weekends!" Sahana raises the ruler again, and Moose throws his hands up.

"Fine! I surrender." His eyes catch mine. "Matt's in! You'll go, won't you?"

"Go where?" I settle on the grass between him and Rae.

"The football game tonight! You know, those guys in helmets

who are always knocking each other over on the field?"

"I don't know." My evening currently consists of writing the weekly report for the Sweep and fielding Dad's phone call, but if Rae's got other plans, maybe I do too. "I'm not really into football."

"Where's your school spirit?" Juan scolds, snatching his ruler from Sahana. "We're playing Lancaster. They'll kick our butts all over the field—they won the division last year—but everyone will be there. Moose can stare at Tyson all night!"

Moose smacks him on the back of his head. "I appreciate football. And Tyson is an excellent wide receiver."

"He is, but we're still going to get crushed." Rae turns to me. "It'll be fun though. You should come."

Mrs. Polly used to scold me for never going out with people my age, and I can almost see her shooing me out the door.

"All right," I tell them. "Count me in."

Rae waits in front of her house when I pull up that evening. The game won't start for another hour, but we're meeting Juan and Moose for pizza first. I already texted Dad that I'll be out late, and his response made the night even better.

Won't be able to come this weekend. Busy with my project. You okay?

Yes, I sent back, and the smile is still on my face when Rae gets in. Mrs. Winter and Cady call goodbye as they head out for their own special night of Chinese food and a movie, and heavy traffic downtown signals a busy Friday night for Mills Creek.

I peer through the windshield at a crowded entrance. "Is that the restaurant?"

"Yup. Look for street parking." Rae scans the curb. "Lot's going to be full."

We park a few blocks away and walk back. People dressed in our school colors spill out the doorway, and we weave through them to a bench where Juan and Moose sit.

"How long's the wait?" asks Rae.

"An hour," Moose says.

She groans. "We'll miss the start of the game."

"Don't worry." Juan waves his phone in the air. "We took care of it."

I raise my eyebrows. "We're going to eat your phone?"

"Nope. We called for takeout when we got here." He glances at his watch. "Fifteen more minutes, and we'll have hot pizza in our hands. Hope pepperoni and sausage is okay."

"We can take it to the park," Moose adds.

He and I volunteer to run to the grocery store down the block for drinks, and by the time we get back, our pizza is ready. We pile into my car since Juan's mom dropped Moose and him off, and they direct me to the park's picnic area. The pizza is cheesy and delicious, and we talk about school and running and the new movie Moose insists I watch with him tomorrow, since Juan and Rae will be busy. Suddenly, I'm glad I came.

"What's your real name?" I ask Moose, reaching for another slice.

Juan hammers Moose's shoulder. "He is officially Mitchell Collins. But to us, he will henceforth be a moose."

"One little mistake," Moose says, shaking his head, "and you're never allowed to forget."

Rae starts laughing. "You know those trails around here? Coach sent us running on them freshman year. The guys were ahead, and all of a sudden, there's this yell. More like a screech, really. We catch up, and Moose is making antlers with his fingers—"

"He thinks he's seen a moose. In the middle of Mills Creek." Juan snorts. "So we go after it, and know what we find? A guy with one of those beer hats. Ever seen one? You stick a can on each side, and there are straws coming out so you can drink. That's what our boy here saw."

Moose cuts in. "Okay, first of all, I didn't say it *was* a moose. I said it *looked like* a moose. Second, that was a very large man. And shaggy! Remember his beard? It was an honest mistake."

By now, I'm laughing so hard my stomach hurts. The sun's setting and the sky is pink and we're jostling each other and it hits me: If this is what normal life is like—life without the Mark and the Sweep and the burnings—maybe it's not so bad.

Maybe this is the life I want.

"You okay?" Rae squeezes my arm. "You got this funny look all of a sudden."

"Yeah. Just thinking." I take a long drink of soda so I don't have to talk. The others finish the pizza with Rae and Juan still laughing at Moose, who cheerfully brushes them off. Across the park, the trees are thicker, and in there somewhere is the network of trails where Moose earned his name.

They're also private, with branches that shield whatever happens inside.

I hate myself for noticing.

Bright lights illuminate the freshly chalked grass of the MCHS football field, and people cram into the area just past the entrance, lining up for concessions and clustering in noisy groups. Lancaster students mingle as well, calling to friends and flaunting pom-poms with red and white streamers. Juan, Rae, and I find a spot beside the field to wait for Moose, who's in line for nachos since he's hungry again, and the blare of the band's trumpets brings a cheer from the stands. The air hums with anticipation, the thrill of darkness settling over a Friday night game. Rae catches my eye and grins.

"What do you think?" she yells, as the band launches into another song.

"I think I like football!" I holler back, and she bursts out laughing.

If Mrs. Polly could see me now.

The teams warm up on the field, but nobody is watching them. Everyone's eyes are on our school spirit squad. Those twelve teenagers have more energy than the entire crowd, and the way they toss their smallest member into the air—a genius from my biology class, who throws in a flip and a 500-watt grin while she's about twenty feet off the ground— and then catch her without missing a beat makes me reconsider all the stereotypes I've read about cheerleaders.

"That's impressive," I tell Juan, who's yelling along with them. "You should have done that instead of cross country."

He snorts. "Like they would be able to throw me. Even worse, I'd be expected to catch someone. Give me the Monster any day."

Rae jabs him. "I'm going to remind everyone you said that. Maybe Coach can—"

She stumbles forward suddenly with a cry, as if shoved from behind. I catch her before she falls, and a girl's voice cuts in.

"Oops. Sorry." Haley stands in Rae's place, a sneer on her face and several girls in Lancaster colors surrounding her. "Guess you were in my way. Again."

"What the hell is your problem?" Rae snaps.

"Oh, my." Haley shakes her head, prompting laughter from the other girls. "Someone is such a sore loser. Where's the Wallflower bitch? I bet she knows all about—"

"Oof!" Moose bumps into her, his hands full of food. Haley turns, a retort forming on her lips, but it turns into a shriek as he trips and dumps his entire plate of nachos onto her gleaming white sneakers.

Juan smirks. "Well, that's a shame."

"You said it." Moose looks mournfully at his empty plate. "I didn't even get to eat any."

Haley explodes, her face reddening as she swipes at the cheese dripping down her ankles. "Watch where you're going!"

Rae smiles at her sweetly. "I think he did."

"Asshole!" Haley snarls before pushing Moose aside and

storming away, her friends following as she heads for the rest-rooms and the paper towels inside.

At least the pleased expression on Moose's face makes it clear I don't have to wonder about the Mark this time. Rae beams at him.

"Thank you," she tells him. "That was incredibly awesome."

"My pleasure." His shoulders are thrown back, and he looks about two inches taller than usual. "Please tell Sahana I de-fended her honor."

"I will," Juan promises. "Want more food? My treat. You've earned it."

We get Moose more nachos, and the whistle blows as we make our way into the stands. Players grunt and yell and fall down, and Moose, Juan, and Rae do their best to explain the rules of the game. I have no idea what constitutes a penalty, since pretty much everything out there looks like it should be illegal, but I join in cheering when Tyson makes a spectacular catch. His opportunities are limited, however, since the Lancaster players usually tackle our quarterback before he can throw the ball.

Mrs. Polly was right. This is the best night I've had since arriving in Mills Creek.

The clock is counting down to halftime when I see Haley shoving her way through the stands, her friends in tow. The Lancaster fans belong on the opposite side of the field, and sev-eral MCHS students cast curious looks her way as she storms up the bleacher steps. Her glare locks on Moose and Rae, and the enormous cup in her hand leaves little question about her intent.

"Uh-oh," Juan mutters. "Somebody is angry."

Rae's eyes narrow. "She better not think she's just going to come over here and dump that on us."

"Hey, don't—" I say as Rae starts toward them, but she shakes off the hand I put on her arm and steps past Moose, fists clenched.

Haley pauses several rows below us. I'm hoping she'll see Rae's expression and be smart enough to flee back to the Lancaster side, but she only scowls and picks up her pace. Water sloshes from her cup as she runs up the last few steps, and her foot lands on the scattered ice of someone's spilled soda. Her leg shoots out from under her, sending her pitching backward with a scream, and the cup goes flying as she tumbles into the girls behind her. A few of them go down like dominoes, and Haley turns a painful somersault before crashing to a halt at the bottom of the stairs.

I suck in a shallow breath, my chest tight as my gaze jumps between Haley and the puddle that sent her plummeting. The bleachers are made of metal, which can get slick when wet, but her foot had to land just right for a fall like that. Then again, her eyes had been shooting daggers at us as she rushed up those steps, so she wasn't looking where she was going. My gaze slides to Rae, her lips pressed together as she watches Haley.

Dad would already be reaching for his matches.

Haley doesn't move, her low moan rising through the sudden silence in our stands. Someone kneels next to her, and she slowly takes the offered hand, wincing as she wobbles to her feet. McNally appears, his face more pinched than usual, and directs a few students to help her to the first aid station intended for football players. The teachers attending the game pass through the crowd, trying to figure out what happened, and my heart skips a little as Ms. Timmult leans over to ask if we saw anything.

"She just slipped." Rae points to the puddle. "No one touched her."

Ms. Timmult frowns. "People really do need to clean up after themselves." We agree, and she returns to her seat on the far side without ever looking back.

"I hope she's not hurt too badly." Rae frowns at where Haley sits on the mat by the school trainer, who presses an ice pack to her head. "She totally deserved it, but that fall could have broken something."

"She seems okay," Juan says. "At least she'll leave you alone now."

"For tonight, at least," Moose adds.

The next minutes reveal nothing more. Haley stays beside the trainer, her shoulders rounded in a subdued posture, and the game continues. Rae cheers along with the spirit squad, the grin back on her face without a trace of guilt or remorse, and I have no idea if I just witnessed an unfortunate accident or the work of the Marked. Moose and Juan start making plans for a postgame visit to the Pit Stop, and I'm trying to fake enthusiasm for it when my phone buzzes with a text from Dad.

Have you checked the house?

The noise of the crowd drops away, drowned out by a new

ringing in my ears. Searching the project's home is a critical part of our job, since early changes often manifest there—torn pictures, ripped cushions, diary entries that reveal a twisted perspective. People show far more of their true selves when they think others aren't looking, though I still wonder if Mrs. Polly's shattered plates resulted from her battle with the Mark or mere clumsiness.

If I tell Dad I haven't searched the Winters' house, he won't be happy. He'd probably do it himself if he didn't think the Sweep would find out. I need to get there soon, and one time I can be certain no one is home is right now.

Putting a hand on my stomach, I hunch down and grimace, the expression coming easily when I think of combing through Rae's room. "Hey, you guys feeling okay? My stomach hurts all of a sudden."

"Yes." Concern knits Rae's forehead. "What's wrong?"

I take a few deep breaths for the benefit of anyone watching. "Not sure. Might be the pizza."

Moose crouches next to me. "Want me to call someone?"

"No." I straighten, steadying myself with a hand on his shoulder. "I think I'll just go home. Sorry I can't drive you—"

"Hey, guys!" Toshi pops up behind Juan, his MCHS cap perched at a jaunty angle and a bucket of popcorn in his hands. "Matt, you all right? You look like you're going to hurl."

"He's not feeling well," Rae says. "Go home, Matt, and sleep in tomorrow. We'll catch up on math next week, okay?"

My Saturday tutoring with Rae. Another casualty of tonight's work.

"You sure you can drive?" Juan asks. "Not dizzy or anything?"

"Yeah. Just need to lie down." I ease past them to the steps. "Enjoy the game." I give a strained smile and start toward the parking lot. A final glance back shows Toshi settling in beside Rae, his grin wide as he offers her popcorn.

The pain in my stomach turns real. I want to make an immediate recovery and kick him down the bleachers, since a trip to the first aid station alongside Haley would keep him away from Rae. If he saw the same thing I did tonight, he just moved a step closer to ending this project.

Still, a burning requires planning. He won't set the fire yet.

He'll try to get closer to her, though. Gain her trust. My feet beg to turn back, to put myself between him and Rae, but I grit my teeth and keep going.

I have work to do.

CHAPTER

16

Quiet fills the streets beyond the high school. A few cars roll lazily past, and darkness blooms from the hills surrounding town. I park a block from the Winters' house and pull on the baseball cap and gloves I keep under my seat. My tools slip easily into my pocket, and I step out and check the road.

Nothing moves. If a Sweeper is watching, he or she keeps to the shadows, which is fine with me. A search of the project's house will be expected and appropriate, just another step closer to passing this test.

Though I try not to think about the ending.

A quick walk brings me to the Winters' front steps. Their car is missing from the driveway, which means Mrs. Winter and Cady must still be at their movie. I can't be seen fumbling at the lock, so I hurry instead through the gate leading to the backyard. Tomato plants grow along the edge of a small lawn, and a picnic table sits in the center of a concrete patio. The barbecue near the side looks clean but well used. Maybe Mrs. Winter cooks with it.

Or maybe it just stands untouched, like a shrine to the cookouts their family once shared.

Behind the patio is a sliding glass door. A simple lever keeps it shut, and I pry it open in seconds and step into a cheerful kitchen with yellow curtains. The lights have been dimmed to a soft glow, and colorful magnets attach pictures and reminders to the refrigerator, a stark contrast to the blank whiteness featured on every refrigerator Dad and I have ever shared. The counter holds a bowl of fruit and a rack full of clean dishes, and four mugs sit on a decorative shelf over a coffeemaker. A square table fills the eating nook near the front window, with a chair pushed up to each side.

Four mugs. Four chairs.

Memories must haunt every meal.

The doorway to the right brings me to the front entryway and a cozy living room, with a comfortable couch and books scattered across a coffee table. Framed photos perch on the fireplace mantle, one of which shows a younger Rae and Cady with their arms wrapped around each other and a wide gap where Cady's two front teeth should be. More photos of the Winters and smiling strangers decorate the top of an upright piano, and I flip through the envelopes stacked on the narrow console table beside the door. They're mostly bills, and the one marked OVER-DUE from Mills Creek Community Hospital makes me cringe.

Death is expensive.

I cross back to the kitchen and the darkened hallway on the other side. A small flashlight is tucked in my pocket, but I flick the switch on the wall, since nothing calls attention to a dark house like a bright spot moving around inside. It's smarter to just let neighbors assume someone came home early, especially with curtains blocking their view. I turn down the hall and start peering through doors. Linen closet. Bathroom. Mrs. Winter's room, judging from the large bed and the wedding photo of her and Mr. Winter on the dresser. Two doors face each other at the end of the hall, and the one on the right stands half open. Inside, Rae's backpack rests against a bed with a pale green quilt.

Stepping onto the soft beige carpet brings a rush of guilt at this invasion into a place that's supposed to be hers. But after Haley's fall tonight, I need answers.

The organized room reminds me of Rae's locker, with its carefully arranged bookcase and clean desk. The faint scent of her shampoo sweetens the air, and a plush beanbag occupies one corner beneath a standing lamp. Above her desk hangs a bulletin board covered with photos, and Sahana grins out from at least half of them.

My gaze falls on a picture at the top, and I draw closer for a better look. Mr. Winter sits beside Rae in one of the orange booths at the Pit Stop, and judging from her beaming face, it wasn't taken more than a few months ago. His arm curves around her shoulders, and both raise their milkshakes in a toast. The camera captured Mr. Winter looking not at its lens but at his daughter, eyes crinkling above his enormous grin, and love shines in every part of his expression.

The photograph feels too personal for my eyes, and I turn away and step toward a lone nightstand beside the bed. A clock and three books are stacked on top, and I'm careful not to knock them over as I open the drawer.

The inside holds an assortment of random objects: braided friendship bracelets; a journal that gets my heart thumping until I realize the last entry is over ten months old; and a stack of postcards from Moose, Juan, and Sahana, their dates ranging from several years ago to this past summer, sent from various places around the country. Maybe that's part of their group ritual—when someone travels, he or she sends mail to the others.

Would they write me postcards too?

I suppose I'll never know. It's not like I can leave a forwarding address.

The dresser in the corner holds only clothes, though I refuse to go digging through the top drawer's delicate materials that I've never seen outside of department stores. If she's hiding something in there, it can stay a secret. I scan the cross-country and track medals on top of the dresser—good grief, she's fast—but nothing screams of importance. Her calendar featuring black-and-white scenes from nature raises no alarms, her books reveal only a love of fantasy and biographies, and the world map on the wall signals an interest in travel, not plans for global destruction.

If the Mark is here, I don't see it.

I save her desk for last. The top is bare except for a pile of history handouts tagged with colorful Post-its, and a blue cup holds pens and sharpened pencils. Markers, scissors, a calculator, and paper fill one drawer, and another contains stationery and half-filled notebooks from old classes. The bottom drawer holds a book of paintings by famous artists, and I pick it up to find a pile of loose papers under it. I turn the top one over, and my breath hitches at the one line that repeats down the entire page.

I'm sorry.

The handwriting is small and tight, not Rae's usual flowing slant, but it's still hers. She pressed the pen down so hard I can feel the impression on the other side, and the edge of the paper is wrinkled, as if her fingers squeezed it too tightly.

A smudge mars one corner, like a dried teardrop.

The next paper is the same, and the next. Each holds more lines of apology, and the question of exactly what she's sorry for rises from every tortured page. I go through the entire stack, apologies written in blue and black and green ink, and find a half-empty jar of dark blue paint lying at the bottom of the drawer.

The same color used by the MC tagger.

A shiver runs through me. Maybe this is why she's not sleeping at night.

I'll think about that later. Right now, it's time to go.

I snap a few photos, tuck the papers back where I found them, and take a final look around the room. Everything appears in place, and I turn off the lights as I make my way back to the kitchen and out the sliding door. The street stays empty as I reach my car, and eleven minutes later, I'm inside the shack without even an encounter with Mr. Garrett.

Success. If you can call it that.

Pulling out the red notebook, I update it with my findings, beginning with the football game and Haley's fall, which replays in my mind as I write. I outline the search of the house next, but my pen freezes at the description of the pages of apology and the blue paint.

When Dad reads this, he'll see nothing but the Mark.

I shove the notebook across the table as my phone lights up with a message from Moose: **got our butts kicked 42-3 heading to the Pit hope ur better.** I should text him tomorrow that I can't see the movie with him, since it will look odd if I make a complete recovery so quickly, and the reminder that I'll miss tutoring with Rae makes the night even worse.

Flopping onto the mattress, I try not to think of her heading to the Pit Stop with Moose, Juan, and no doubt Toshi, who would have offered them all a ride. When they finish, Juan's mom will pick him up, along with Moose. Rae will be alone in the car with Toshi, who will take full advantage of the drive home. He'll draw her into conversation, make her laugh, take his time pulling up to her house and turning off the engine.

And then . . .

Anger roars over me like a raging fire, and my fist shoots out, punching right through the shack's thin plywood wall. The splintered wood catches at my knuckles, leaving the skin scraped and bloody, and the sharp pain is all that stops me from doing it again. Fury still pulses through me, and Toshi's not its only target.

I hate this life. The projects. These choices.

It should be like flipping a switch—an immediate change from friendly Matt Watts, who jokes and laughs with his friends, into Dad's cold and calculating Matthew Watts of the Second Sweep, here to uncover the Mark and burn Rae Winter. Yet each passing day makes it harder to shift between the two, especially when I'm starting to like only one.

And it's not the one that got me sent here in the first place.

CHAPTER

17

I text Moose the next morning. **Still not feeling great. Gotta stay home sorry**

He sends a sympathetic response and promises to wait to see the movie he talked me into watching. I wouldn't mind missing the film, but his words make me smile.

It's almost like I have a real friend.

Juan texts as well—**how u feeling?**—and my morning would be far better with one of Sahana's coffee creations. Rae might be with her at the Wallflower right now, unless she stayed home for a lazy morning with her mother and sister.

Either of those beats sitting alone in this shack.

My watch shows just past ten when I finish the weekly report. I flip through the red notebook, thinking a quick drive past the Winters' house couldn't hurt, and someone knocks on my door.

I must have offended Mr. Garrett. Biting back a groan, I open it.

"Hey," Rae says. "How are you feeling?"

A bag dangles from her hand, and judging from her clothes and the sweat beading on her forehead, she either just finished a run or is halfway through. Behind her, Toshi bounces on his toes.

"You look all right." He grins. "Just surprised."

"I'm good!" I sputter. "Well, better. What are you doing here?"

"I was coming to see you and ran into Toshi," Rae says. "He came along to say hi."

I glance at him. "You were just hanging around?"

"Nope." He jogs in place. "Doing Coach's run."

His easy answer infuriates me. He wears his usual workout gear, though he looks more like he's been out for a leisurely stroll than someone who's been exercising, and the fact he just happened to meet Rae can't be coincidence. I want to give him a hard shake that rattles the truth right out of his lying mouth, but all I can do is nod.

"Want to come in?" I ask Rae.

"Please." She glances at the house, where Mr. Garrett watches from the window. "I rang his doorbell first since I didn't want to just come back here, but he's kind of creeping me out."

"Yeah. He's like that." I move aside to let them enter. The shack looks about a step above a prison cell, but at least it's clean.

The red notebook lies closed on the table, my laptop open beside it.

Rae sets her bag beside the notebook and taps the bright cover. "Doing homework?"

"Just finished." I grab it and shove it deep into my backpack as my other hand slams the laptop shut. "Sorry I couldn't drive you to the Pit Stop after the game."

"Don't worry about it," she says. "Toshi didn't mind."

The anger from last night flares up as Toshi starts laughing. "That drive home took forever. I didn't think the human body could hold so much liquid."

I shoot a questioning look at Rae. "Moose and Juan had a lemonade drinking contest at the Pit," she explains. "Toshi had to stop three times on the way to my house to let them out."

"Then twice more on the way to Juan's, and Moose needed one more after that," Toshi adds. "Kind of gives a whole new meaning to Pit Stop, you know?"

The smile spreading across my face has nothing to do with Moose and Juan squirming in their seats. "Who won?"

"Juan, but I think he learned his lesson. He almost popped." Rae pulls two cans of chicken soup from her bag. "Here. They're not exactly homemade, but Mom thought they might be good since your dad's out of town. Does that stove work?"

"Sometimes." I turn the knob, and it clicks a few times before a feeble blue flame appears. "It's fine once it gets going."

Rae looks unconvinced, but she doesn't argue. "I should go, or I'll be late for work."

"Me too. Well, not work, but I'm supposed to help my mom fix the fence in our backyard." Toshi glances at his watch. "Think I can count this as part of my running time?"

"Definitely," Rae says. She opens the door and nearly crashes into Mr. Garrett. "Oh! Hi. We're just leaving."

Ducking around him, she jogs out the gate, and Toshi hurries after her. Hopefully, they'll part ways quickly, with Rae rushing to get ready for Charon's and Toshi plodding home alone. I can't watch him, however, because Mr. Garrett still glowers at me from the cardboard mat.

"Not a party," I say quickly, gesturing to the chicken soup. "They were just dropping some stuff off."

His eyes flick around the shack. "Wanted to make sure everything was all right."

"It's fine," I say. "Haven't been feeling so well, that's all."

Something flashes in his eyes—either suspicion or concern, I can't be sure which—but then it vanishes and his hard stare returns. "Your dad around?"

"No. He's working." Though next time Dad shows up, maybe he can assure Mr. Garrett he's keeping an eye on me so my landlord will leave me alone. "I'm okay. Really."

"That so?" Mr. Garrett brushes past me as he storms inside. I'm trying to come up with an excuse for the new hole in the wall when he opens the cupboard in the kitchen. "No pot. How are you going to heat that soup? You even got a can opener?"

The same questions already crossed my mind, since my usual cereal and peanut butter sandwiches require neither a pot nor a can opener. "I can go to the grocery store. They have that stuff, right?"

"You're sick," he reminds me with a scowl. "You're supposed to be in bed."

He stomps out of the shack. I stay where I am, basking in the fact Rae brought me soup and wondering what to do about Toshi.

"Here." Mr. Garrett's back. He slaps a pot, ladle, and can opener onto the table. "Keep them. It's a wonder you haven't starved."

"Oh." I'm not sure what to say. "Thank you. I can get my own—"

"Loretta always bought extras." His mouth curves in the closest thing I've seen to a smile. "I've got others."

Then he's gone, sliding his hand across the oak's trunk before disappearing into his house.

Loretta must be the late Mrs. Garrett. Maybe when she was alive, Mr. Garrett wasn't the grump he is today.

I have hot soup for lunch and again for dinner. The canned noodles taste surprisingly good, though maybe that's because each spoonful reminds me of Rae. I text her Sunday afternoon that I'm feeling better and can pick her up tomorrow, and a smiley face pops up in response. It sends a grin over my own face until I see the red notebook still in my backpack. I haven't added Rae's visit, or the news that I'll be her ride to school.

Are both relevant to the project? Dad would say yes. They show my growing closeness to Rae, which means greater access and better insight. It's data.

The word sounds cold and impersonal. Which, as he would remind me, is what this project is supposed to be.

In the end, I compromise, skipping one but writing the other. Toshi or anyone watching might tell the Sweep both, but until I know for certain, some secrets are mine to keep.

Picking the project up tomorrow. 7:30 a.m.

CHAPTER

18

I pull up in front of Rae's house two minutes early the next morning. The front door opens, and Mrs. Winter appears wearing light green scrubs.

"Rae will be ready in a moment," she calls.

"I didn't know you were a doctor," I say, crossing the lawn.

She laughs. "Of animals. I'm a veterinarian, which is why all I can do when you're sick is send canned soup. Feeling better?"

"Yes, and the soup was delicious. Thank you."

"Any time," she says, as Rae appears behind her. "Got your homework, hon?"

"Yup." Rae plants a kiss on her cheek. "Good luck. She's still in bed."

Mrs. Winter sighs. "Don't worry about her. You have a good day, okay?"

"I will. Love you." Rae follows me to the car, and Mrs. Winter stays in the doorway, watching as we pull away from the curb.

"How's Cady doing?" I ask.

"Pretty much the same. Some days are better than others." Rae hugs her backpack to her chest. "It's just hard, especially right now."

"Why now?"

"Halloween's coming." Her face wilts, and she swallows hard. "Dad loved Halloween."

Nothing makes loss sting like a holiday. I keep my words gentle. "What did your family do?"

"We'd dress up. And then we'd go there." She points to a new orange banner hanging over the street.

I crane my neck for a better view as we pass under it. Wavy black letters spell HALLOWEEN SCREAM! along with JOIN US IF YOU DARE! 7:00 P.M. IN MILLS CREEK PARK. A white sticker, probably covering up dates from years past, shows next Friday.

"Most of the town goes. There's music, games, food—that sort of thing." Rae's voice breaks, and the pain creeping through each word coils something inside me so tightly it might snap. "We always did a family costume. Last year we went as s'mores. Mom and Dad were graham crackers, Cady was a chocolate bar, and I was a marshmallow. Totally silly, but Dad sewed them all himself. He always got into it."

She stares out the window at something I can't see. We pull into school in silence, and my car creaks to a stop.

Rae jumps out, shaking back her shoulders like she's brushing off our conversation. "Did you finish McNally's homework?"

We chat about classes on our way to her locker, and the day resumes its usual rhythm. From the chatter I hear in the halls, however, Rae isn't the only one thinking of Halloween.

"It's Moose's favorite day of the year." Juan grins wickedly as we meet for lunch. "He gets to wear a mask so no one knows who he is, which means Tyson might actually talk to him."

"Very funny." Moose snatches one of Juan's chips. "I'll have you know we talk every day. He's got Anderson's class right after me."

Juan smirks. "Is that why you're always late to French? Hanging around for your daily dose of Tyson Walsh?"

"No!" Moose shoots back, a little too quickly. "And you're lucky some of us have actually been planning for Halloween. I'm going to save you from your stupid sheet."

Juan raises his eyebrows. "What's wrong with my sheet? I'm a ghost."

"Every Halloween since you got here! But no more. This year"—Moose places his arms grandly around our shoulders—"we are the Kitchen Zombies."

Juan's eyebrows shoot up. "We are?"

"Yes!" Moose beams. "Now that Matt's here, we've got three. It fits."

"Are those special zombies?" I ask. "Or do they just live in a kitchen?"

Moose shakes his head sadly at me. "They're from a movie. You really need to get out more."

He pulls up a photo on his phone. The Kitchen Zombies look like your basic zombies—pale, decaying figures with bad teeth—except they're wearing chef hats and colorful aprons.

"It's hard to succeed in the food industry when you're undead," Moose says, "but they're trying."

"What do you think?" Juan points to the photo as Sahana and Rae join us. "Halloween costumes. Not my fault. Moose picked."

Sahana wrinkles her nose. "Lovely, and no thank you. We'll do something else. What are you dressing as?" she asks Rae, who hunches over her sandwich. I catch Sahana's eye, trying to send a telepathic reminder of past Halloweens, and it actually works, probably because she's been with Rae every year since they were little. Regret darkens her face, and she bites her lip. "I'm sorry."

"It's okay." Rae forces a smile. "You should totally dress up."

Sahana puts an arm around her. "We'll do something together that night, okay? Whatever you want."

"Us too," Juan adds. "Though I apologize in advance for our attire."

"We're Kitchen Zombies," Moose protests.

"That's what he meant," I tell him. "But don't worry. I'm sure Tyson will appreciate the effort."

"Really?" He whacks me with his backpack, and even Rae cracks a smile. "You too?"

I zombie-walk at him, moaning and swinging my arms, and Juan somehow gets sucked into our wrestling match. By the time McNally hollers across the courtyard to cut it out, I'm almost looking forward to Halloween.

We head to our separate classes when lunch ends, and any excitement fizzles as Rae drops her smile and leaves with shoulders sagging and eyes distant. Between her sister's overwhelming grief, the upcoming holiday, and the agonized lines of *I'm sorry* I still haven't figured out, the weight on her must be crushing.

If the Mark lurks inside, she won't have much energy to fight it.

When I come home from school Thursday afternoon, Dad's SUV is parked in front of Mr. Garrett's house. He told me on the phone last night he would come, but my body still tenses as I cross the yard and open the shack's door.

Only emptiness greets me.

He can't be at the Winters' house, since the late hour means they could arrive home any moment. The grocery store is too far away to walk, and I didn't see him out roaming the sidewalks. The minutes tick past, and I'm about to go for a drive—just a quick check past Rae's house—when his voice comes through the window. He's telling his story about a fishing trip that never actually happened, which means he's not alone. I plaster on a smile and open the door. His audience is none other than Mr. Garrett.

"Sounds wet," he says, when Dad pauses for a breath.

"Sure was!" Dad's eyes fall on me, and he brightens even more. I swear the man can outshine a light bulb when he wants. "Matthew! There you are. Thought you might have gone to dinner with your friends."

"Practice ran late." My fingers grip the doorknob. "When'd you get in?"

"About an hour ago. I got us some hamburgers," he says,

holding up a bag from the Pit Stop, "and then Allen here was nice enough to let me bore him with my stories. He claims you've been a good tenant. No wild parties so far."

Though I did have a visit from Rae and Toshi that never made it into the red notebook. My pulse jumps, but I keep my voice calm. "Just homework and stuff."

"That's it?" Dad's tone is teasing, but his eyes are as sharp as ever. "To be honest, I was a little worried. Hanging out all by yourself."

"He's been fine." Mr. Garrett shrugs. "I'll leave you to enjoy dinner." His gaze meets mine for the briefest of moments, and then he heads inside.

Looks like my landlord won't report me after all.

I hold back a sigh of relief as Dad puts a hand on my shoulder. "It's good to see you. Everything going well?"

"Yes." I duck free of his touch, and he follows me into the shack, nearly tripping over my backpack. The small space squeezes us together, and I retreat a few steps to the kitchen. "You don't need to check on me, you know. Shouldn't you stay with your own project?"

His eyebrows arch, and he sets the Pit Stop bag on the counter. "A seventeen-year-old boy living alone draws attention in a town like this. People notice. It's important they see me sometimes." The easy smile he held for Mr. Garrett falls away, replaced by that stern watchfulness. "Besides, your test is far more important than my project. Tell me about the search of the house."

"Again?" I busy myself with the hamburgers, and the crinkle

of paper fills the room. "There's nothing new. I told you every-thing on the phone."

Everything except what I found in Rae's drawer. I may not know what the pages and paint mean, but Dad won't hesitate to see them in the worst possible light.

More signs of the Mark. More reasons to burn.

"Are you sure?" he asks, and something in his tone sends a warning rippling up my spine.

I keep my eyes on the food. "I think so. Nothing too inter-esting in her room, and the house seemed normal. Why?"

Wordlessly, he opens the red notebook to a new entry and pushes it across the table. By the time I finish reading, my knuckles are white on the pages.

"What are you doing?" I demand. "You can't just go and search her home! If the Sweep finds out you're interfering, they'll fail me!"

"I went straight there when I arrived. I didn't even tell Kendrick I'd be in town, and there's no reason anyone would be watching an empty house." Dad's voice stays even. "Did you really miss that drawer? You didn't mention the writing or the paint."

He phrases it like a question, but the hard line of his jaw says he already knows the answer.

I lie anyway. "I guess I must have."

"Really?" He taps the page where he's drawn the graffiti we've seen around town, with its infinity symbol and the cross above. "Surely you've noticed the similarity between the street paintings and the Leviathan Cross. She's leaving Lucifer's sign all over town, Matthew, and the *I'm sorry* she wrote on those pages . . . she's feeling the change. And she can't stop it."

"You don't know that." The words jump out. "You're guessing."

"And you're *lying!*" His accusation blisters the room with unexpected fury, and I stumble back as he slams his palm against the flimsy table. "Matthew, you know better! You're letting the project get too close. You can't judge her correctly if you care about her!"

"I don't—"

"You do, and if I see it, the Sweep sees it as well. Have you forgotten everything I taught you?" His voice rises, a jarring break from his usual calm, and the panic radiating off him sweeps over me like a hurricane. "You need to pass this test!"

"Dad, I will! Okay? I'll pass it. I promise." Assurances pour from my mouth, though the horror the words send writhing through me nearly chokes them off. "I just need to make sure before—you know. I don't want to make a mistake."

He stares at me, his hands clenched like he's trying to hold back the fear still spilling across his face. When he speaks again, his expression is taut but composed, his usual stoicism almost believable.

"They are watching, Matthew. Kendrick is watching. You need to act before Toshi does, and you must do it soon." His shadowed eyes meet mine. "Or I will not be able to protect you."

CHAPTER

19

I'm exhausted when I arrive at school on Friday, since I spent most of last night huddled in my locked car, watching Rae's house in case she snuck out to wreak havoc on the world. The hours passed without her ever appearing, though every noise made me jump and I clutched my knife the entire time in case any Sweepers arrived to declare my test a failure and drag me away. No one came, and the terror brought about by Dad's panic receded to a dull worry by the time morning dawned, bringing a fresh realization.

He's rushing me.

Dad may have more experience, but I know the timing for a project just as well as he does. His impatience is a far cry from his usual careful approach, and I remember those early days with Ms. Rivera, when Kendrick urged Dad to act after an art critic who disparaged her work suffered an unfortunate bike accident that hospitalized him for a week. Dad stubbornly refused, even gathering reports of other accidents that happened on that same trail, and time had proven him right. It must be hard to be on the sidelines for the first time, especially with Toshi lurking so close, and a quick burning would end Dad's worries.

But we've never struck the match so early, and I won't start now.

I spend the day yawning through classes, sleepwalking through the monotony of lessons and hallways and homework, and my legs feel so heavy I barely make it to the end of the cross-country workout. For once, I don't need to fake my slow plod behind Toshi.

"Don't forget to run this weekend!" Coach calls as we arrive back at school, and I can't even nod.

"Tired?" Rae asks as she stops beside me, and I groan. She laughs. "Going to recover in time for tutoring tomorrow?"

"Absolutely." At least if we're together, I'll know she's not out tagging the neighborhood.

And that Toshi isn't anywhere near her.

We say goodbye and I take my time driving home, since Dad will be waiting at the shack for an update. There's not much to share since he's not interested in my classes, and I'm certainly not telling him about our lunchtime Hula-Hoop contest. Juan had brought the toy for a physics club project, and he and I tied for last place at two seconds apiece. Moose lasted four, Rae made it almost half a minute, and Sahana finally quit when the bell rang.

"It's really not hard," she said, catching the hoop in one hand as it whipped around her waist. She handed it to Juan, who stared after her admiringly as she left for class.

No, Dad doesn't need to hear about that.

He still insists I keep watch on the Winters' house, which means once again I'm parked down the block though it's past midnight, my car doors locked against any approaching Sweepers. The moon's glow leaves too little light for whittling, so all I can do is sit here and wish I were in bed. My eyelids are falling closed when a sudden movement slaps me wide awake.

The Winters' side gate opens, and a slight figure rolls a bike out. The hood of her sweatshirt hides her face, but I recognize Rae's familiar outline as she adjusts her backpack and pedals off.

This can't be good.

She turns away from me, and I start my engine and keep my headlights dark as I ease the car after her. There aren't any other people out at this hour, and I give her as much distance as possible, slowing whenever I can. She passes the movie theater and the hardware store, and I start to think she might be going to Charon's when she turns suddenly and vanishes into an alley between buildings. My car would stand out like an elephant in the deserted passage, so I park and follow on foot.

Businesses on both sides use the narrow alley for storage and garbage, and the dumpsters lining it stink of rancid food and spilled beer. Discarded trash and fallen boxes slow her speed, and I keep to the shadows and sneak after her. Halfway down the block, Rae dismounts. Her head turns, and I dive behind a stack of boxes just in time.

When I peer out, her bike leans against the wall, and a flashlight tucked into the backpack on the ground illuminates a light green building with **WALLFLOWER** painted above its closed door. A metal canister flashes in Rae's hand, and the sound of its rattle bounces off the dumpsters as she shakes it.

She reaches up, and the spray can hisses.

The blue infinity symbol starts at shoulder height and stretches almost three feet across, making this the largest one I've seen. Rae works methodically, finishing the symbol before dragging an empty crate over and flipping it upside down. Her new step raises her another two feet, and she reaches up to begin the cross. She doesn't add the second line—doesn't quite make it Lucifer's sign—but the similarity is undeniable.

My fingers touch the matches in my pocket. Dad made me bring them tonight, and the dumpster in front of me beckons as an easy option for a burning. Kendrick used one once. He had knocked his project unconscious, tossed him inside, and set the whole thing alight.

"Trash worked as kindling, and the metal contained the flames." He sounded pleased when he recounted the story to Dad and me. "No mess, no fingerprints, and no more Marked."

Rae's distraction presents the perfect opportunity, and a cold sweat breaks over me. What if Dad's right and I'm waiting too long? My heart jumps to my mouth as I take out the matches, my hands shaking so badly I nearly drop them, but my feet root to the ground. I can't even move as Rae finishes, tosses the spray can aside, and backs away from her work. Her shoulders jerk, and her hood slips off as she begins to cry.

The tearstained face makes my stomach lurch. My body goes numb, the matches frozen in my fingers, and my eyes can't move from the girl in front of me.

Not Rae, but Cady.

In the night's gloom, their figures were similar enough that

I saw exactly what I had been looking for—Rae sneaking out to paint Lucifer's symbol. Now I notice her sneakers are pink, not black, and the sweatshirt Cady wears features the logo of her middle school.

I almost burned the wrong sister.

Cady staggers back against the far wall as her sobs wrench out, jagged and mournful like the hard edge of grief itself. Her body sags to the pavement, and she pulls her knees to her chest and cries.

I can't just leave her.

My hands still tremble at my mistake, every part of me sick with horror, but I hurl the matches away and yank out my phone. **U awake?** I text Rae.

Her answer appears almost immediately. **Yes. Can't sleep.**

Cady must have been quiet as she snuck out, though perhaps she's had practice. Maybe this is why it's so hard for her to get up in the mornings. As quickly as I can, I tell Rae what's happening.

Stay with her pops up as soon as I finish. **I'm coming.**

The minutes crawl by, and still Cady doesn't rise. When at last her sobs run out, another bike clatters over the debris at the mouth of the alley. She jumps to her feet as Rae rides toward us, and I step out from the shadows.

"What are you doing?" Rae hisses as she reaches her sister. Her eyes dart to the symbol on the wall, and her face falls. "Damn it, Cade! You promised to stop!"

"I'm sorry!" Fresh tears trace their way down Cady's face. "I couldn't sleep and I just— I don't know."

Rae picks up the spray can and shoves it into Cady's back-pack. "We need to get out of here."

"My car's close." I grab Cady's bike and start wheeling it down the alley. "This way."

Rae hustles Cady along, and the three of us silently jog to the street. We manage to balance their bikes in the trunk of my car, and both girls scramble into the back seat. I start the engine, all of us grimacing at the sudden noise, and pull away slowly enough that the bikes don't fall out.

"You're the one painting that symbol?" My voice wavers, and I take a breath to steady it as we creep down the block. "I've seen it all over town. Does it mean something?"

Cady's head dips. When she speaks, sadness laces her voice. "It's for Dad. The *T* stands for Timothy. And infinity . . . well, he's with me forever. Even if he's gone." She lets out a heavy sigh. "The Wallflower was Dad's favorite coffee shop. I didn't want them to forget him."

Her words sink in, and the explanation seems so obvious I can't believe I missed it. Dad and I saw the Mark, but nothing could have been further from the truth.

Maybe when all you do is look for signs of Lucifer, that's all you see.

"No one's going to forget him, Cade." Rae hugs her sister close. "But you can't keep doing this. You need to stop."

Her phone buzzes, and she winces as she looks at it. "Crap. Mom's up. I better let her know we're okay."

Rae texts back, her sister curled miserably beside her, and I catch Cady's eye in the rearview mirror. "Just tell her the truth," I suggest. "She'll be mad, but she loves you. It'll be okay."

She rests her head on Rae's shoulder. "How did you find me anyway?"

I was waiting for your sister to go spray-paint the town and almost lit you on fire instead.

"Couldn't sleep. I went for a drive and saw you on your bike." I shrug. "Didn't think I should let you go biking around at two in the morning."

"Thanks for texting me," Rae says. "Apparently, none of us sleep anymore."

"Including your mom." I nod at their house as we approach, and Cady whimpers at the sight of Mrs. Winter standing in the doorway, arms crossed. I pull to the curb.

"Come on." Rae climbs out and stretches her hand to Cady, who takes it slowly. "We'll tell her together. Matt, you should go. No need for her to yell at you too."

I agree, whispering an encouraging "Good luck!" to Cady as I help them unload their bikes. Rae's fingers graze mine, and I give them a quick squeeze before jumping back in the car. Mrs. Winter's voice murmurs as I close my door, anger drawing her words tight, and the three of them disappear inside.

Cady's in trouble, that's for sure, but maybe some good will come of tonight. If Mrs. Winter knows how much her younger daughter is hurting, she might be able to help. I guess we have Dad to thank. He was right about keeping watch on the Winters' house tonight, though he couldn't possibly have suspected what I would see.

Cady, the MC tagger.

I almost found out too late.

Bile sours the back of my throat, and my fingers burn with the memory of the matches in them. My eyes land on my reflection in the mirror, and a wave of disgust hits me.

What have I become?

Cady designed a symbol to honor her lost father, and I saw none of it. Not a grieving young girl, not a drawing born from pain and love, not a cry for help. No, I saw a sign of the Mark, and I believed it so strongly I stood and watched as she painted, matches in my hand and murder in my heart.

Dad's head pops up from his sleeping bag the moment I open the door to the shack, and his expectant "Well?" makes me collapse onto the mattress. I gulp a deep breath and take him through the night's events, stumbling over the moment I reached for the matches.

His brow only furrows deeper.

"The project's Mark could be amplifying the younger girl's moods," he murmurs, almost to himself. "They're so close it's a possibility."

"Dad! You're not listening." I haul myself up, open the notebook, and jab my finger at the symbol he drew. "That's not the sign of Lucifer, and Rae didn't even draw it. Cady made it for her dad, all right? It's not the Mark at all!"

"If the project is changing, Matthew, she could affect those around her." Dad stands and reaches for the notebook. "We need to document this. Her actions and moods are becoming more potent, and a younger sister is especially vulnerable."

"What are you talking about?" I practically spit the words

at him. "Rae had nothing to do with it. Cade is just really sad, that's all!"

His eyebrows shoot up. "Cade?"

"Cady. The sister. Whatever!" I throw my hands in the air. "We were wrong, okay? We missed it. That's why I can't rush this. I need to be careful!"

"Don't assume the project wasn't involved, Matthew." Dad frowns. "She knew what was happening and did nothing to stop it. Remember, physical accidents are only part of the change. The Marked can manipulate in other ways as well— goading the innocent, planting ideas."

His reasoning makes me want to shake him. "You're not giving Rae the chance to be innocent! You're twisting everything we see. You want her to be Marked!"

"And you're doing the opposite!" A flush of red colors his cheeks. "You're ignoring the signs right in front of you."

I want to argue, but I'm too tired. Shaking my head, I turn my back to him and crawl under my blanket for a few hours of sleep before I meet Rae for tutoring, assuming Mrs. Winter hasn't grounded both her and Cady. Dad mutters something, the notebook thumping on the table as if he's tossed it down, but he soon slides into his sleeping bag.

At least we're done for tonight.

He'll just start back up tomorrow though, because the truth I should have seen long ago crystalizes with crushing clarity: Dad made up his mind the moment I accepted this project. For him, the only way this ends is in flames.

What if he's right? a part of my mind whispers, and my

stomach sinks as I remember the incidents with Mrs. Archer, with McNally, with Haley.

Maybe there's hope even if Rae is Marked. Dad may refuse to trust it, but love can be as powerful as Lucifer. When Mrs. Polly first started to change, I asked if we could make an anonymous phone call to tell her son of the danger she faced. Just one call to bring him to her side. To try and save Mrs. Polly.

Dad said no. And I listened.

I won't make that mistake again.

Lying in the darkness, I make a promise. I'll continue the project, stay close to Rae, watch for signs of her Mark. But if she changes—if that trickle of evidence becomes a flood—I won't reach for the matches.

I'll turn to our friends.

Sahana and Moose and Juan may not believe me when I tell them about the Mark, but I'll point out the changes and ask them to hold Rae even closer, to watch over her and support her and let her know she's loved. They'll think I'm crazy, but they care enough about her to listen.

And if Toshi tries anything . . . I can take care of him too.

I'll do it for Rae. For Cady and Mrs. Winter.

And for me, because I should have made that phone call for Mrs. Polly.

CHAPTER

20

"Is Cady all right?" I ask Rae as she slides into the passenger seat the next morning. She asked that we do tutoring at a different café today, one far away from the spray paint her sister left on the Wallflower, and I offered to pick her up. "What did your mom say?"

"She was furious." Rae rubs her eyes. Dark shadows under them tell of a long night, and the papers sticking out of her backpack hint at a rough morning as well. "But sad too. She said Cady should have talked to her earlier. Now they've got to fix all the damage she did, and they may have to deal with the police. Mom's contacting a friend who's a lawyer for advice."

"That's smart. Hopefully the places she painted will understand." I can't imagine anyone in Mills Creek pressing charges against Cady after everything she's been through, but people can surprise you. "How are you doing with all this?"

"I'm okay." She leans back in her seat and closes her eyes. "Just worried about her. Maybe now that Mom knows what's going on, it will get better."

I hope so too, especially since an improvement in Cady's behavior might make Dad ease off his idea that Rae's Mark is somehow manipulating her sister. The early morning hours had passed with stiff silence between us, Dad staring at his newspaper and me working on an essay for English, and any conversation with him that lies ahead makes Cady's talk with her mom look like a party in comparison.

The café Rae chose sits near the edge of town, with a drooping canopy and dusty windows. Its drinks aren't as good as the Wallflower's, but the inside holds only a few strangers and no reminders of spray paint. Rae takes me through the week's math lessons patiently, and we work quickly enough that there's even time to talk.

"We should drive out and see the hills around Mills Creek. They're beautiful this time of year," she says, her face brightening as we finish the drinks and gather our books. "It's one of my favorite things about this place."

Savoring autumn trees would be another first for me, since the changing seasons usually just indicate the passage of time in a project. I don't even remember if the leaves in Mrs. Polly's town turned to fall colors. Then again, our nine months there began in December, when the trees likely held only barren branches, and the leaves were still green when we finished.

I wonder how Mills Creek will look when I leave.

We drive to Charon's, where Mr. Yamamoto's polished bench sits ready for another day of customers. The freshly cleaned windows gleam, and a few flyers decorate the glass.

One makes me jump out of my car for a better look.

"What is it?" Rae follows me. "Did you see that dog?" She gestures at a "Lost Pet" poster.

I shake my head and point to a flyer from an art gallery just off the main street. "I know the artist. She used to live right down the street from me."

The painted birds featured in the newest exhibit—some poised in midflight, others surrounded by colorful flowers—brim with vibrant life. A photo displays the artist at work on her porch, but I don't even need to look at it. I would recognize those birds anywhere.

After all, I spent a year watching Abby Rivera paint them.

The Sweep gave Dad and me her name after a small plane crash left the pilot dead and her unharmed, and we spent a year as friendly neighbors before judging Ms. Rivera free of the Mark. The early accidents that happened near her faded until even Dad dismissed them as coincidence, just like I'm hoping will happen with Rae. Bad luck seems to come in spurts, and if he weren't so impatient this time, he would see that too.

"You should go to her exhibit and surprise her!" Rae says. "What are the chances you both wound up here?"

I feign a perplexed look. "Mills Creek is such an exciting place. Who wouldn't want to come?"

She leaves me with a laugh, and I drive home to tell Dad that our old project is in town. The timing is actually perfect, since she's due for her annual visit in just a few weeks. The fact she's touring with her art seems like a positive sign, and I'm hoping any threat of Lucifer's Mark is far behind her.

"Or," Dad says, his forehead crinkling when I tell him, "I was wrong, and the Mark has manifested. Kendrick cautioned me about this possibility. Now she's found a way to spread that evil further."

I pause, studying his face to see if he's serious. "Ms. Rivera always talked about taking her work to galleries around the country, remember? Maybe she's actually doing it. Let's go see her, and then we'll know."

He nods slowly. "When will she be here?"

"This evening." The flyer promised a "Meet the Artist!" event at the gallery tonight. "We'll just say we saw she was in town and came to say hi."

Dad agrees, the lines of worry deepening, and I spend the next hours finishing my homework and trying to carve a rabbit from a chunk of wood. I cut off its ear when Dad pulls up Ms. Rivera's website, frowning at the list of cities featuring her exhibition, and the sickening feeling in my stomach makes me grab my keys for an escape.

"Be right back," I tell Dad. "I need to check on the project." It will help pass the time, and I can talk with Rae while I eat a cupcake. Triple win.

He raises an eyebrow. "I thought seeing her at the bakery would be too aggressive?"

I just shrug. "Things change."

His eyes narrow slightly, but he stands. "Want me to come?"

"I'll be fine. Solo project, remember?" I say, and hurry out the door.

Escape brings a breath of fresh air. I drive slowly through Mills Creek's downtown, avoiding the many pedestrians out to enjoy the sunny afternoon. The parking spaces in front of

Charon's are full, and I take my time walking over from a spot I find two blocks away. I'm about to cross the street when its door opens, and a familiar figure emerges.

Ms. Rivera settles on the boat bench and pulls a brownie from a white bag. Rae must have sold it to her, and the thought of the two of them standing just a counter's width apart—one old project, one new—brings a heaviness that makes my feet slow.

Dark sunglasses hide Ms. Rivera's eyes.

Mrs. Polly wore them as well once the Mark shuttered those windows to her soul. Dad's apprehension slithers through me, and I duck behind a tree and text him. His response pops up immediately: **No contact. On my way.**

I keep my phone out, trying to look like I'm checking messages instead of watching the woman across the street. Ms. Rivera relaxes on the bench, nibbling the brownie, and the neon blue frames of her sunglasses make me think more of her colorful sense of style than the Mark. Most people around me wear sunglasses as well, and I'm starting to feel foolish behind my tree when an older man with a cane hobbles down the sidewalk. Her head snaps his way so quickly the hairs on my neck rise.

Ten yards from her, he stumbles, his hands flying up as he pitches forward. The cane clatters to the side, and he lands hard on the ground.

I sprint across the street, Dad's order to wait forgotten. Ms. Rivera jumps to her feet and rushes toward him as well, and I yank the knife from my pocket. If this is the work of the Mark, she might not be finished.

We reach him at the same time, Ms. Rivera on one side and me on the other, but she doesn't look my way. She crouches next to him, her hand on his shoulder.

Has she really not noticed me? Or is this a trick?

The door to Charon's flies open, and Rae bolts outside. She drops to her knees beside Ms. Rivera.

"Is he okay?" She pulls out her phone. "Should I call an ambulance?"

Ms. Rivera finally looks up. Her sunglasses reveal nothing behind the dark lenses, but her hand rises, fingers spreading like claws.

No.

I reach out and shove Rae back, nearly sprawling over the man. My knife falls to the sidewalk, and Ms. Rivera lifts her sunglasses.

"Matthew?" She blinks at me. My heart seizes, but her brown eyes stay clear, her quizzical smile holding nothing but friendliness and confusion. No malice. No harm. Her fingers aren't claws at all, and her hand is gentle as she helps the man to his feet. "My goodness. What are you doing?"

"Yeah!" Rae scolds, brushing dirt from her clothes. "What was that for?"

"I—sorry." At least I don't have to fake the sheepishness in my voice. "Lost my balance."

"Better be careful," the man says, rubbing his knees, "or you'll wind up like me."

"Are you all right?" Ms. Rivera gestures to the uneven sidewalk, where the roots of a nearby tree have pushed up the concrete. "I tripped right there too! The city should really fix that before someone gets hurt."

"I agree." The man reaches for his cane, and Rae hands it to him. "Maybe I'll file a complaint. Thank you for your help."

He continues on his way, and Ms. Rivera picks up my knife. "Still whittling?" she asks cheerfully.

Before I can answer, a car screeches around the corner and skids to a stop, its bumper inches from a curbside fire hydrant. Dad leaps out and races toward us, sending pedestrians scrambling out of his way as his panicked gaze bounces between me, Ms. Rivera, and the knife still in her hand.

Rae catches my arm. "Is your dad okay?"

"Yeah, he just—" *He just thinks this nice lady has been Marked by Lucifer, and she's here to kill everyone.* "I don't know."

I step in front of Rae, blocking him from her wide-eyed stare, and pour reassurance into my voice.

"Hey, Dad, look who's here!" I give him a broad smile and turn to Ms. Rivera. "I told him about your exhibit. We were planning to go to the gallery."

"Well, that's sweet! It's so good to see you, Jonathan." Ms. Rivera hands me the knife as Dad reaches us, sweat shining on his forehead. "Such a nice coincidence I had a showing here. I wondered where you two ended up. You never wrote that letter you promised, Matthew."

"I'm sorry." I offer an apologetic wince. "I've been really busy." Busy with the projects that came after hers, but I leave this out. We talk about painting and whittling, and I introduce Rae, who still casts sidelong glances at Dad.

"I really love the drawing of the owl in the gallery window," she says. "The one with the white face shaped like a heart?"

Ms. Rivera beams. "The barn owl. That's my favorite too."

Her eyes twinkle as she talks, and no hint of the Mark tarnishes her words as she mentions how she had read about Charon's in a food review and couldn't wait to try their desserts. The normalcy of the day resumes—the man's fall resulted from a broken sidewalk, Ms. Rivera is just an artist here for an exhibition, and our unexpected meeting is nothing more than a happy coincidence.

In fact, the only thing that looked unusual on this beautiful afternoon was Dad.

"I should get back to work," Rae finally says. "It was great to meet you. Nice seeing you again, Mr. Watts."

Ms. Rivera and Dad say goodbye, and I walk Rae the few steps to Charon's and follow her inside, as if a closed door can shut out the memory of Dad's frantic approach. I can't shake the look on her face as he careened toward us, and embarrassment heats my cheeks.

"Sorry about my dad." My gaze sticks to the floor. "He gets a little crazy sometimes."

"It's okay." Rae nudges me with her shoulder. "I've met his son, so I guess it runs in the family."

She sends me off with a slice of cake I won't be able to eat, because her words strike too close to home. The idea I might someday become the crazy one, seeing the Mark where there is none, festers all afternoon. Dad and I attend Ms. Rivera's exhibit that night, and her easy laughter as she circulates among the guests assures us our initial judgment stands. At the end of the showing, she hugs me goodbye, and Dad leaves soon after since he needs to meet his project for a photo shoot early tomorrow.

I should be celebrating as he drives away. Not only am I free of him again, but Ms. Rivera passed her annual check with flying colors, shrinking even more the possibility she bears the Mark. Despite all this, something inside keeps buzzing like a fly trapped in a jar. What's bothering me, besides Mr. Garrett watching from his window?

I escape to the shack, where the events of the day fill the small space like a swirling cyclone, and the moment that makes my head pound most has nothing to do with Ms. Rivera. No, it's the expression on Rae's face when she saw Dad charging toward us in such a frenzy he almost ran over a few people. The unease digging through me goes beyond embarrassment. Dad saw us standing with the Marked, but Rae saw . . .

What did Rae see?

Ms. Rivera, a talented and pleasant artist.

An elderly man who tripped over an uneven sidewalk.

And Dad, half crazed out of his mind, when all around him was an ordinary day.

Rae didn't see the Mark, never even suspected it might be there, because the rest of the world is blind to Lucifer's touch. She doesn't know how that curse creeps into our lives and devastates the innocent. For Rae, the Mark doesn't exist.

She's wrong, of course.

Isn't she?

Nausea swells through every part of me as the uncertainty

born during Mrs. Polly's burning rises once again, rattling that tiny corner where I locked the questions away. When I was younger, I simply believed Dad—believed him from the moment he first told me about Lucifer and the Second Sweep— and Kendrick's involvement only cemented his role as the coolest uncle ever. The Mark resonated with my eight-year-old mind, and the proof they presented, of accidents and changes and Evil, seemed obvious each time they pointed it out. Dad and Kendrick trapped me in a bubble, like our own little cult of three, and I never questioned them. Never doubted.

Not until Mrs. Polly.

And then it was too late. So I just closed my eyes and hoped I was wrong.

But now . . .

Everything that seemed so clear when I got up this morning shivers and blurs, Dad's lessons slipping from my mind like sand. The certainty I'm reaching for won't come, the questions howling too loudly to ignore. I can't hold on to the teachings, can't see Lucifer when I view the world through Rae's eyes.

A world without the Mark.

But if that stain isn't here—if it's not Rae who sees the world wrong, but me—then all the years of spying and judging have been nothing more than make-believe. But the burnings . . .

The burnings were real.

CHAPTER

21

I spend the night on the cold tiles of my bathroom floor, heaving up dinner and scouring the internet for any shred of proof the Mark exists. It's a search I've done before, and as always, I start with the Sweep. The first hours yield nothing new, only images of random men named "James Trainer" and a run-down strip mall in McLean, Virginia that houses the PO Box where we send our reports.

The name on the rental agreement remains a mystery.

I dig deeper, chasing chat rooms and message boards about Lucifer, diving down rabbit holes of cults and exorcism. My eyes blur, my brain throbs, and still—nothing. Well, nothing more than what I started with: Dad and Kendrick.

I launch a new search, skipping over websites of Kendrick's security firm to pore through older articles about him. He holds a degree in computer science from a prestigious university, where he led the football team as their star quarterback, and left to do overseas work with the military after graduation. The stories contain few details about those contracts, but the death of his wife became a national headline, both because of her beauty and the devastating honeymoon. The grisly accident makes me cringe even now. Not only had the nail gun misfired as she walked past the construction site, sending a three-inch nail through her heart, but the trigger stuck, riddling her body with metal piercings until the ammunition ran out. The wedding photo beside the grim words shows the widest smile I've ever seen on Kendrick's face, and I doubt it's been there again since the day she died. Maybe, like Dad, he became an easy recruit for the Sweep.

Or maybe his broken mind dreamed up the whole thing.

By the time I crawl into bed, the sky outside lightening to gray, I'm no closer to the truth than when I started. Countless sites spin theories about Lucifer, but the Mark I've spent my life hunting appears nowhere in the writings. Nothing—no web pages, no articles, not even a wayward comment in a chat—even hints at the Sweep's existence, which is exactly what I would expect from an organization fighting to remain secret.

Or one that doesn't exist.

Questions still ricochet through my brain in the morning when I approach Rae, who sits beside her father's grave as the church organ swells with the opening hymn.

"Hi," I say. "Can I sit?"

"Sure." She scoots over, and I settle on the grass beside her. "Is your dad here?"

"He left yesterday." The thought of Dad makes my head hurt even more. "How are you doing?"

Her face brightens, and she shares her plan to see Ms. Rivera's art exhibit with her mom later that week. I nod along, trying to pay attention, but Rae isn't fooled.

"You okay?" she asks. "You seem kind of out of it."

"Long visit with Dad." I stare at Mr. Winter's grave, with a fresh bouquet of daisies in its vase. What kind of father had he been? Nothing like mine, I bet. "He said some things that got me thinking."

"Like what?"

I have to be careful. It's bad enough to be discussing this with someone outside the Sweep, and even worse that the person I'm talking to is my project. Who knows what alarms I might set off? But I need to talk to someone who is smart and rational and outside the fire-happy duo of Dad and Kendrick. Moose would be too ready to believe it, Juan would demand facts and figures, and Sahana would ask how much television I've been watching. It has to be Rae.

I want it to be her.

My fingers crush the grass, and I glance around to make certain no one, especially Toshi, is near. "Dad said Lucifer—the Devil—seizes souls in this world. He makes people do terrible things."

The moment the words are out, I wish I could pull them back. I hold my breath, but no look of horror appears on Rae's face. Instead, she gestures toward the church. "That's not weird. I bet most people in there would agree."

"It's more than that." I hesitate, but she waits with no hint of wariness or unease, so I plow ahead. "He thinks Lucifer

Marks people's souls so they start wreaking havoc here on Earth. Like—remember that man who tripped yesterday? Dad might say Ms. Rivera had been Marked and turned evil, so she shifted the ground to make him fall. That kind of thing."

The words sound ludicrous when said out loud, but I've seen it. I watched Mrs. Polly change with my own eyes.

I helped burn her for it.

"Sometimes accidents happen." Rae gives me a perplexed smile, like she's trying to figure out if this is a joke. "That man just tripped."

"Yeah. I know. Stupid, huh?" I force a laugh, but her forehead wrinkles.

"Okay. Say Lucifer can take over people." She pauses. "Do they fight back?"

She's humoring me, but at least I can play along. "Maybe for a little while, but eventually, the Mark begins to win. The people affected start to cause trouble, like making others fall or tipping a bowl of soup into someone's lap, but then their power grows and the damage escalates. Soon, the accidents can kill."

I pause, waiting for gravestones to topple, a wayward car to careen through the fence, the ground to open up and swallow me whole for revealing what no one but a Sweeper should ever hear.

Rae just nods. "So how do you get rid of it?"

"Maybe you can't." I keep my eyes on Mr. Winter's grave, since whatever she reads in my expression will reveal too much. "Maybe once someone is Marked, there's nothing to do but get rid of that person."

I don't mention how.

She shakes her head. "I don't believe that. Lucifer might make it harder to do the right thing, but people always have a choice. You just have to decide there's a line you won't cross, no matter what, and stick to it."

"I guess." Her words make sense, their simplicity rendering the idea of the Mark even more ridiculous. What would Rae have seen with Mrs. Polly? The accidents that happened around her, the deaths that followed—in Rae's eyes, they would have been coincidence and misfortune, more bad luck Mrs. Polly couldn't escape. Add in the fact she survived a horrific accident, and of course she changed. But maybe the tragedy scarred her mind, not her soul.

Maybe there is no Mark.

My head spins, but Rae weaves her fingers through mine, a reassuring pull against the thoughts whirling through my brain. She tucks herself in against me, and I rest my head on hers and close my eyes, as if Dad and the Mark and the burnings would all disappear if I just never let go.

All too soon, Cady's voice drifts across the graveyard. "Rae! Come on!"

We make our way through the parking lot, and I do my best to sound normal as Mrs. Winter greets me, though my stomach feels like I ate cement. When they drive away, the idea of returning to the shack with only my questions for company sends my feet hurrying in the opposite direction. I spend the day roaming Mills Creek, wandering the streets and seeing for the first time in a long while a world without the Mark. It's like I borrowed a pair of glasses with different lenses, ones that make the sun shine brighter and people's smiles more genuine and lurking shadows nothing more than patches of shade. This world is better than the one I know, a safer place without Lucifer and His Mark that makes monsters.

Except for me. Maybe I'm the monster.

I run into Moose outside a music store, and we go to the Wallflower. Sahana isn't working, which means the coffee isn't as good and no one stops our conversation from devolving into talk of aliens and demons, courtesy of Moose's latest movie interests. At least that makes it easy to slip in the same questions I asked Rae.

Moose's face glows. "Yes! That would be awesome. And then someone has to hunt down the people Lucifer possessed and burn them alive!"

My heart jumps, and I glance quickly at the other customers. The man at the closest table seems absorbed in his book, and I can only hope he isn't a Sweeper. "Is there a movie like that?"

He shakes his head. "But there should be. It'd be crazy."

Crazy. That's what I'm starting to think.

I open my mouth to ask more, but Moose waves to someone behind me. "Hey, Toshi! Over here!"

Any words die in my throat as I turn. Toshi grins at us from the register.

"Hey, guys!" He orders his drink before making his way over. "What's up?"

"Matt's telling me how Lucifer infiltrates our world," Moose says cheerfully. "Possibly through people, which means I was right about McNally. Better watch out."

My ears burn so hot they're probably giving off smoke. If Toshi didn't know I was a Sweeper before, he does now. I mumble something about movies, but Moose is on a roll, running through a list of people who are likely possessed.

"My fourth-grade teacher, Mr. Raymond." He nods seriously. "And Mrs. Jameson! She lives in the apartment below us, and she always complains I walk too loudly. Maybe Lucifer has super hearing."

Toshi chuckles. "What do you think, Matt? Who else is touched by Lucifer?"

He used the word "touched," not "Marked," but his steady gaze keeps panic ringing through my head. "I don't know," I stall. "Definitely McNally. Sometimes Coach, depending on the workout." That gets a laugh from Moose, and the sound emboldens me. Might as well dig a little. "But you have to think, if Lucifer really is out there, there must also be people watching for Him. Right?"

"Ooh!" Moose's eyes widen. "Good hunting evil. Classic."

I keep going, my eyes glued on Toshi. "Only no one knows who the hunters are, not even those on the same side. But maybe one of them starts to figure it out."

Toshi tilts his head. "And then?"

Good question. "I don't know. Guess it depends on what they do next, right?"

I'm hanging on his response, but the barista calls that his coffee is ready, and he pushes back his chair and stands. "Nice seeing you guys." He takes his drink and pauses at the door to wink at us. "Watch out for Lucifer."

Moose bursts out laughing, but I can't even fake a smile. Toshi's timing couldn't have been worse.

Or maybe whatever role I've invented for him exists only in my head, and this hunt for the Mark is nothing more than a gruesome game. The Second Sweep could have sprung from Dad's and Kendrick's broken minds, and they carried me into their twisted world with such conviction I never noticed when reality blurred and slipped away.

I have no idea. But I know someone who does.

When Dad calls that night, I answer like always, chatting about my day and the upcoming week. The noise in the background nearly drowns him out, since he's calling from a jazz club where his project is performing. I tell him I finished my weekly report and do my best to sound casual as I ask, "Hey, who actually reads those things? Will I ever get to meet him? Or her?"

Cymbals clash as Dad reminds me of one of the Sweep's cardinal rules: No contact with any Sweeper except mentor to mentee, which leaves Kendrick as our sole connection. "We don't want everyone knowing us, remember? We can trust Kendrick. No need to bring in others."

"Yeah, but . . ." I swallow hard. "There *are* others, right?"

He laughs. "Of course," he says, before telling me his project is waiting and he needs to go.

Any chance of sleep flees with the click of Dad hanging up, and I settle in for another long night of whittling under the oak tree. At least I won't be tired in class tomorrow. School is closed so teachers can attend a training session or whatever it is teachers do when students aren't around. My Monday is wide open, which means I have plenty of time to pay Dad a visit.

He owes me some answers.

CHAPTER

22

I slip out Monday morning before Mr. Garrett wakes. Rae will soon head to Charon's since she picked up the extra hours, and talking to Dad feels more important than watching her work at the bakery. She thinks I'm meeting him for lunch somewhere near his latest photo shoot, which I set in the opposite direction. It was as close to the truth as I could come, and it's still a long way off.

I hate lying to her.

The drive offers time to organize my thoughts, but my head is still muddled as I near Dad's city. He doesn't know I'm coming. I didn't want to give him the chance to tell me to stay home.

Came for a visit, I text. Where ru?

A moment later, his reply appears. He's at a nearby coffee shop, but he warns me not to approach. I park down the street and spot him sitting on the patio. He holds a cup in one hand and a newspaper in the other, but his gaze is locked on a man and woman browsing at the magazine stand across the street.

Looks like Dad is working.

The scene shifts, my view slipping to Rae's world without

Lucifer, and suddenly the project is no longer the threat. It's Dad who turns sinister—his eyes fixed on the unsuspecting couple, his head ducking behind the newspaper as they make their purchases, the chilling casualness with which he stands and saunters after them as they leave. I've read about this kind of behavior.

In a book on serial killers.

I wait until he turns the corner before jumping out of my car. We form a strange procession, with Dad following his project and me trailing Dad, and we zigzag across several blocks before the man and his friend enter a small store. It's a music shop filled with old records, and Dad finds a bench down the street. He pulls out his phone, and a moment later, a text pops up on mine.

Monitoring the project, it says. **Be back soon.**

When the couple emerges from the store, Dad buries himself behind his newspaper once again, keeping it raised until they cross the street to an apartment building. He glances at his watch, and I can practically see his brain taking notes: how long the project was in the store, the expression on the man's face when he exited, where he went next.

Before I would have just seen a Sweeper doing his job. Now I don't know what I see.

Dad stands, and I hurry to my car. He appears a few minutes later, which means he must be confident the project will be inside for a while.

"Hi." I climb out. "Hope I'm not interrupting."

"You're not." He motions me back behind the wheel. "Let's

drive. Might be hard to introduce you if anyone sees us."

His words make perfect sense, since having a teenage son show up would certainly complicate Dad's story. Still, I doubt Moose or Juan have ever heard anything like that from their parents. I guide the car away from the busier parts of town, assuring Dad everything is fine and I just missed him, and we drive through the outskirts as I update him on Rae.

I don't mention our talk in the graveyard.

"How do I know if I'm passing the test?" I ask instead, keeping my tone light. "Will the Sweep give me a progress report or something?"

Dad shakes his head. "They'll be watching for the end. But they read your reports, so make sure you do a good job on those."

"Who's 'they'?" I keep my eyes ahead. "If I'm part of the Sweep, it feels like I should know who I'm working for. This blind loyalty stuff is crap."

My face heats at the intensity of Dad's stare, and I almost wish I had kept my mouth shut. But I can't.

I should have asked the questions long ago.

"Watch your language, Matthew," Dad finally says. "I understand, though. When Kendrick first told me about the Mark, it sounded insane. Then I started watching, and the more I saw, the more it made sense. You've seen it too. Remember how Mrs. Polly changed? And you didn't see Mr. Whittmeier as much, but he did as well. As for the Second Sweep . . . well, the secrecy makes sense. But Kendrick has seen others."

This is news to me. "Really? When?"

"Long time ago. Someone ran into trouble, and Kendrick got a call to drive to a gas station a couple hours away. He went, and a woman got out of a van and climbed into the back of his truck. His phone rang again and a man gave him an address, and he drove another few hours to some roadside diner where a car was waiting. It's the only time I've heard of the emergency number being used." Dad taps his chin, his eyes faraway. "He said she smelled like smoke."

There it is. The proof I've been hunting. Except . . . "Did you see her too?"

Dad shakes his head. "Just Kendrick. He told me about it the next time we met."

The answer works, as always. But it feels a little too convenient and entirely dependent on Kendrick, like everything else about the Sweep. Dad must read the skepticism on my face, because his next lines come with more urgency than usual.

"Matthew, this is no time for doubt. Your test is very important." His jaw twitches. "You need to bring the project to its proper end."

The words wrap around me like a straightjacket. "I don't have enough evidence."

"She popped a woman's tire," Dad reminds me. "She knocked that girl over with a shopping cart and then sent her falling down the bleachers, and she made her sister paint Lucifer's sign on the wall."

"That wasn't Lucifer's sign! And she didn't—"

Dad cuts me off. "That's a lot of coincidence, Matthew. At some point, it becomes something else." His tone is harsh.

Unyielding. "If Kendrick asks, you tell him you're close to the finish. Understand?"

I open my mouth to protest, but his stern expression silences any argument. Whatever questions I had about the Sweep wither as well, but it doesn't matter. I wouldn't believe his answers anyway. Neither of us speaks again until I pull to the curb near the coffee shop.

"I'll come visit in a few days." Dad waits until I meet his gaze before continuing. "Take good notes, and keep a close eye on the project. The Sweep is watching, Matthew. Now isn't the time for questions."

Now is exactly the time for questions, before it's too late. It's already too late for Mrs. Polly. But all I say is, "I know. They'll like what they see."

His frown relaxes. "All right." He gives my arm a quick pat. "Drive safely. I'll call tonight."

"Sure. Thanks."

He strides down the street, arms swinging like he just ventured out for a brisk stroll, but I know better. He'll park himself near the project's apartment, watching once again, and his unwavering confidence in our work only rattles mine more.

How can he be so certain? Maybe his years of experience taught him things I still need to learn.

Or maybe he never recovered from Mom's death, and Kendrick found him at his most vulnerable. A cracked mind is easier to sway than one that's whole, and nothing weakens a person like grief. The Mark could have given Dad something to hold on to when everything else came crashing down, and he's been clinging to it ever since.

Blind faith, a pocketful of matches, and a trail of bodies behind him.

A wave of nausea hits, and I close my eyes and wait for it to pass. When I open them again, Dad has disappeared, along with any hope of getting answers from him. I toy with the idea of calling Kendrick, but I'm not ready for that conversation, especially with Dad's warnings ringing in my ears.

But maybe there's someone else I can call.

The phone number for the Sweep is supposed to be for emergencies only, but I think this qualifies. I punch in the number and wait, my heart beating in my throat as I listen to it ring. Once. Twice. Then—

"Jim's Deli," a voice chirps. "How can I help you?"

I check the number on the screen. Dad's made me repeat it hundreds of times over the years, and I'm certain it's the right one. "Um—this is Matt Watts. I'm looking for the Sweep?"

"You want the Streak? It's got ham, salami, pickles, and cheddar. Bolt of flavor!" the woman says cheerfully. "White bread or whole wheat?"

"No." I hesitate. "I'm a Sweeper. It's an emergency."

"Oh." The woman sounds confused. "What kind of emergency?"

"It's—I need help. My dad and Kendrick keep saying my project's Marked, but they're wrong. You have to stop them." I bite my lip and wait.

There's a long pause. "You want the Market sandwich?" she finally says.

I hang up. My heart still pounds, and I wait for it to slow before I look up the deli online. Its website features a cute storefront in Maryland, a full menu, and photos of both the Streak and Market subs.

And the phone number I've been repeating half my life.

CHAPTER

23

Tuesday brings a throbbing headache as my mind jumps between the world with the Mark and the world others see. Last night's surveillance outside the Winters' house, dutifully recorded in the red notebook, felt like playing a role in someone else's script, and I spent the remaining hours whittling under the oak until my eyelids refused to stay open and my brain quit asking questions that have no answers. A shadow passed in Mr. Garrett's window a few times, but he didn't bother me.

He asks this morning if everything is okay.

I say yes.

My mind keeps spinning the entire week, even as I haunt the Winters' street for signs that never come. Each night, I pour over the scant evidence I have for Rae's Mark, and it's like dueling pianos in my brain as her voice counters each one.

1) The door to Charon's smacked that woman who had been asking those insensitive questions. Could that have been the beginning of Rae's change? *No, that's what happens when someone doesn't open the door wide enough.*

2) Mrs. Archer's tire popped as her car passed Rae, whose furious glare had followed the woman down the street. Was that the Mark breaking through? *That wasn't the Mark. That was a nail puncturing an old tire, because Mrs. Archer never bothered to change it.*

3) McNally's pencil landed with amazing precision in his mug. Did Rae somehow guide it? *Given how McNally kept yelling and jerking his head, it's no wonder that pencil went flying. It could have landed anywhere. Just happened to be in a great place for the rest of us.*

4) The shopping cart struck Haley while Rae watched, and the fall down the bleachers happened as she stormed up the stairs with that giant cup of water. Did Rae cause those accidents? *Nope. Someone bumped that cart, which rolled across the slanted lot, and Haley slipped because she was too focused on revenge to be careful.*

5) Cady chose that symbol, which she claimed she made for her father. Could it be a warped version of Lucifer's sign, manipulated from the shadows by Rae? *That's ridiculous. Cady explained what it meant. If you still see the Mark, you're no better than your dad.*

The last thought makes me shudder, especially as I remember Dad's frantic sprint toward Ms. Rivera. I can't become that. I won't.

The questions go around and around in my head each night, bouncing between Dad's Mark and Rae's logic. Neither can drown out the other, and those tortured lines of *I'm sorry* only add to the confusion. I'm never any closer to the truth when morning arrives.

On Thursday evening, I head for Rae's house. It's just supposed to be a quick drive by, but I end up parking a block away to watch. In the deepening shadows, the porch light casts a circle of warmth around the front door, and lamps glow softly behind the curtains. Inside, Mrs. Winter might be calling Rae and Cady for dinner in that comfortable kitchen, and the three of them will gather around the table.

How does it feel to end each day like that? No scheming, no red notebook, no lies—just a quiet meal with people who care about you. I rest my forehead against the steering wheel, trying not to compare the scene inside to my own nights, and my phone buzzes. Dad won't ring for another hour, so I expect Juan or Moose as I pull it out. The "Kendrick" on the screen makes me pause.

If anyone knows the answers to my questions, it's him.

Kendrick may not be my uncle by blood, but I've called him that as long as I can remember. This is the man who rented a tuxedo for my kindergarten graduation, took Dad and me to our first baseball game, and showed up with a giant cake on my thirteenth birthday. I used to think I could talk with him about anything, but the memory of that gun in his waistband makes me reconsider.

Knowing Kendrick, he's an excellent shot.

The phone buzzes again, and I bite my lip and press the green button. "Hey, Uncle Kendrick."

"Hey there, kiddo." His voice rumbles through the phone. "Just wanted to see how you're doing. Anything new?"

"Not really. I'm outside the project's house right now." Wondering what they're having for dessert. "Just checking on things."

"Good. Keeping your notebook current?"

"Yes. I sent the weekly report too."

"All right." A beat of silence follows, during which Kendrick is probably running through a mental checklist of my project. "You're staying close? Able to watch the girl outside of class?"

"Rachel." Rae's given name sounds too formal coming out of my mouth, but maybe it will help him see her as something more than a project. "She tutors me every Saturday. And I drive her to school in the mornings."

"Good," Kendrick says. "Any other ways to get closer? You've got classes and the running team . . . you've both lost a parent. Did you try using that?"

The idea of using Mom as a way to get close to Rae almost makes me drop my phone. We might have talked about her in the graveyard that day, but the painful honesty of that conversation is a far cry from whatever Kendrick has in mind. Even Dad, who would have certainly noticed both Rae and I were missing parents, never suggested I use Mom in that way.

"I think I'm doing okay," I tell Kendrick.

"You're doing a great job, Matthew," he assures me. "But more connections never hurt. Keep it up, and give me a call if you need anything. I'm not far."

"Okay. Hey, Uncle Kendrick?" I choose my words carefully. "Does the Sweep need to interview me or anything as part of my test? Maybe the leaders want meet me?"

"Nope. I've told my mentor about you, and she passed it up the chain. They seem satisfied, especially since you've done such good work with your dad." He pauses. "Why?"

If Kendrick can tell me something that will let me sleep tonight, I have to try. "It's just . . . I wish I could meet other Sweepers. Maybe swap stories so we know what others have seen. That way, we could be sure"—I gulp and plunge ahead—"that it's the Mark causing changes in people, and not some-thing else."

My mouth goes dry by the time he speaks again. "You're wondering if the whole thing's real, aren't you?"

Any response dies in my throat. He goes on.

"That's all right, son. The solo test always brings out the big question. Your father once asked me the same thing, and I asked it myself years ago. The Sweep is real, Matthew, and so is the Mark. If you let that Evil grow, let it feed on a soul until it becomes too strong, good people die." He doesn't mention his wife, though from the bitterness sharpening his voice, it's clear who he's talking about. "Don't wait too long, or that sweet girl just might kill someone."

The warning in Kendrick's words makes me take another

look at the Winters' house, its warm light growing colder in the graying dusk. If he's right, it's only a matter of time until bodies start falling.

Though if Rae had heard him, she would say he's nuts.

"Tell you what," Kendrick says, when my silence stretches too long. "You keep watching and tell me what you see. I know it's hard, and asking questions is fine—it shows you're thinking, and that's good—but the answer is right in front of you."

"All right," I say, and we hang up, though the conversation plays in my head the entire way home. It's the same lesson I've heard a million times, and the old beliefs (*Watch—Judge—Burn*) rise up like embers reigniting. Yet that reasoning turns foggy when I think too hard, and the friendly streets of Mills Creek make it difficult to see the Mark anywhere.

It's like staring at two versions of the same world, and I have no idea which one is real.

On Halloween morning, I arrive at the Winters' house to find Cady sitting outside in the swing. Her feet drag on the ground, and she wears a sweatshirt far too large for her featuring the faded name of an out-of-state university. Judging from the way she rubs her eyes with its sleeve, it's not hard to guess the person it once belonged to. Rae comes out, slinging her backpack over her shoulder, and pauses. Her own head dips, and she walks to her sister.

Cady doesn't look up, but Rae strokes her hair gently, lips

moving with words too soft for me to hear. Her face mirrors the grief on Cady's, but I can't tell if it's for her lost father or the little sister slowly drowning before her. At last, Cady reaches up to wrap her arms around Rae, who coaxes her from the swing and steers her to the porch, where their mother waits. Mrs. Winter gathers Cady close, and the door shuts behind them as Rae climbs into my car.

Her eyes are wet, cheeks damp.

"Are you all right?" My voice rasps, and a grief that should belong to someone else leaks out.

She slumps back in her seat as we drive away. "Dad always used to make this special Halloween breakfast for us. Pumpkin pancakes, sausages wrapped in pastry like mummies . . . Mom offered to do it, but we said no. Cady's been crying all morning. She misses Dad." Rae bites her lip as the banner for the Scream comes into view. "So do I."

I wish I knew what to say to ease the grief shredding those words, but all I can do is reach for her hand. The drive passes in silence, because she is thinking of her dad and I am thinking that even though I keep looking for the Mark, all I see is heartache haunting a girl who deserves better.

Luckily, reinforcements wait at school. Sahana leans against Rae's locker, and one look at us makes her fold her friend into a tight hug.

"I'll see you in math," I tell Rae, and leave them to talk alone before class.

Lunch brings the liveliness of our little group, though Rae's sandwich sits untouched the entire time. At least she nibbles the cookie Juan insists she take, since his mom sent him to school with enough Halloween sweets even Moose can't finish them.

"Do you want to go to the Scream tonight?" Juan asks Rae. "We're up for anything. Just name it."

"I can pick you up." Sahana jostles Rae gently. "Want to go see what these guys are dressed like? I think zombies might be an improvement."

"Hey!" Moose objects. "But that reminds me. Here." He hands Juan and me packets of ketchup from the cafeteria. "Zombie blood. Just squirt it on tonight."

Juan groans. "Next year, I pick our costumes."

A small smile creases Rae's face. "All right. I'll go."

Halloween night looks like a movie set exploded on the street outside the Winters' house. Bands of witches, skeletons, and superheroes roam the sidewalk, and honking cars crawl past. I'm parked in my usual spot, though my zombie face stands out more than I'd like. The white and black paints hadn't been easy to apply—I scrubbed off the first two attempts—but I finally ended up with something that resembled the character on the movie poster. The scar on my leg appears worse than usual thanks to some extra paint and the ripped leg of my pants, and ketchup stains my white apron.

Moose will be proud.

Several costumed figures pass, and I slouch lower in my seat.

Behind the masks and shadows, others may also be watching, and they need to see a Sweeper at work. I still don't know what to believe, which means I need to play both sides until I figure out which is real—the world where I may have to burn Rae, or the one where Kendrick, Dad, and I killed innocent people.

Either way, I lose.

A group of tiny vampires approaches the Winters' bright porch, and one knocks. Mrs. Winter feigns terror as she opens the door, a large bowl in her hands, and the children holler "Trick or Treat!" before gathering around like vultures in a feeding frenzy. After a quick flurry, they back away, dropping candies into their bags and calling thanks as they head for the next house.

Mrs. Winter leans against the doorframe, rubbing a hand across her face in a way that makes my own eyes blur. Today must be as hard for her as it is for her daughters. Another group approaches, however, and she steadies the bowl and greets the children with a smile.

She's strong. I guess she has to be.

A yellow VW bug parks just past the house, and Sahana climbs out. She grabs a large pirate hat off the passenger seat and crosses the lawn to Mrs. Winter, who offers her the candy bowl. Sahana plucks one out, and the door closes behind them as they disappear inside.

Except for a few more trick-or-treaters, the house stays quiet for the next fifteen minutes. I send Rae a text I'm running late, but no response comes. Maybe she's having second thoughts.

My phone finally buzzes with her answer: **Me too.**

The door soon opens, and Sahana appears. Rae follows slowly. Her pirate costume looks great, but her steps are heavy, and she reaches for the car as Mrs. Winter jogs toward her. Rae turns, and her mother wraps her in a gigantic hug. They stand locked together for a long moment, neither speaking, and wipe each other's cheeks when they finally let go. Rae climbs into the car with Sahana, and I blink hard, let a few others drive past, and follow them to the park.

By the time I arrive, several texts from Moose light up my phone.

Where ru?

Zombie trio means 3 not 2 so sad

No candy for u!

U ok?

Almost there, I write back.

I wind through the park, squeezing between groups of people and keeping my eyes open for Rae and Sahana. Finding them feels impossible in the costumed crowd, and the scattered lights leave too many pockets of darkness. Moose texts that he and Juan are waiting near the tables full of jack-o'-lanterns, and I head that way. Hopefully, the girls are doing the same.

"Sorry I'm late," I say when I reach them. "Which pumpkin's yours?"

Moose shakes his head. "None. I refuse to lobotomize squash. Juan, however, has no problem with it."

"You're just jealous." Juan points to a jack-o'-lantern with an intricately carved snarl. "You're looking at first prize. I'm calling it right now."

"Oh yeah?" It's Sahana, hefting her own jack-o'-lantern. She chose a scene instead of a face, and the cat arching its back will definitely give Juan a run for his money. "Don't count on it."

"Ooh, pumpkin smack talk." Rae is right behind her, with her smile back in place. I have to hand it to Sahana; whatever she did in the car worked. "I love it."

"Nice costume," I tell Rae. She's certainly the best-looking pirate I've ever seen. Her jeans are tucked into tall brown boots, and the red sash at her waist complements a frilly white blouse. A thick rubber band fastens a stuffed parrot to her shoulder, matching the green bird perched on Sahana.

"You too," Rae says. "Excellent face."

"Pirates versus Zombies!" Moose's eyes light up. "Who would win?"

"Give me that cleaver"—Sahana points at his cardboard weapon—"and let's find out."

Rae shakes her head, but her lips twitch. "You guys are ridiculous."

"I'm not the one wearing a parrot," Juan says, waving his mace at it. "Polly want a cracker?"

"Actually, Polly does." Rae jabs him with her plastic sword. "Let's get something to eat."

We make our way through the park, checking out booths full of food and games as ghostly music plays. Dusk turns the corner to night, and the landscape becomes the perfect Halloween playground, with shadows and haloed lights and people moving in and out of darkness. Judging from the crowd, at least half the town is here. I'll never be able to pick out a Sweeper, and every mask stares back. The police roam the park as well, and Rae nods politely at a tall, uniformed woman with dark brown skin and a polished badge that says "Walsh."

"Hi there, Rae," the woman says. "I love your costume."

"Thank you." Rae's cheeks redden, and she looks down at her boots. "And thanks for helping Cady with her—crimes."

"I call them mistakes." Captain Walsh pats the parrot on Rae's shoulder. "You should too. Hang in there, okay?"

Rae looks up. "I will. Thanks."

"Tyson's mom?" I ask as we join the others in a line for ice cream.

She nods. "Mom reached out to her about Cady's spray-painting. Captain Walsh was really great; she talked to the store owners and convinced them not to press charges as long as we pay to have the walls repainted. Cade is going to volunteer at Mom's work to help earn the money, so it'll keep her out of trouble as well."

"That's smart." At least I won't have to worry about Cady painting the town anymore. Hopefully, Dad will forget about it as well, along with Rae's imagined dark influence.

Though he'll probably find something else to blame on her.

A voice booms over the speakers, announcing the start of the costume contests, and we get our cones and gather around a stage in the middle of the field. Music blares as the first contest begins, sending miniature monsters and cartoon characters parading past. The speakers call "Pets!" next, and people line up their costumed animals in a flurry of fur and tails.

"Is that a hamster?" Sahana squints at the stage. "We need a new rule. If we can't see your pet, it can't be in the contest."

"How many categories are there?" I ask. This could go on forever.

"A lot. But the best are at the end. We"—Moose raises his cleaver—"are in 'Spooky.'"

The parade of pets ends, and the speakers spark to life again. "Family Costume Contest!"

Parents and children make their way to the front. One family wears matching baseball uniforms, and another joins together to form a caterpillar. They gather by the announcer, eager for their walk across the stage.

Last year, the Winters had been part of that group, full of grins and giggles as they arranged themselves into their graham cracker s'more. They assumed they'd be back this year with a new theme. New costumes.

Same four people.

Beside me, Rae ducks her head—an island of misery in the cheering crowd. Sahana wraps an arm around her waist, and Moose and Juan draw close, biting their lips as the first family strides jubilantly onto the stage. My own chest aches, an echo of the sadness pouring off her.

She doesn't need to watch this. I tug her hand gently. "Let's go for a walk."

Rae nods without looking up.

I catch Sahana's eye and motion that we'll be back. Concern lines her face, but she gives Rae a final squeeze and lets go. I guide Rae to the edge of the park, find an empty picnic table, and pull her down to sit beside me. When she lifts her head, tears stain her cheeks.

"I miss my dad, Matt." She draws a shaky breath. "I miss him so much."

Her pain cracks something inside me wide open, and I forget to even check for watching Sweepers before putting my arms around her and pulling her close. "It's okay," I murmur over and over again as she cries, even though we both know it's not.

Her sobs soon quiet. She stays in my arms, her face buried against my chest.

"What did your family dress up as?" I ask. I don't want to make it worse, but talking sometimes helps. "I know about last Halloween, but what about before?"

She tells me about the years of Mrs. Winter's rabbit with three carrots, of milk and cookies, of cardboard boxes turned into a fleet of race cars. "Dad would stay up late working on the costumes. Mom always said it was silly, but I think she liked it just as much as the rest of us." She sighs, and her body shudders against mine. "I hope she's okay."

I run my hand through her hair, wishing I could brush some of her pain away. "She's probably thinking the same thing about you."

Rae tilts her head, and her eyes catch mine. Tears trace down her cheeks, and I wipe them away gently. Her nearness steals my breath and sets my heart pounding, and the sounds of the Scream recede to faraway chatter. My fingertips graze her skin as she lifts her chin, lips parting slightly, and I lean forward to close the space between us.

At the last possible moment, she looks away, and my nose bounces off her cheek.

"I can't." Rae speaks so softly I would have missed it if my face hadn't been hovering centimeters from hers.

"You don't have to." I pull back, my skin hot with embarrassment. "It's fine if we don't. I'm sorry."

"Don't be. It's my fault." Her body sinks a little with those words, and she pulls her hand from mine. "It's all my fault."

The lines of *I'm sorry* flash before me. "What are you talking about?"

Her voice comes in a strangled whisper: "The accident."

Guilt thickens those two words, and despair clouds her face. She turns away, but I catch her chin, drawing her gaze back.

"Rae, no. It wasn't. It was the other driver. He was drunk, and he hit you." Her desperate expression doesn't change, so I keep pleading, trying to make her understand. "You have to stop blaming yourself. Your dad would want you to be happy—"

"He wanted me to drive!" The words burst out in a torrent, and she doubles over, tears spilling down her face with each ragged breath. "He asked me to drive that day when he picked me up. I was supposed to be practicing; I had my permit. But I told him no, I was tired and didn't feel like it, so he didn't make me. I hardly even talked to him, I was on my phone the whole time, and then that car hit him so hard . . ."

"Rae, stop. Please," I beg, but she can't hear me, not over the sobs racking her body.

"I always drove home. I should have been in that seat." She

jerks away from me and lurches to her feet. "That should have been me!"

"Wait!" I reach for her, but she turns and stumbles away. "Just stop, okay?"

She doesn't listen, shaking off my hand as I touch her arm, and a figure dressed like a mad scientist comes jogging toward us. It's not until he's close that I recognize Toshi beneath the white wig and bright green goggles.

"Rae?" he calls. "Are you okay?"

Wonderful. I don't know if he's a Sweeper—if the Sweep even exists—but I do know his timing couldn't be worse. "Go away, Toshi. Not now, okay?"

He ignores me. "Rae?"

She stops, rubbing her hands over her eyes. "It's all right. We're fine."

He steps closer to her. "Are you sure?"

My face heats up. The guy can't take a hint. "She said it's fine!"

His lip curls. "Doesn't seem fine."

I storm toward him, ready to rip his goggles right off his face. "What?"

"Matt, don't," Rae says, but hot anger already clouds my vision, and I barely feel her fingers on my arm.

Toshi glares at me. "You heard me. She's so upset she can hardly stand, but everything's *fine*—"

The frustration that had been building this last week explodes, a volcano erupting with white-hot heat. My fist shoots out and connects with his chin, knocking his wig side-ways as he staggers back.

"Leave her alone!" The words spew from my mouth. "She's not your project, understand?"

"What?" Toshi winces as he touches his jaw, but I raise my fists again, and his eyes narrow. He launches himself forward, hands crashing into my chest. Anger crackles over me, filling my ears and drowning out Rae's shout, and we tumble to the ground. I land another punch on his cheek, but he returns a blow that makes my head ring. The world dims, sharp lines turning hazy, and then more hands are on me, pulling me up.

"Matt, stop it!" Moose's voice cuts through the buzzing in my ears. "Come on, relax."

I blink, and the shapes around me take form. Juan holds Toshi, who glares daggers in my direction, and Sahana stands beside Rae. The dismay on both their faces spurs a wave of shame that swallows my fading anger.

"What's going on?" Captain Walsh demands, pushing through the crowd that has gathered. Some people even point their phones in my direction, recording the fight.

Dad is going to love this.

CHAPTER

24

"What happened, boys?" Captain Walsh frowns at Toshi and me. "Are your parents here?"

"My mom—" Toshi begins, but a shrill voice cuts him off.

"Toshi! Are you all right?" A woman shoves her way through the crowd and points an accusing finger at me. "Officer, arrest that boy—"

"Mom, stop it." Toshi pushes her hand down. "No one's getting arrested." He turns to me, anger replaced by wariness. "But you need to chill. All right? Are we good?"

If he really was my competition for the Sweep, he would have gleefully let Captain Walsh haul me away. Instead, he's helping, which makes me feel even worse about the bruise purpling his cheek. "Yeah. We're good. I'm sorry."

"It's not *good*!" Toshi's mom snaps. "You should be suspended. Kevin McNally is here. He'll do something!"

"He can't." Juan steps away from Toshi to join Moose and me. "We're off school grounds. And it's not a school event."

"Practicing for that career in law, Mr. Esparza?" McNally shoulders his way past a group of gawking witches. "You're right, unfortunately. I'd be happy to give Matthew's father a call, but I think the boys are done here tonight." He crosses his arms, and I take it as a signal to go.

The others slowly follow me to the front of the park. "I'm sorry," I tell them, though I'm mostly talking to Rae. She hasn't said a word since the fight. "I shouldn't have done that."

"You think?" Sahana shoots back. Rae nods, and the last of my anger winks out.

Moose punches my shoulder gently. "At least now we know you have a wicked right hook. Not bad for a zombie."

Kendrick taught me that punch, but I doubt he ever thought I would use it in a situation like this. My cardboard axe is gone, lost somewhere in the bushes, and a new hole decorates the knee of my jeans. I touch my sore chin, and my fingers come away smeared with paint and dirt. If I didn't look undead before, I do now.

"McNally can't touch you with anything official, but he'll definitely call your dad," Juan says. "Probably haul you into his office too. Better have an explanation ready."

I nod. "Thanks. And thanks for helping me back there."

"No problem." He elbows me. "We zombies need to stick together."

His words soothe the shame that aches worse than any of Toshi's blows. "I should go. Sorry about the costume contest, Moose."

"That's all right." He taps my shoulder with his cleaver. "Sure you're okay?"

"Yeah." I look at Rae, though it's hard to meet her eyes. "Sorry again."

She doesn't answer, her face still shadowed with sadness as I trudge away. Halfway down the block, she calls my name.

I turn to see her hurrying toward me, leaving the others standing where I left them. Sahana's expression sends a clear warning, and my shoulders automatically straighten.

"What is it?" I ask, when Rae reaches me. "Are you all right?"

She nods. "Can you give me a ride home? I don't really feel like staying."

"Sure." I don't know if this means I've been forgiven for fighting or if she just wanted to let Sahana stay and enjoy the party, but it's something. She falls into step beside me, and we walk to my car in silence. When I open her door, she pauses.

"Don't do that again." Her sharp tone pierces the quiet. "I mean it, Matt. Especially not because of me."

"I won't," I say quickly. "I promise. It was wrong. I just got so mad, and then . . ." My voice trails off. There's no explanation, no reason for punching Toshi like I did. Already, the fight itself is a blur, and only a feeling of utter stupidity remains.

"I won't," I repeat, but the look on her face doesn't change.

It's a long ride.

I park in front of her house, and Rae unbuckles her seat belt. She reaches for the door, but I can't just let her go, not after hearing that terrible guilt she's been carrying since the accident.

"What you said about how you were supposed to drive that day . . ." I bite my lip as she stills, her fingers frozen on the handle. "Rae, it wasn't your fault. None of it was. Nobody knew what was going to happen. It's awful your dad died—so much worse than awful—but you have nothing to be sorry for. If you want to blame someone, blame the guy who hit you. All you did was survive, and you can't blame yourself for that."

Her eyes fill, and she eases back in her seat. I wait for her to speak, but she doesn't, and it's like we're back behind the church, sitting in front of her father's grave with that silence settling between us. The minutes slip past, and then she leans across the seat to me.

I don't move. "You don't have to. That's not what I meant."

Her eyes glint in the porch light. "I know."

Our noses bump as I meet her halfway, and she tilts her head and kisses me. Her lips are soft against mine, and she tastes like ice cream and tears. I pull her closer, my hand slipping into her hair, and her touch on my skin sets my heart thumping in a whole new way.

All too soon, she lets me go. Her fingers graze my cheek once more, sending a jolt right down to my toes, and she opens the door and climbs out.

"Thanks, Matt." Rae bends down to look at me. "What you said—thank you." Her smile trembles, and I squeak a "Bye!" as she turns and goes inside.

My head spins, and I fumble for the ignition as a wide grin stretches across my face. The drive home passes in a daze, my skin still humming from Rae's touch and the kiss replaying in my head. Did she know it was my first? Did I do it right?

It sure *felt* right.

The walk to the little shack seems different, as if the world is smiling back at me. Even the bench Mr. Garrett pulled across his front steps, sending a clear message to any potential trick-or-treaters, only makes me chuckle. My room doesn't feel so empty, and the chill seeping through the cracks lacks its usual bite. I toss my keys onto the table, and they land next to my laptop, which I left out after working on this week's report for the Sweep.

All it needs is tonight's update.

The thought shatters my joy like a bullet through glass, and a hail of remorse hits. I slump into the chair. Our kiss only complicates the project, deepening the mess I'm making in Mills Creek. What was I thinking?

Best-case scenario: Rae remembers me as a nice guy who moved here for a year. It's not like we're going to stay in touch.

Worst-case scenario: Dad orders me to burn her on my way out.

At least now I'm convinced Toshi has nothing to do with the Sweep. He hadn't been faking that confusion, and he saved me from a jail cell when a competing Sweeper would have left me to rot. The realization lifts the fear Toshi will ever harm Rae, sending a wave of relief through my aching body. My bed beckons, but there's one more thing to do tonight.

Despite the late hour, Dad picks up on the second ring. "Matthew? Is everything okay?"

The alarm in his voice brings a rush of guilt. "It's fine. I just need to tell you something." I launch into the events of the evening, starting with the Scream and ending with the ride home.

I leave out the kiss.

When I finish, the line is silent. "If your teacher calls, I'll handle it," Dad finally says. "But Matthew, you need to be careful. Nothing to draw more attention, understand? Absolutely no more fights."

"Yes." My finger already covers the "End" button. "Thanks. Sorry I woke you."

"One more question." He pauses. "Exactly what caused this? You didn't want the other boy to interfere?"

I did my best to gloss over this part, but of course he found it. "That's right. I even thought Toshi might be a Sweeper, remember? But he's not," I add quickly, in case Dad decides to dispense with my competition for me. "He's just a regular kid."

"I see," he says slowly. "So this was a rational decision for the project?"

Even miles away, he sees it. "Yes. I'm just doing my job."

The lie tastes bitter, but it works.

"All right," he finally says, and hangs up.

I uncurl my fingers from the phone. My face leaves paint smudges on the screen, and the mirror shows a zombie who has seen better days. I scrub myself clean and tumble into bed.

The report can wait.

My jaw throbs where Toshi punched it, but the tingle on my lips from Rae's kiss makes the pain fade to nothing. Dad might scold me for being foolish tonight, and Kendrick would call it worse. Both might be right.

Still, I want more.

I toss and turn, trying to get comfortable, but the memory

of Rae's sobs echoes in my ears. Burying my head in the pillow does nothing to drown them out, and the raw pain in her voice makes my chest throb. Kendrick told me to watch for signs, but I didn't see the Mark tonight. I saw a girl being crushed by tragedy and the ocean of guilt it spawned.

Perhaps if Dad and Kendrick had heard her, if they had felt the pain bleeding from every inch of her, they would know Lucifer missed too. But they didn't, and I already know it wouldn't matter. To them, Rae's wrenching confession would become nothing more than a disguise, another piece of the Mark's deception, since they would rather set people on fire than try to understand their pain.

What else have Dad and Kendrick missed—not just with Rae, but with Mrs. Polly and all the projects who came before? The question ricochets through me, an internal hurricane raging for answers, until at last Rae's calm logic breaks through.

Except this time, the voice is mine.

Accidents change people. A brush with death could shift anyone's perspective, and some, like Rae, lost loved ones on those horrible days. Our projects may have survived, but they didn't walk away untouched. The scars just lay deeper.

An accident might mark a soul, but Lucifer's not to blame.

Mrs. Polly's screams stab through me, bringing the agonizing realization that most of my life has been based on nothing more than a madman's tales. Though I try, I can't blame Dad for this. He may have set the fires, but he's as much a victim as I am, recruited to judge and burn when he was at his most vulnerable. His grief for Mom must have been overwhelming, and it made him an easy target for the man who spawned the Sweep and its dreadful purpose.

Dear old Uncle Kendrick.

CHAPTER

25

Monday morning, I pull up in front of Rae's house, and my heart quickens with the memory of the kiss that happened the last time I parked here. We skipped tutoring on Saturday after the late night at the Scream, and she took the weekend off from Charon's as well. She texted that she had spent some time at her dad's grave site and talked with her mom about the accident, but aside from a few messages from Moose and Juan to make sure I was all right, my phone remained silent except for Dad's calls. I assured him each time the project was fine and I was watching closely, which was the truth.

With him and Kendrick convinced of Rae's Mark, leaving her alone isn't an option.

I haven't figured out the whole plan, but my priority is keeping Rae safe. At least I know now that I have no competition for this project, which means Dad can no longer rush me. I have ten and a half months to fill with reports of Rae's excellent behavior and the ordinary events of her day. Dad and Kendrick won't hear of a single accident or questionable encounter, so they won't be able to argue when I judge her among the lucky ones. In the meantime, I'll work to pry Dad free from Kendrick's grip.

As long as he doesn't burn his project along the way, we'll be fine.

Once the year ends, Rae will be safe. Dad and I will tell Kendrick we're done with the Sweep, and maybe he'll let us walk away.

If he doesn't, then it's a good thing I've been such an excel-lent student. He won't even see it coming.

"Hi, Matt," Mrs. Winter says as she answers my knock. The smallest furrow appears on her forehead, and I can feel her examining me more closely than before. "Rae told me what happened at the Scream. Are you okay?"

My gaze drops to my feet. "Yes. I'm sorry. It won't happen again."

I half expect her to tell me to stay away from Rae, but her voice stays kind, though it holds a firmness that says she's serious. "Maybe use words from now on, all right?"

It's the same thing Dad said—words, not fists—though her reasons couldn't be more different. "I will," I promise.

Footsteps hurry toward us, and Rae appears. The look she exchanges with her mom suggests more had been said about me that weekend, but Rae just asks, "Did you talk to him about dinner?"

"Not yet." Mrs. Winter smiles at me, her eyes still watchful. "Rae tells me you've been surviving on cereal while your dad travels. Why don't you come eat with us tomorrow night?"

A dinner invitation is the last thing I expected. She's

making this too easy, though part of me suspects she might want to know more about the boy who drives her daughter around, especially after my fight on Halloween. I suppose this is what normal parents are like—always trying to meet their kids' friends, feeding and watching over them when their own parents fall short, even forgiving them when they mess up.

Not analyzing them for signs of Lucifer.

"That would be great," I tell her. "Thank you."

"Thanks, Mom!" Rae follows me toward the car. "Bye, Cade!"

"Wait!" Cady runs through the door carrying Rae's forgotten lunch bag. "I put in a cookie. Chocolate chip."

Rae takes the bag and pulls her sister into a hug. "You're the best. You know that?"

"Yup." Cady hugs her back. "But you're okay too."

She and Mrs. Winter stay in the doorway, watching as we drive away. Rae rolls down her window to wave before tucking her lunch bag into her backpack.

"That was nice of her," I say. "Was the weekend okay?"

"Better than okay. I told Mom and Cady what happened the day of the accident, and they didn't get mad at all. They both actually cried." Sadness creases Rae's face. "Mom said none of it was my fault, and that if Dad were here, he would tell me the same thing. Cady agreed. It feels good they know the truth and don't blame me."

Maybe whatever wound opened in her that day can finally start to heal. "Think you can stop blaming yourself too?"

Rae nods slowly. "Mom keeps telling me she loves me, that Dad loves me too, and it's okay to be sad or angry or whatever. Cady just hugs me. It still hurts, but it doesn't feel like I'm hiding this horrible secret anymore. I can finally breathe again."

Good. If Rae's behavior keeps improving, it won't be hard to convince Kendrick she escaped the Mark. "That's great."

"Yeah." Her voice softens. "Thanks for helping me, Matt. I really appreciate it."

"All I did was get in that stupid fight," I say, but she shakes her head.

"You listened to me talk about Dad, you took me home, you told me it wasn't my fault. That's a lot."

A sudden thought pinches me. "Is that why you kissed me? To thank me?" I brake at a stop sign, and the car jerks. "You didn't have to do that."

She smiles. "No, Matt. I said 'thank you' to thank you. I kissed you"—she leans over and does it again, and my lips hold hers until she pulls away—"because I wanted to."

A wave of heat sweeps through me. "Okay. Just checking."

Not everyone is ready to forget the fight, however. McNally delivers his entire math lecture standing a foot from my desk, calling on me for every other answer, and keeps me after the bell to berate me for my behavior at the Scream. Coach holds me in at lunch to shake hands with Toshi, which we both sheepishly do, and the idea this skinny boy with a lopsided grin could be part of the Sweep now seems ludicrous. Lunch makes up for it, however, as Rae sits close enough that her knee brushes mine, and an invisible current hums between us like a spark only the two of us can see.

At least that's what I think until cross country ends, and Moose elbows me in the side.

"Spill it," he says.

"Ow!" I rub my ribs. "Spill what?"

"The story behind that goofy look you've been wearing all day." Juan nods to where the girls are finishing their workout. "Does it have something to do with a certain friend of ours? What happened after you left the Scream?"

"Rae was upset." I shrug. "I took her home."

Moose crosses his arms. "And?"

"Nothing! Well, not really. Just—" I hesitate. "Nothing."

His eyes grow round. "You totally kissed her."

"Um—" I glance at Rae, who watches us as her team gathers around Coach. From the looks Moose and Juan are casting her way, she knows exactly what we're talking about.

"Do not lie." Juan points at me. "Did you, or did you not, kiss Rae?"

"Not exactly." They're going to find out anyway. "It's more like she kissed me."

"Oh, man." Moose throws his arm around my shoulders. "Our little Matt's all grown up."

"Cut it out." I squirm free. "It's nothing."

"What's nothing?" Rae comes up behind me.

"Matt's just telling us about Friday," Juan says innocently. "When he wasn't busy punching Toshi, it seems he had a good time."

"So did I." Reaching up, she gives me a quick kiss before heading toward the locker room. "See you guys later."

Moose's mouth hangs open, and it's my turn to elbow him. "Maybe I can give you some tips for Tyson."

"Yeah." His face breaks into a grin. "Maybe."

Juan chuckles. "Poor Toshi. He's been crushing on Rae ever since he got here, and all he gets is a zombie punching his jaw. At least maybe now he'll stop staring at her. I think it was driving her crazy."

I laugh along with them, though I can't help feeling silly for all the moments I suspected Toshi had been analyzing her for the Sweep—a fictional competitor for an imaginary organization. I've been so wrong. He's just a classmate, Ms. Timmult is merely a teacher, and all the people I've seen around Mills Creek are nothing more than regular people.

The only one who doesn't belong is me.

CHAPTER

26

Tuesday passes quickly, with the usual McNally sunshine and a hilly workout from Coach. I finish before Rae and head for the shack, ignoring Juan's and Moose's wide grins since they know where I'll be going for dinner tonight. After a quick shower, I grit my teeth and call Dad, who made me promise to phone for last-minute instructions.

"Hi," I say when he answers. "Just letting you know I'm leaving."

"Make sure you're presentable," he instructs, and I roll my eyes at my reflection in the mirror. "Watch your manners, and maybe they'll invite you back."

"Dad—"

"And bring flowers. Or chocolates. Don't show up empty-handed."

"Dad! It'll be fine, okay? It's just dinner."

"It's access," he corrects. "Try to engage the project and make a stronger connection. That will help you see the Mark more easily."

"I'm going to be late," I tell him, and hang up before he can say more.

The Winters' car is in their driveway when I park, and I straighten the collar of my shirt before knocking. Rae opens the door.

"Thanks for inviting me." I hold out the flowers I bought on my way over. All the bouquets in the market looked the same to me, but a clerk assured me these would be perfect. Rae's smile tells me the man chose well.

"They're beautiful," she says. "Thank you."

She carries them into the kitchen, where Mrs. Winter calls hello from the stove as she stirs a steaming pot. A delicious smell—chicken, I think—hits me, and freshly chopped vegetables sit in a bowl beside a cutting board. For the briefest moment, the feeling of home wraps around me, though it's certainly not like any home I remember.

"Matt, that's so thoughtful of you," Mrs. Winter says, when Rae shows her the flowers. "I'll put them in a vase. Why don't you two get some homework done? Dinner won't be ready for a while."

"Thanks, Mom," Rae says, and points me down the hall. Cady's door is open, and I peek inside to see her lying on her bed, nose in a book.

"Hi," I say, and she looks up, says hello, and smirks at her sister, who shoots her a glare.

"Ignore her," Rae tells me, leading the way into her room.

My last visit to this space had been a terrible invasion, and I try to block out the rising guilt as I enter. At least I'm here now by invitation, so I take my time absorbing the touches that make this room hers. The photo of Mr. Winter and Rae catches my eye again, and I stop in front of the bulletin board.

"That's from my last birthday." Rae straightens the photo with a gentle touch. "We went every year. Kind of like our own tradition."

"That's really sweet," I say.

"Yeah." Her mouth curves in a small smile. "I'd always get a peanut butter and chocolate shake. He'd get banana."

"A banana milkshake?" I cringe. "Sorry, but that's . . . kind of gross."

She chuckles. "That's what I told him."

She settles at her desk, and I flop into the beanbag, both of us opening our laptops as we discuss the essay Ms. O'Brien assigned. The room grows quiet except for the click of our keyboards, and analyzing literature with Rae only a few feet away suddenly becomes an excellent way to spend the afternoon.

When Mrs. Winter calls us for dinner, Rae stretches. "I've got four pages. What about you?"

"Three." I shut my laptop. "But they're brilliant."

She rolls her eyes, the corners of her lips twitching, and guides me to the table, which now holds roast chicken, mashed potatoes, and garlicky green beans. I hesitate to choose a seat, since one of them belonged to Mr. Winter, but Rae gestures to a chair as she and Cady pour drinks and grab plates. Everyone digs in, and the food tastes better than anything I could find in a restaurant. Stories about school and work flow easily, the best of which is Mrs. Winter's tale of a misbehaving guinea pig that escaped its owner in her waiting room, and I'm miles from my usual dinner routine, words and laughter filling every space.

Meals with Dad are never like this.

When we finish our ice cream sandwiches, Cady delivers her plate to the sink and makes a beeline back to her room, but Rae and I tell Mrs. Winter to enjoy her tea while we clean up. She finally agrees, selecting the "Best Mom Ever" mug from the shelf over the coffee maker, and Rae scrubs pots as I carry dirty plates and silverware to the counter. I drop a fork along the way, and it skitters under the table with a clatter.

"Oops." I set down the rest of the dishes. "I'll get it."

I kneel and reach for it, and a small device attached to the underside of the table catches my eye. Tape fastens it behind a wooden leg, nearly obscuring it from view, but I recognize the audio transmitter immediately since it's identical to the one I put in Mrs. Polly's bedroom. The last time I saw it, the bug had been in Dad's hand.

"Find it?" Rae asks.

I grab the fork as my throat seals shut, since anything I say will end up in Dad's ears. Not that my sudden silence matters. He's already heard our entire dinner conversation, as well as anything else said in this room today. I want to tear the bug free and smash it, but there's no way to do that without Rae and Mrs. Winter noticing, so I pull myself to my feet, set the fork on the counter, and begin rinsing the soapy dishes. Mrs. Winter asks when my dad will be back, and my brain fumbles to answer knowing he'll hear every word.

"What did you say?" Mrs. Winter comes closer and leans against the counter. "Sorry, Matt. I couldn't catch that."

Probably because I'm whispering, which won't help anyway

since the kitchen is too small and the table too close.

"Tomorrow," I repeat. Dad had told me this during his call last night, and I thought the midweek visit meant my behavior on Halloween worried him more than he let on. Now I know the real reason, since he can't just leave the bug sitting there. "Only for the day, and then he has to leave again."

I analyze everything that comes out of my mouth, wondering how Dad will interpret each word. A chill splits the house as if someone cleaved it with an axe, and the windows suddenly offer too many views of the rooms inside. I finish the dishes without breaking any, which is an accomplishment since I've been rattling them to try to cover our conversation, and retrieve my backpack.

"You can stay longer," Rae offers, but I plead exhaustion from Coach's workout. Leaving the transmitter in the house makes me fume, but there's no way to extract it without drawing attention. She walks me to the porch, and Mrs. Winter gives me a hug as I thank her once again.

"Come anytime," she tells me. "I mean that, especially when your dad's gone. You're always welcome."

They watch as I drive away, and the calm demeanor I held together through the last hour evaporates the moment I turn the corner. A garbled yell bursts out, and my fist hammers the steering wheel. By the time I kick the door of the shack shut, frustration burns through me, and the frigid room swallows any lingering warmth from my visit.

In this bleak space, there is no hiding.

Tonight's dinner is just another entry for the red notebook, my carefully chosen outfit is a cunning disguise, and even the bouquet I brought was nothing more than a pretty lie. The shack is a hideout, not a home, and my promise to fill Dad in when I returned feels like I'm on the wrong side of an inside joke, since he already knows exactly what happened. I should call him and yell, but I can't even do that, not with my stomach still full from Mrs. Winter's dinner.

Taking my knife, I settle beneath the oak and start carving, as if I can cut away the parts of me I no longer want and create something new. I finish hours later with nothing but splinters and slivers, which I suppose is fitting.

If I cut away all the pieces I don't want, there's not a whole lot of me left.

My phone vibrates through class the next day, since I never talked with Dad last night. I had let his many calls go to voicemail and finally sent a short text: Went fine. Tired. Talk tomorrow.

Looks like tomorrow is here.

I don't know what to say that doesn't end in an argument, but then again, one feels long overdue. He's not supposed to arrive until later this evening, but his footsteps sound outside the shack minutes after I get home.

Guess there's no hiding any longer.

I open the door. "Hi, Dad."

"You should have called last night." He frowns at me before brushing past, dropping his suitcase as he sits at the table. His fingers drum its stained surface. "Tell me about it."

"Don't you already know?" I should stop, but my mouth keeps going. "I found the bug, so don't pretend you didn't hear every word."

I hold my breath, waiting for him to deny it, but his fingers pause and his frown deepens. When he speaks again, the words come tight and clipped.

"I didn't plant a bug, Matthew."

His face shows alarm, not deceit, and I know him too well to misread it. Coldness ripples over me. "We used one just like it for Mrs. Polly . . ."

"Tell me what you saw," he says.

I describe the small black transmitter taped beneath the table. It's not as if the person who left it signed his name, but if it wasn't Dad, there's only one other guess. "How did Kendrick know I was going to be there? I didn't tell him."

"I did." Dad rubs his chin, and it's clear whatever Kendrick is up to, he left Dad out of the plan. "I thought it might help if he knew how well you were doing. I never suspected . . . Did you say anything he shouldn't have heard?"

I replay the night in my head. "No. We just talked about class and Mrs. Winter's work, stuff like that. I put it all in the notebook, and I'll send it in the weekly report too."

"All right," he says, but his voice doesn't relax, and my throat goes dry as he leans over and peers under my table. "You need to make certain Kendrick likes what he sees. And hears."

"I will," I assure him, and the evening passes under a new cloud.

Kendrick is watching more closely than I thought.

The next day comes too soon, since I spent most of the night either sitting outside the Winters' house or lying in bed with my eyes open. My usual escape to the branches of the oak would have left me exposed, and the thin walls of the shack provide a poor barricade against anyone lurking outside. Even Dad's nearby snores offered little comfort, though the thought of being here alone almost makes me wish he would stay.

We leave at the same time that morning, me to pick up Rae and him to return to his project. At least he assures me he's not certain whether the musician is Marked, which means he won't be burning anyone soon. My mind is a jumbled mess through school that day, and I spend the night turning the shack inside out for any more of Kendrick's bugs.

I find nothing.

Worry claws at me, but I turn it into fuel for running, channeling all the craziness churning inside to my legs on longer morning workouts. I even let loose a little more in cross country and leave Toshi far behind in Thursday's meet. My new PR shaves a minute off my old time, and Coach skips all the way to the bus.

"Matt!" he hollers the moment I step onto the track for Friday's practice. "What a run! Did everyone see him?" Heads nod, and Moose lets out a whoop. "The biggest improvement of the season! And that's not all. Eleven other PRs got set yesterday. Raise your hand if you're one of them!"

Hands go up, along with shouts and cheers. Coach beams. "In honor of a spectacular race, I've brought punch."

More cheers. I nudge Rae. "Punch?"

"It's this blue drink he gets at the grocery store," she

whispers. "A gallon for ninety-nine cents. We have no idea what's in it, but the man loves it."

"It will be waiting for you at Boulder Park," Coach announces. "Better hurry, or there might not be any left!"

Like a herd of cattle, we make our way off campus and start jogging. Boulder Park is only two miles away, which must be Coach's idea of a celebratory day off. Everyone bumps together—boys and girls, Varsity and JV—and I find myself with Moose, Juan, and Rae.

"What are you guys doing this weekend?" Rae asks. "I'm off Saturday. Mr. Yamamoto's bringing someone in to fix a plumbing problem, so Charon's is closed."

"Plumbing problem?" Juan pants, wrinkling his nose. "That sounds . . . unpleasant."

She whacks his arm. "It's a leak. No toilets involved."

"I've got it!" He grins. "Apple picking at Walsh's Farm. The perfect fall activity."

"Sounds great," I tell him.

"Yes!" Rae flashes me a smile. "Sahana has relatives visiting, so she won't be able to come, but it'll be fun."

"Definitely," Moose says, and his ears turn pink as Juan snorts. "What? You're the one who suggested it."

"I'm trying to help your love life." He dodges Moose's elbow and grins at me. "Did you know Tyson's dad owns the orchard? He helps out every weekend. Apple picking for the rest of us, and time with Tyson for our boy here."

"I don't need your help!" Moose shoots back as we reach the park. "Matt, can you drive? My mom asks too many questions whenever I want to take the car out, and some of us"—he rolls his eyes at Juan—"are too young for a license since we couldn't be bothered with second grade."

Juan shrugs at me. "I skipped. Not really rocket science, you know?"

I laugh, but my eyes cut to Rae, whose gaze remains fixed on the ground. She hasn't gotten behind the wheel since the accident, though she told me her mom promised to take her driving whenever she felt ready. I let my shoulder bump hers, scrunching my forehead in a silent *Are you okay?* when she looks up, and she gives a reassuring nod.

"Sure, I'll drive," I say. "Meet at Mr. Garrett's?"

The others agree, and I follow them to the park's picnic tables, where Coach is pouring punch.

"Great race yesterday!" he says, handing each of us a cup.

"A toast!" Moose raises his electric blue drink. "To apple picking."

"To Matt's PR," Rae reminds him.

"How about to all of you?" I suggest. "Because if you weren't there, I would have quit the first day."

"To us!" Juan announces, and we tap our cups together.

To us. I like that.

I jog to the front of Mr. Garrett's house at ten the next morning. The street is still empty, so I settle on the curb, resting my elbows on my knees.

Behind me, the door creaks.

Mr. Garrett shuffles down the steps, his bathrobe pulled around him, and bends to retrieve the newspaper lying on the sidewalk. His gaze falls on me, and I can't pretend I'm invisible any longer.

"Hey, Mr. Garrett," I say.

He straightens, newspaper in hand. "What are you doing out here?"

A typical Mr. Garrett greeting. "Waiting for some friends. We're going apple picking at Walsh's."

"You're late. Season's almost over." He frowns at me, like it's my fault the apples aren't cooperating. "Go up the north side. Everyone else goes the other way, so those trees get picked over first."

Who knew Mr. Garrett was an apple-picking expert? Maybe this is from the days of Loretta. "Okay. Thanks."

He grunts and heads back inside. Without looking, I already know he's watching from the window.

A few minutes later, a black hybrid sedan pulls up, and Juan and Moose scramble out.

"Thanks, Dad," Juan calls to the man behind the wheel. "Hey, Matt. You ready?"

I nod. "Just need Rae."

"Here she comes," Moose says, as the Winters' car turns the corner. Rae climbs out, and Mrs. Winter rolls down her window.

"Have a great time, everyone." She gives me a worried smile. "Drive carefully, Matt. Okay?"

Coming from her, this is more than normal parent worry.

She knows better than anyone what happens when people don't drive carefully.

"I will," I promise. She blows Rae a kiss and pulls away.

"Shotgun!" Moose hollers. He scrambles into the front seat, and Juan and Rae settle into the back. There's general chaos as everyone finds their seat belts, and then we're off.

The drive is like a picture out of some scenic movie, with the leaves showcasing the fall colors, and even Moose stops talking long enough to enjoy it. We crest the hill, and the valley spreads out below us, its green fields punctuated by barns and corrals and the apple trees in the distance. By the time we pull into the dusty parking lot beside the orchard, the gorgeous view and cheerful chatter even lets me set aside my worries about Kendrick.

For just a few hours, I'm going to pretend all this is real.

We make our way to a line of people waiting in front of a wooden stand and pass Ms. Timmult, who's just exiting with her own bag of apples. She calls a greeting, and we return a chorus of hellos. The old Matthew would have panicked to see a possible Sweeper. Now it's just nice my history teacher actually gets out and does things besides grade papers on the weekends.

"It's beautiful," I tell Rae, as a giggling group of children spill over the white picket fence surrounding the orchard. "I'm glad we could come."

"Me too." She smiles, gazing around us. "I needed this."

"So did I," Moose says, and Juan elbows him.

"Especially since . . ." He nods pointedly toward the stand,

and I peer around a group of people to glimpse a blue MCHS sweatshirt moving behind the counter.

"Stop it!" Moose hisses, as the family in front of us gathers their bags and leaves.

"Hey, guys," says Tyson. His wide smile shows off a dimple on his dark brown cheek, and the bulky sweatshirt doesn't hide the athletic frame beneath. "Hi, Moose. You here to pick apples?"

"Yup!" A blanket of blush hides Moose's freckles. If he turns any redder, his face will catch fire. "Absolutely. I love apples."

"Me too! Good thing we've got a whole orchard here." Tyson winks, and Moose practically melts. "How many bags do you want?"

"Five," Moose says, nodding emphatically. "You guys have the best apples ever."

Tyson laughs and hands us the bags. "Thanks. That's really nice of you."

"He's a really nice guy," Juan tells Tyson. "How much do we owe you?"

We pay for the bags, and Moose gives a final wave to Tyson as we head into the trees.

"I can't believe you said that!" he scolds Juan, darting a glance back to where Tyson chats with the next people in line.

"Said what?" Juan widens his eyes innocently. "I think we need to work on your conversational skills. One can only say so many things about apples."

"Like you're one to talk. Maybe you wouldn't be single if you'd just ask Sa—"

Whatever Moose was going to say turns into a yelp as he

hops on one foot, since Juan just kicked his other shin. Rae's abrupt coughing fit sounds suspiciously like laughter, and Juan's teasing and Sahana's returned sarcasm suddenly make a lot more sense.

"Let's go this way," I cut in, steering them up the north slope. "Is that a hawk?" I point to a bird circling overhead, and Moose and Juan stop bickering long enough to look. Rae gives me a grateful nod, and we take our time scuffling through leaves and fallen apples. Most people move around the other side of the orchard, with fewer groups heading in our direction, and soon fruit hangs heavy in the branches above.

Mr. Garrett was right.

"Look at all these!" Rae reaches for an apple, but it's too high. So is the next one. "Is there a ladder?"

"Here." I crouch. "Climb on."

She clambers onto my back, her hair grazing my cheek as I boost her higher. Leaning close, she brushes a kiss on my ear, and I almost wish Juan and Moose would go pick apples somewhere else.

"Can you reach them?" I ask. I'm trying not to blush, though from the way Juan smirks at me, I'm failing.

"Yes!" She drops an apple into her bag and stretches for another. The others climb the trees, and soon, our bags are full. Rae slides to the ground. "Thanks."

"No problem." I toss her an apple. "Here. You earned it."

"I sure did." Moose jumps down, plucks the apple from her hand, and takes a bite. "This is great. Way better than the ones you buy at the store."

"That was mine!" Rae protests, and pulls another from her bag. The sound of her biting into it makes my mouth water, and I reach for one as well. Soon, we're all sitting against the wooden fence, eating the fruit down to its core. Rae leans against me, and I steal a quick kiss before slipping an arm around her shoulders. The sky overhead is a beautiful blue, with wisps of clouds sweeping across like cotton, and autumn paints the hills around us in shades of red and orange. It's a perfect kind of quiet, with just the crunch of our apples in an offbeat percussion, and all of a sudden it hits me.

I don't want to give this up.

But every moment marches me toward that day I declare Rae free of the Mark, pack my bags, and leave. I can't stay, not without raising Kendrick's suspicions. I'll go somewhere new with no Rae, no friends at all, and try to finish this nightmare.

Halfway up the hills, something flashes, like sunlight bouncing off a mirror.

"What's wrong?" Rae asks. "You twitched all of a sudden."

"Nothing." I jump to my feet. "I'm hungry. Let's get lunch."

"You just ate an apple," Moose points out.

"Not enough." I prod his leg. "Come on."

Grumbling, he drags himself up. The others follow, and we make our way to my car.

"Slow down, Matt." Rae tugs my hand. "I'm dropping apples."

"Sorry." I force my legs to slow and keep my eyes ahead. Only when everyone is inside the car do I let myself look up the hill again.

The glint is gone, but the figure hunched among the trees remains. His cowboy hat blends almost perfectly with the brown bark of the branches, and he must have parked his truck farther down the road. I can't see them from here, but I know Kendrick's binoculars have been watching me all morning.

CHAPTER

28

M y face hurts from the smile I keep glued on through lunch. The others don't seem to notice, though Moose has to ask twice if I'm really going to throw away half my sandwich. I hand it to him and try to pay attention to the conversation, but my gaze keeps jumping to the window.

First the bug, and now this.

Judging from Kendrick's hiding place, he didn't plan on getting caught. I want to take Rae home, away from his prying eyes, and my forehead nearly smacks the table when Juan suggests we stop by the abandoned barn past the orchard.

"Really?" I ask Rae, as she nods along with Moose. "You want to go see some guy's barn?"

"Why not? Maybe"—she points at Moose—"this will make you stop going off about the noose that totally isn't there."

"Is too!" Moose lowers his voice and leans closer to me. "Just dangling from the rafters all these years after Old Man Pryor hung himself that night . . ."

Juan shakes his head. "You're a dork. You know that, right?"

The short drive to Pryor's barn feels like an eternity, and I watch the road and rearview mirror the entire way. Kendrick never appears, though with years of practice under his belt, it was sheer luck I spotted him earlier. It doesn't matter. Anything he saw only proves I'm doing my job, and he should be pleased at how close I am to the project. When I declare Rae's soul clean, he'll have to believe me.

I hope.

The noose, if it ever existed, is gone by the time we push through the barn doors. Time and termites have mottled the thick wooden walls, and the stale air retains the smell of animals long gone. Sunlight filters through high, dusty windows that haven't been cleaned in ages, and straw and crumpled newspapers cover the floor. Outside, nothing moves, but the surrounding trees and bushes provide enough hiding places that Kendrick could be anywhere.

I duck under a wooden beam, and cobwebs catch my hair. "Can we go now?"

"Matt, relax! We'll protect you from any ghosts." Juan points to the far end of the barn, where a rickety ladder leads up to a hayloft. "I bet that's where he did it."

Moose scrambles forward. "I want to see."

"Be careful!" Rae calls. "It looks old. And wobbly."

"Yes, ma'am," he drones, and begins to climb. Despite the creaking that accompanies each step, he reaches the top without falling. "This is great! You can see everything up here."

A view of the countryside, including any blue trucks that might be nearby, sounds perfect. "I'm coming up," I tell him, and grab the ladder. It sways as I climb, the rungs trembling with each step, but I make it to the top and haul myself up.

The loft feels spacious under the pitched roof, stretching the entire width of the barn, and its height shrinks the others standing at least fifteen feet below. A scattering of hay litters its floor, and boxes of empty mason jars that might have once been used for canning occupy one corner. I edge closer to the window in the back wall. It's really more of a square hole, since no glass keeps out rain and dirt, and the wooden frame feels worn and smooth. A sturdy tree grows in front of it, so close I can reach out and touch the rough bark. Its leaves have fallen, leaving a clear line of sight right through the bare branches. Walsh's orchard appears tiny from here, and the bumpy road leading to Mills Creek is nothing more than a meandering strip of dirt.

I almost miss Kendrick's truck, hidden behind a cluster of bushes with only a dented bumper sticking out.

"See something?" Moose asks.

"Just a bird." The truck can't be more than two hundred yards away, and the idea of Kendrick watching—not just Rae and me, but spying on Juan and Moose as well—makes me bristle. Who does he think he is? "Ready to head down?"

Without waiting for his response, I swing myself onto the ladder. I forget to be careful, to test each step before putting my full weight on it, which explains why the fourth rung from the bottom splinters under my foot. I plummet downward, and a jolt of pain shoots through my left leg as I hit the ground.

"Matt!" Rae crouches next to me. "You okay?"

"Yes," I start to say, but it comes out as a moan. I meant

to get us out of here, to escape Kendrick's prying eyes, and instead I'm sitting on the floor with a throbbing ankle.

"Hold on to me." Juan grips my arm and pulls me to my feet. "Anything broken?"

I ease more weight onto my foot. It hurts, but the pain is bearable. "I don't think so."

Juan and Rae flank me, and I put my arms around their shoulders as we begin to walk. Moose climbs down, careful to skip the broken rung still hanging in place, and moves in front of us to open the barn door. Both the truck and Kendrick are invisible from here.

I feel him, though. He's watching.

We make our way to my car, me hobbling between Rae and Juan, and Moose apologizing for his idea of climbing the ladder in the first place. I finally tell him to knock it off and stop blaming himself.

"Can you drive?" he asks, watching me hop to the driver's seat. "I can do it if you want."

"It's my left ankle. I'm fine," I lie, since Kendrick's presence makes me so far from "fine" we're basically on different planets. Ushering the others into the car, I take one last look around, lock the doors, and head for home.

The edge of the sun hovers near the horizon as Rae slips inside her house, and I pull away from the curb, still scanning for any sign of Kendrick. Juan and Moose are already safe in their homes, and all that remains in the car are me, my apples, and a whole lot of paranoia.

No blue truck followed us on the roads, but Kendrick already knows the Winters' address. He certainly knows mine. I search the streets for an hour, checking parking lots and scanning sidewalks. Once, I even chase a blue bumper around a corner, nearly crashing into it as the truck brakes in front of the dry cleaner. The elderly lady in the driver's seat honks at me, and I raise my hand in apology as I drive past. Finally, I give up and head home.

The only car parked on our street belongs to Mr. Garrett. I limp to the backyard, my ankle protesting the entire way, and swing open the shack's door.

Empty.

Setting down my apples, I sink into the chair. Outside, a breeze rustles the oak, and one of the branches scrapes against the roof. The scratching swells until it vibrates through my skull.

What do I do now?

Kendrick didn't see anything wrong. In fact, he should be impressed at my progress. As far as he knows, I'm doing the same work I've always done.

Then why do I feel so different?

Maybe my ankle hurts more than I realized. Maybe the strain of living in Mr. Garrett's shack is getting to me, or McNally has worn me down. Maybe uncovering Kendrick's awful lies finally broke me. Whatever it is, a new pain erupts as the truth—the one I've been trying not to see, the one that makes each day harder than the day before—rolls over me.

Here, in stupid little Mills Creek, it's real. The laughter. The friendships. The person my friends let me be, who is nothing like the son my father expects.

And I will have to leave it all behind.

The walls lean in, and there's suddenly not enough air inside the shack. I hobble out the door and trip over the cardboard mat I keep meaning to throw away. My ankle buckles, and my knees hit the dirt as a strangled cry slips out. I snatch the cardboard with both hands, letting frustration and rage take over as I rip it to shreds.

"I think you won." Mr. Garrett leans against the oak and surveys the mess on the ground. "Congratulations."

I drop the last pieces and rub my damp cheeks. "Sorry."

"Just clean it up." His eyebrows furrow at me. "What's wrong?"

The last thing I need is Mr. Garrett asking questions. Still, his concern seems genuine, even if it comes with his customary scowl. At the moment, it's almost enough to make me like him.

I shake my head. "Nothing. Hold on a sec."

Inside the shack, I set aside some apples and hop out carrying the rest. "Here. I can't eat them all."

Mr. Garrett eyes the bag like I'm offering him roadkill, but he finally takes it and peers inside. "You pick small ones."

"You're welcome," I tell him, and a corner of his mouth twitches.

"What happened to you?" he asks.

Admitting I fell in Pryor's barn seems like a bad idea, especially since trespassing is illegal and he already views me as a delinquent. "I tripped. Just clumsy."

He squints at my foot. "How bad is it?"

"It's not great." I try to stand on it, and the pain that rockets up my leg makes me grab the doorframe for support. "But I don't need a doctor or anything."

"Up to you," he says, still frowning. "If it gets worse though, you better get it looked at." He turns and heads for his house, crunching into an apple as he goes.

I gather the cardboard pieces and toss them in the blue recycling bin, pausing to study the fence surrounding the yard. The tall planks block out any snooping eyes, but every shadow now carries a threat, and the rustle of leaves comes like a whisper from someone just out of sight. My gaze falls on the lock Kendrick installed on my door.

Dad and I might not be the only ones with keys.

At least the hardware store is still open. The dead bolt I choose is better suited to a fortress than the shack, but by the time I put the last screw in place, no one will be coming through the door without an invitation. Even if Kendrick finds a way inside, it won't matter. He can have my T-shirts and jeans. The red notebook will stay safe in my backpack, since I can't stand the idea of him settling into my chair to read it while I'm gone. If he asks nicely, however, he's welcome to it. He can read all about my well-behaved project any time he wants.

He just better stay the hell away from Rae.

CHAPTER

29

I keep my ankle elevated most of Sunday, but it still swells to the size of a grapefruit. By next morning, walking feels like torture. I open the door, wondering how to make it past the backyard, and knock over a pair of old crutches leaning against the wall. No one is around to claim them, so I pick them up, find an easy rhythm that carries me to my car, and drive to Rae's house.

"Where'd you get those?" she asks, gesturing to the crutches as she climbs in.

"They were outside this morning," I tell her. "Maybe Moose or Juan?"

She turns in her seat to examine them, and then points to their padded tops. "Nope. Mr. Garrett." For the first time, I notice the faint black marker tracing the letters *AG* in the worn material. "That's kind of sweet."

I agree. "He's still totally grumpy, but it's like old-grandpa grumpy. Not mean grumpy."

"Old-grandpa grumpy. I like that." Rae's smile fades. "Guess you won't be going to practice today."

I cringe at the thought of disappointing Coach. "Next Friday's the last meet, right?"

She nods. "Back at Jansford. One more shot at the Monster."

My legs twitch. "Gee, I'm so sorry I can't run."

Rae pokes me. "You know you love it."

"Maybe a little," I admit. Reaching into my pocket, I pull out my latest carving: a cheetah I finished last night when sleep refused to come. My face warms as I hold it out. "Here. For luck."

"You made this?" Rae takes it, turning the sleek cat in her hands. "Wow. It's really good. Thank you."

"You're welcome." Yesterday, I almost decided not to give it to her. Now I'm glad I did.

"You should come to the meet." She sets the cheetah on the dashboard, its small ears pointing toward us. "You're still part of the team, you know."

Am I? Was I ever really?

"I'll ask Coach," I promise.

When Coach sees my crutches, his face sags like he went tumbling down the ladder right alongside me. He spends the next minutes alternating between scolding and worrying, finally sending me to my seat with instructions to see the school athletic trainer and assurances that of course I'm welcome at the meet. I make it through classes, Ms. Timmult excusing my lateness when I hobble in seconds after the bell, and wave to my teammates as they head to practice.

Juan pauses beside me. "What'd the trainer say?"

"Crutches for another week." The woman had expertly probed my ankle, declared nothing broken, and ordered me to ice and elevate it for the next few days. "But I'm out for the rest of the season."

"I think I'm jealous." He gives my crutches a mournful gaze.

"Go on." I pat his back. "Do it for Stanford."

He groans. "Why isn't it enough to just be smart?"

"Because you're not *that* smart," Moose calls as he jogs by.

"Hey!" Juan sprints after him, and I'm alone, with the afternoon to myself.

I head to the Wallflower to pass the hours with coffee and homework, and Sahana grins at me from behind the counter.

"I guess falling off a ladder is one way to get out of running. Want the iced special?"

"Sure." A sign by the register describes her newest concoction, which includes coffee ice cubes guaranteed to never dilute a drink. I tap the paper. "Clever."

"Thank you. I even used daisy molds, so they look like our flower. Hey, did you see?" She pauses pouring long enough to gesture to a framed drawing behind the counter: Cady's symbol for her father, drawn not in blue paint but with gold and silver ink. "Rae and I talked to Mrs. Batra, the owner, and she said this would be fine. Cady still has to pay to have the wall outside repainted, but Mrs. Batra knew Mr. Winter. She thought it would be a nice way to honor him."

"That's really sweet. Cady must have been happy." Her drawing shows a sophisticated hand, with lines that thicken around the curves and thin at delicate intersections. "She did a good job."

Sahana hands me my drink. "She's actually a really great artist. This guy in a cowboy hat even asked if he could take a picture of it."

"What?" Panic roots in my gut, and my hand begins to shake, sending coffee splashing across the counter. I grab a napkin and swipe at my mess. "Did you let him?"

"Sure." She shrugs. "Why not?"

Because he'll use it as evidence of Rae's Mark, just like Dad. If Kendrick collects enough of these meaningless signs, nothing I write in the red notebook will save her.

"Thanks for the drink," I say, and leave quickly, any plans to study at the coffee shop scrapped as I hurry outside and speed back to MCHS. The cross-country team will be finishing Coach's workout soon, and making certain Rae gets home safely is my new priority. I complete my math homework in the car, parked just out of sight near the front of school, and don't relax until Mrs. Winter drives away with Rae beside her.

No blue truck crosses my path on the way home, and my new lock appears untouched when I reach the shack. Still, given how Kendrick keeps showing up in places he's not welcome, it would be nice if I had a guard dog or a security camera to tell me for certain.

Come to think of it, I kind of do.

For once, Mr. Garrett isn't spying from his window when I

knock on his door. Feet shuffle on the other side, and the warm smell of apples and cinnamon drifts out as it opens.

"Hey, Mr. Garrett." I hold up a crutch. "Just wanted to say thanks. They really help."

He frowns at me. "Sure that ankle's not broken?"

"Yeah. It's already a lot better. But can I keep the crutches a little longer?"

He gives a curt nod and begins closing the door, but I put out a hand to stop him.

"Has anyone come to see me? Maybe that guy in the cowboy hat?"

Mr. Garrett shakes his head. "No cowboy hat, and not your dad either. He going to be in town for Thanksgiving?"

"I think so." We haven't planned anything, but Dad and I have been together every Thanksgiving since I was born. Despite the tension between us, the day would feel wrong without him. "We'll be quiet if you're having people over."

Mr. Garrett grunts. "Do I look like someone who throws parties? I just want an adult keeping an eye on you. Lots of drunk driving that weekend, and I don't need trouble."

The words come just as gruff as always, but the wrinkles around his eyes deepen, as if the idea of me alone on Thanksgiving actually bothers him. "I'll be fine," I assure him. "Thanks for asking."

Mr. Garrett gives me a look like he expects to have to bail me out over the holiday and then disappears, leaving the door open. A minute ticks by before he returns with a jar of golden-brown mush.

"Loretta's recipe," he says, and holds it out. I take the jar, and the door closes in my face.

The mush turns out to be applesauce. Specks of cinnamon are swirled among chunks of fruit, and I eat it straight from the jar. The warm food settles in my stomach, pushing away the worry over Kendrick's lingering presence. Maybe Mr. Garrett can even help separate my father from his mentor, giving him a friend who doesn't see the Mark everywhere he looks. It's not an ideal starting point, but right now, it's all I've got.

When Dad calls that night, I mention the crutches and applesauce, making Mr. Garrett sound almost friendly. "What do you think of inviting him to Thanksgiving dinner with us? Might be fun to get to know him."

Dad pauses. "It's a nice suggestion, Matthew, but we'll have to do it another time. Kendrick invited us over."

I press the phone hard against my ear. "Kendrick?"

"Yes. An in-person report will be good, and he's not far from you. He's got some work to do nearby."

I bet he does. Dinner with Mr. Garrett suddenly looks downright pleasant. Still, a meal with Kendrick will give me the opportunity to plant the seeds of Rae's innocence, even if the idea of the three of us sitting around a table feels like Pryor's noose tightening around my own neck.

If I'm not careful, it may be tightening around Rae's as well.

CHAPTER

30

The next two weeks creep by. My ankle heals enough that I feel only a slight twinge with each step, but I get a cramp in my neck from constantly peering over my shoulder. Even Coach asks if everything is okay.

"You look tired." He stops me as my teammates scurry past, their chatter rising as they board the bus for Jansford Park. "Are you sleeping enough? Ankle feeling all right?"

"I'm fine," I tell him, and escape onboard. Rae beckons me toward the empty space next to her, and Moose and Juan sprawl into the seat behind us. Even Toshi gives me a nod from near the back, and the excitement building for our final meet erupts in a raucous rendition of our school song as Coach bounds up the steps. He joins in, directing our singing like an orchestra conductor, and I holler along with everyone else. The energy buzzing off the walls lifts the gloom that has clung to me these past few days, and our poor bus driver does her best to ignore us as we rumble away from MCHS.

Still, if Coach noticed my behavior, Kendrick will spot it in an instant. Maybe that explains why I haven't caught a glimpse of him since that day at the orchard. Either what he saw satisfied him and he's done spying, or he's slipped farther into the shadows.

Knowing Kendrick, it's the latter.

"Are you looking for someone?" Rae peers out the window. "Is your dad coming?"

"No." Dad told me last night he was busy with his project, and I assured him all was well and not to hurry back. "He'll be here next week for Thanksgiving. Are you doing anything for the break?"

"We'll go visit my aunt." Rae's voice quiets, just like it did at lunch when she told me her father's gravestone had finally been installed, and I slide my arm around her. "She doesn't want Mom to be alone, and it'll be nice to see our cousins."

"Good." I brush a kiss across her temple, and she leans into me. "And I'm just a text away if you need anything."

A small smile brightens her face. "You going to come to my rescue?"

"You bet. I'll save you from too much turkey, and we'll take off for Vegas. I hear it's fun there."

This gets a laugh, and Moose pokes his head over the seat. "I want to come."

"Road trip!" Juan crows.

"We totally should." Moose grins. "Not Vegas, since my parents would never let me, but somewhere cool."

"Yosemite," Rae suggests. "Or the Grand Canyon." She elbows me. "This summer. What do you say, Matt?"

"Absolutely!" But I can't, and neither can she. Not for a year, at least.

The bus empties quickly once we park. Rae slows as she looks around the course and gestures at a group of adults, all wearing bright yellow T-shirts with letters that scream **RACE OFFICIAL** across the back.

"Why are so many people here?" she asks. When Juan, Moose, and I don't answer, she narrows her eyes at us. "What's going on?"

Juan sighs. "We didn't tell you since we knew you'd say no. But we might have mentioned to Coach that dirty runners cheat on the backstretch, and maybe they should monitor it for league finals."

"We didn't mention you. Or Haley," Moose chimes in quickly.

Though Coach probably figured it out, judging from the way he looked over at Rae when we talked with him after practice last week. Still, he just nodded and said he'd take care of it, and it looks like he did.

"We didn't rat on anyone," I tell her, "and now it's a fair race. So just beat her, okay?"

Rae watches the officials head for parts of the trail that usually lie out of sight. "Fine. And . . . thanks, guys."

She joins the other girls to stretch, and Coach sends the JV boys on a warm-up jog. I catch sight of Haley with her team, but she doesn't seem to notice us, and it's probably better that way. Moose and I settle amidst the mountain of MCHS backpacks and sweatshirts, where he pulls an entire loaf of French bread from his bag, rips off a chunk, and holds out the rest.

"Want some?" he offers.

By now, I'm used to Moose's prerace eating habits. "No, thanks. You need it more than I do."

"True." He takes a bite and speaks through his full mouth. "So how does it feel to be here and not run? You're crying inside right now. Admit it."

He's right, though I'll never tell him. Cross country made me part of something in a way Kendrick's Sweep never did. My teammates created a Matt-sized space for me, and they cheered me on through every slow, plodding run.

And I learned to do the same for them.

Moose waves a hand in front of my face. "Earth to Matt. If you miss it that much, feel free to hop in. I'm sure Coach will appreciate your dedication."

I push my thoughts away and return his grin. "You got me. Maybe this running thing isn't so bad after all."

"Told you." He jumps up, bread still in hand. "Let's go cheer them on."

We arrive at the crowded start as my team lines up. Most schools in the area have turned out for the event, and everyone is jostling for position, even the spectators. I slap Juan's shoulder, wishing him luck, and then hold out a fist to Toshi.

"Sorry," I tell him, and this time I mean it. "You were right. I was a jerk."

"You were." He grins as he knocks my fist with his own. "But you've improved."

Juan shakes his head sadly at my injured ankle. "Next season, Matt. We'll crush it together then."

I force a smile, but there is no next season in Mills Creek. Not for me. "Run fast" is all I can say.

By the time they finish their race, my throat aches from yelling, and I almost tripped twice as I hurried around the course to cheer. Juan ran his best time of the season, even beating out a runner in his final steps, and Moose is practically doing cartwheels beside me.

"Not bad," I say as Juan limps over, still panting.

"Best part? I am *done*." He beams at Moose. "And you are not."

Even Moose can't hide a grin. "Nice finish," he says, and they exchange high fives. "Almost looked like you had fun out there."

"Did not," Juan retorts, but he glances at the course, and a satisfied smile crosses his face.

The Varsity girls race next, and Mrs. Winter and Cady arrive just in time. We gather near the start in a solid wall of MCHS blue and white, yelling as the gun fires and runners thunder down the hill. Rae emerges in third around the turn and tears up the path, and our team jumps and screams as she sprints past.

Haley stays right at her heels.

"Where do you want to go cheer?" Moose asks me. "Can you make it to the Monster?"

I shake my head, since my ankle already throbs. "I'll wait at the finish line. Go yell at Rae to run faster. She could win this whole thing."

"I know!" He takes off after Juan and Toshi.

I join the rest of the team in our usual spot to cheer for Rae, craning my neck for a glimpse of that blue-and-white uniform. When she bolts around the final curve—the very first runner to appear—the explosion of cheers makes my eardrums hurt. She flies toward the finish line, only a few feet ahead of Haley and another girl, whose black braid bounces with each furious step. With a hundred yards left, Haley begins to close.

"Go, Rae!" Juan shouts.

"Pick it up!" Moose screams in my ear. "Rae, you gotta go!"

I join in. "Come on! You can do it!"

Everyone hollers and yells as we hold on to each other, trying to make her run faster by sheer force of will. Rae doesn't look back, but she shifts her weight forward and pumps her arms harder.

So does Haley.

But a sharp gasp rises from the crowd, and I see it too—the lace on Haley's right shoe snaps, sending one long string flapping with each stride. She keeps running, two more steps, and then her left foot lands on the broken shoelace. Her leg crumples and she crashes down, hitting the dirt ten yards before the finish line as Rae sprints across.

First place.

Spectators murmur and yell, and the girl with the black braid flies by to claim second. By the time Haley stands and hobbles across the finish line on bloody knees, seven more girls have passed.

"That looked painful," Juan mutters. "Even I feel kind of bad for her. Rotten time to break a shoelace."

Not for the runner Haley was chasing. A chill drips down my back.

Rae makes her way through the finish chute, frowning as she sees the cluster of coaches rushing to help Haley.

"What happened?" she asks, and Juan sweeps her into a bear hug.

"What happened?" Moose echoes. "You just won league finals! That"—he pounds her shoulder—"was *awesome.*"

A grin spreads over her face. "Thanks." Rae glances at Haley again. "But what about her? She was right behind me."

Juan tells her about the broken shoelace and harrowing fall, and I can't help studying her as she listens, searching for any hint of smug responsibility. Only pity pinches her face. Haley limps past on scraped legs, tears streaking her dust-covered face, and Rae casts her a look of sympathy.

"That sucks." She shakes her head. "Don't get me wrong— she's still terrible—but that's a crappy way to finish a season."

"You would have beaten her anyway," Moose says, and I agree, shoving aside any doubt. Evidence of the Mark is exactly what Dad would have seen, and I'm not like him.

Not anymore.

"No way was she going to catch you." I lean over to plant a kiss on her forehead. "You were incredible."

Mrs. Winter joins us, her smile brilliant as she wipes her eyes. She holds her arms out, and Rae steps into them.

"Dad would be so proud." Mrs. Winter's voice cracks, and she hugs Rae close. "He's watching, you know. He'll always watch over you."

Rae buries her face in her mother's shoulder, her back heaving from either exertion or the agony that her father missed this day—that he will miss every day to come. Cady shuffles next to her, and Rae reaches out to pull her into the embrace. The course quiets, people pausing in an impromptu moment of silence for the father who should have been celebrating with them, and a lump hardens in my throat.

When they let go, my eyes are as wet as everyone else's.

Moose joins his team for warm-ups while the officials gather in a quick huddle to tally scores, since the top two Varsity teams will advance to state championships. Dejected groans rise as they announce MCHS in third place, but a cheer goes up when they call Rae's name as one of the few who earned an individual trip to the state meet.

"Guess you're not done yet," I tell her, as Juan breaks into a jubilant dance.

The smile on her face grows. "Guess not."

Haley's team falls short as well, though she would have placed if she hadn't fallen. She hangs her head as attention turns to Moose's race, and we gather to cheer (and jeer, in Juan's case) for him and the other runners. Coach's tough training pays off with a first-place finish that earns the team a trip to the state meet alongside Rae, and we celebrate all the way to the exit. The Winters say a cheerful goodbye, and I board the bus and gaze out for one last look around Jansford. Funny how this barren, hilly place has wormed its way into some of my best memories.

My gaze wanders to the people still flowing toward the exit, and I spot Haley limping beside a teammate. A man slows to let her through the gate, and his brown cowboy hat hits me like a kick to the stomach. I hadn't seen him on the course, but the crowd provided enough cover for anyone who didn't want to be noticed. Kendrick lifts his head, and I can see him studying Haley's injuries as she passes.

He watched her fall, and I know exactly who he'll blame.

CHAPTER

31

I panic every time my phone buzzes throughout the weekend, dreading any word from Kendrick. It never comes. I dodge Dad's messages with texts and project-related excuses, and my weekly report highlights Rae's focus on the finish line and her surprise at Haley's accident. Our Saturday tutoring session passes in a fog as worry eats a hole through me, and it doesn't help that I spend both nights sitting in my car with my gaze bouncing between the Winters' quiet house and my rearview mirror.

At least Monday and Tuesday keep me too busy to worry, since teachers try to cram everything in before the Thanksgiving holiday. McNally breaks his record for the amount of homework given in a night, and even Coach hits us with a pop quiz. By the time Wednesday arrives, my brain hurts.

"What shall I do this afternoon?" Juan wonders aloud as Moose and I meet him in the courtyard after the last bell. "Maybe a movie. Or a nap. Or both. What about you?" he asks Moose. "Oh! That's right. Varsity's still got practice." He smirks.

"You're just jealous." Moose adjusts the duffel bag hanging

over his shoulder. "Hey, I bet Coach will take you to the championships as an alternate in case one of us gets injured. You should work out with us."

"No chance of that," Juan says smugly. "Coach will take someone fast."

"What's the deal with state championships?" I ask. "It's not at Jansford, is it?"

Moose shakes his head. "It's in Fresno. We'll drive down Friday after Thanksgiving and race Saturday morning. Probably get back late that night."

"Are you stuck on the bus with this guy?" Juan asks Rae, as she and Sahana join us. "That's the problem with qualifying as an individual. You have to go with whatever other jokers are running."

Moose catches Juan in a headlock, and they struggle for a moment before Moose lets go. "Good thing you're not an alternate," he tells Juan. "Don't have to worry about injuries."

Rae bites back a laugh. "I'm driving with Mom and Cady. We'll leave from my aunt's house and meet everyone at the hotel."

I wish I could go as well, but Dad will be in town, and the last thing I want is to accidentally bring him—and Kendrick—along. "You guys are going to do awesome."

"Pretend I'm yelling at you all around the course." Juan sighs. "I will be enjoying family time in Colorado. Gonna freeze my butt off."

"Skiing?" Sahana asks.

He shakes his head. "Grandparents' house. I'm the oldest kid, so I get to babysit all the cousins."

She raises an eyebrow. "People trust you with their children?"

"Ha," he shoots back, and we say our goodbyes and Happy Thanksgivings. Sahana will be staying in town as well, but her house will be packed with family the whole time. Mine too, I suppose. I wish Moose luck, and Rae and I linger in the courtyard after the others leave.

"Have fun at your aunt's house." I pull her close, and she wraps her arms around my waist. "Text me anytime. I'll miss you."

"I'll miss you too." She brushes her lips against my cheek, sending a thrill through me. "When's your dad getting here?"

"Tonight." I should probably clean the shack before he arrives, or at least hide the stack of comics Moose loaned me. "He'll stay for the weekend."

"That's great. He's gone so much."

"Yeah." At least some time alone with Dad will give me a chance to start raising questions about Lucifer's Mark, poking holes in all the lies Kendrick has fed him through the years. "Eat lots of turkey and pie, and good luck at state. Run fast."

"Of course. I've got my cheetah, remember?"

Her kiss makes the idea of not seeing her for four whole days almost unbearable, and she leaves me staring after her as she heads to the locker room. I make my way to the car and check my phone.

The only message is from Dad. His car is acting up, and he needs to take it in for repairs. He won't be here until tomorrow, just in time for dinner with Kendrick, which kills any chance of talking with him first.

It's going to be a long Thanksgiving.

The morning arrives in a shroud of gray and gloom. Rain hammers the roof of the shack, and I huddle under my blankets as long as I can before a crash of thunder drives me to my feet. Water drips onto the table through a crack in the ceiling, and I eat my cereal standing up. When I finish, I take the red notebook from my backpack.

Dad asked me to bring it today.

My entries focus on Rae's emergence from the crushing guilt brought about by her father's death, but given what Kendrick saw Friday, his trusty lighter could already be sitting on the table when I walk in. Any confrontation over the bug he planted in the Winters' kitchen or his spying will have to wait. Getting through dessert without orders to burn Rae will be enough.

Lunchtime passes, but I'm not hungry. I try carving a penguin out of a chunk of wet oak I find in the yard, but it ends up resembling a lumpy potato. Dad should be on his way soon, though getting his car fixed on a holiday might have taken longer than he planned. Hopefully, we can still drive to Kendrick's together, which would give me a chance to put the best possible spin on Haley's fall before our old mentor starts in.

An hour later, my phone rings.

"I'm stuck," Dad says when I answer. "The guy at the repair shop isn't answering his phone, and my car's locked inside. I called Kendrick, and he said you should head over. I'll send his address."

My fingers grip the phone. Dad might not agree with my decision about Rae's Mark, but he's more likely to listen than Kendrick. "I'll wait for you."

"No, go ahead. I have no idea when I'll get my car. Be sure to update Kendrick on the project and show him you're watching closely." He pauses. "Sorry to miss Thanksgiving dinner, Matthew. I'll be there as soon as I can."

He hangs up, and a moment later, an address appears on my phone. Time ticks past as I stare at it. Finally, I tap it, and a map opens. Less than an hour away.

Guess if Kendrick plans to spy on me, he might as well make it convenient.

I tuck the notebook inside my jacket to protect it from the rain and hurry past the television noises blaring through Mr. Garrett's closed windows. His voice rises inside, yelling at some team, and part of me almost wants to join him. I should at least stop by and wish him a happy holiday, but my brain can't handle both him and Kendrick right now.

Besides, he'll just be mad I interrupted his football game.

The streets are quiet, with most people already having braved the storm to reach their holiday celebrations, and I soon arrive at a small apartment building. An inflatable turkey bobs outside, but its cheeriness does little to calm the worry rollicking through me. I take the elevator to the third floor and knock.

"Matthew!" Kendrick booms as he opens the door. "Glad you made it."

"Hi," I say. "Happy Thanksgiving."

"Same to you. I hear Jonathan's missing a car, so it looks like it'll just be the two of us." He beckons me inside. "Hope you're hungry."

I follow him into a neat living room with a small sofa and bare side tables. Nothing about the place hints at home except his cowboy hat, which hangs on a hook near the door.

"Keep going." Kendrick waves me through another doorway. "Gotta check the bird."

I lead the way into the kitchen. The smell of roasting turkey fills the air, and the table is prepared with a pitcher and three place settings. I sit, watching him stir cranberry sauce and slice sweet potatoes. The feast doesn't surprise me. In addition to burning the Marked, Kendrick is an excellent chef.

"What kind of work are you doing here?" I ask as casually as I can. "Still opening that new center?"

"Watching you, actually." He pours a glass of water and hands it to me. "Just seeing how your project's going."

I take my time sipping the water, buying an extra minute as I study his face. The last thing I expected was the truth. "So how am I doing?" I finally ask.

"Got your notes?"

He didn't answer my question. My fingers feel stiff as I set the notebook on the table, and he seats himself across from me and begins to read.

He's slow. Deliberate. I try not to fidget, but each passing minute makes my skin crawl and my scalp itch. I refill my glass, empty it, and fill it again, and he's only made it to the third page. At last, I give up trying to sit still and wander the apartment until Kendrick finally closes the notebook.

I rejoin him at the table. "Well?" My hands clench, and I bury them in my lap. "What do you think?"

"You've got some good work here. You're organized. Detailed." He taps the notebook. "Still, it feels a bit thin. Lots of writing, but not a whole lot of evidence. Though I guess that might be changing. Tell me about the race."

My pulse quickens. "Didn't you see it yourself?"

He just shrugs. "You were closer."

The scene plays out again as I take Kendrick through each moment: the exciting finish, Haley's fall, and Rae's surprise when she heard what happened.

"I don't think she was faking it," I add, putting as much certainty into my voice as I can. "Shoelaces break. The project wasn't even looking at her."

"Or the project snapped it with a thought and wasn't even aware of what she did," Kendrick counters. "You asked for evidence the Mark exists, Matthew. You can't disregard it when it appears."

"Her eyes—"

"Are the last to change. When you reach that point, you've

already waited too long." His gaze hardens. "Sounds like you better get those matches ready. Know how you'll do it?"

The question steals my breath, strangling the air between us. Maybe this is why Dad is late; the "repair" is nothing more than an excuse to allow Kendrick to grill me alone, pushing for an outcome they both want.

I match the edge in his voice. "There's not enough proof."

"Seems like a lot to me." He tips his chair back, studying me with an intensity that makes my own gaze flinch away. "I suppose you can wait a little longer, but you need to prepare yourself. Remember, this is the hardest part of the job. You've got to be close enough to see the change, but you can't care so much you miss it. Never forget: She's a project."

"She's a person." The words jump out before I can stop them. "With a mom and a sister and friends who love her. If she really is fighting the Mark"—maybe his own lies will sway him, since the truth obviously won't—"they might be able to help. Right?"

Kendrick scratches his chin, and his calloused fingers make me wonder how many fires they've sparked. "Lucifer's a lot stronger than any of us, especially someone so young. If the girl is Marked, no amount of love is going to save her."

"You don't know that!" My voice comes out too sharp. "Maybe it's saving her right now."

"Or maybe she's losing the fight, and you're missing it," he argues. "Leave out all the guessing about whether the car's tire was old, or if that teacher's pencil slipped on its own, or if the shoelace just snapped at the wrong time. That's all speculation. It's you putting your spin on events, or worse, letting the project put her spin on them." He frowns. "And back off the boyfriend angle."

The hair on my neck bristles. "What's that supposed to mean?"

"It means we don't have time for some fairy-tale romance!" he shoots back. "Sorry to break the news, but these stories don't get happy endings. Don't be naive."

"I'm not—"

"You are!" He closes his eyes and draws a heavy breath. When he opens them again, his voice is calm but earnest. "Look, Matthew, I get it. She's pretty, she's nice to you, and you're having fun. You haven't had an experience like this before, and that's partly my fault. We can fix all that later, but right now, you've got to focus. You're a Sweeper, and there's a job to do. Your dad and I are here to support you, but you need to finish this on your own."

"I still have time." I swallow hard. "I need more evidence."

"This isn't enough?" He taps the notebook, and the frustration building inside spills out.

"I see bad luck and crappy situations. That's all!" I throw up my hands. "It's not like people are dropping dead around her."

"Is that what it would take?" Kendrick asks quietly, his face drawn, and I sink lower in my seat as I remember his wife. "The goal of the Sweep is to protect the innocent, Matthew, not wait for the Marked to strike first. That's why we're here. And even when it hurts—even when there's so much about a project to like, or even love—if that Mark lurks inside, they're already lost. The kindest thing to do is let them go."

The lines around his mouth deepen in a way that suggests the burnings don't come so easily to him either, but fervor shines in his overly bright eyes. Whatever I say won't make the Mark any less real in his mind.

"We waited with Mrs. Polly" is all I can muster.

"And I'm sure the people she killed would have appreciated if you had acted sooner." He rubs his neck and sighs. "Your father is overly cautious, but I was too when I started. Once enough people die because you're afraid to make the hard decision, you'll move faster. The last time I hesitated, my project nearly killed a nine-year-old girl. And the woman who murdered my wife?" I startle, because he's never spoken of her. "A Sweeper had been watching her for seven months. The project already killed two others, and she should have been dispatched by then. Elaine would still be alive."

There's no reasoning with those bitter words. "You said I could wait."

"I did. But not long." He stands and turns toward the stove, his back to me as he stirs the pot. "We can't save the Marked, Matthew. All we can do is save everyone else."

The rain has stopped by the time I wave goodbye to Kendrick, who stands at the front door of the building watching me climb into my car. Dinner passed with struggling con-

versation, though we both worked to avoid any further dis-
cussion of Rae. We talked about the new center he's opening
for his security company, and he asked about classes and life
without Dad. He even raised the idea of me taking a break after
this project to actually go to school and sample life as a regular
teenager.

"Really?" I had asked. "I wouldn't have to be a Sweeper?"

"You'd come back eventually, of course." Whether Kendrick
missed the hope in my voice or just chose to ignore it, I wasn't
sure. "But there's no harm in you trying out an ordinary
existence. Might help you better understand the importance of
your work and who you're saving."

The meal ended with a chocolate soufflé since he remembered I never liked pumpkin pie, and several containers full of
leftovers sit next to me on the seat. My stomach feels heavy
as I drive away, not just because I'm stuffed but because I'm
exhausted from trying to reconcile friendly Uncle Kendrick
with the crazy man bent on burning people. I suppose they
were always both there, but the part consumed by the Mark
seems to be swallowing the other.

If I don't burn Rae, he might do it himself.

The thought sends a torrent of panic crashing over me that
lasts all the way home. My tires bump the curb as I park, and I
grab the containers of food and push through the gate to where
the shack waits, leaning a little to the left like always. The
familiar sight nearly sends me to my knees, and the leftovers
go tumbling to the ground. Kendrick said I have time, but he
won't wait long. If I refuse—even if I go to the police and spill

the truth—he'll find a way past them. They won't save her.

No one will.

Defeat crushes down, and I want to punch something, break something, but all that's here is the shack and the oak, so I grab a branch blown down by the storm and hit the tree as hard as I can. The impact sends a shudder through my arms, but I do it again and again. Someone screams, and only when the wood splinters and I sag to the ground do I realize the sound came from me.

Kendrick crouches beside me as the last whimper scrapes out. "It's okay, son. Let's go somewhere and talk."

I blink at him, confused, and my words come in a hoarse mumble. "What are you doing here?"

"You forgot your notebook." He holds it up, and I can only stare at its red cover as he pulls me to my feet. "Come on. I'll drive."

"Hold on there!" Mr. Garrett's voice thunders across the yard. The old guy really can yell. "Matt, what the hell is going on?"

I look at the broken branch and the fresh scars on the tree. He must have heard me, even over his football game.

"Sorry." Something inside me cracks. He can't know. No one can. "I'm sorry."

Mr. Garrett stomps off his porch, and I'm ready for him to order me off his property when he stops and faces Kendrick. "Why don't you leave? Seems like Matt's not feeling well."

"I'll take care of him." Kendrick tries to steer me past, but Mr. Garrett plants himself in front of us, and I squirm free.

"I'm fine," I tell them both. "I just want to go home."

I've never called the shack that before.

Kendrick's hands fall to his sides, eyes flicking between Mr. Garrett and me. He weighs more than the two of us put together, but Mr. Garrett's stubborn glare makes it clear he won't back down.

"All right," Kendrick finally says. "But we have to talk soon. Call me when you're ready." He holds out the notebook, and I force one hand up to take it. With a final pat on my shoulder, he strides out the gate, and relief sweeps through me.

Mr. Garrett frowns. "Want to explain why you were beating up my tree?"

I hang my head. "I shouldn't have done that. I just— I'm really sorry."

He stares at me a long moment before bending to gather the containers of leftovers lying in the dirt. "Well, it's been here a long time and survived worse, so I think the tree's going to be fine. It's you that's got me worried. What set you off?"

I can't tell him. Not about Rae or Kendrick or any of it, though it feels like my secrets are growing too big to handle alone. "It's nothing. Just being stupid."

"You or your friend?" Mr. Garrett eyes the gate. "Think he'll be back?"

"I don't know." I watch as he stacks the containers beside my door, though I know I won't eat another bite. "Probably."

He straightens. "Where's your dad? Thought he was coming."

"Car trouble. He should be on his way." Though when Dad hears what happened, anything he says might make me wish he stayed home. "Sorry to interrupt your game."

Mr. Garrett holds my gaze. "Matt, I'm not going to pry. Whatever's going on with you is none of my business. But if you're in trouble, you need to talk to someone. Your dad, a teacher, whoever. But someone. You understand?"

I nod. "I will. But it's okay. Really."

"Didn't look okay from where I was standing. Want to sleep in the house tonight? Walls are a lot sturdier."

The offer tempts me, but the last thing I should do is involve him further. "I'll be fine. Besides, I already put a new lock on the sha—um, guesthouse." A sudden worry hits, since the shack still belongs to him. "Is that all right? Sorry I didn't ask first."

His lips twitch. "Just give me a key. And tell your friend I don't want him wandering around here, understand? If he comes to visit, he knocks at my door first. I don't want strangers on the property." He studies me once more. "Sure you're all right?"

Not at all. "Yes. Thanks again."

He gives a short nod and turns toward the house, muttering to himself. I catch something that sounds like ". . . better have scored that touchdown . . ." and then his door slams and I'm alone.

At least dinner had gone well enough, and while I want to kick myself for forgetting the notebook, there's nothing to be done about that now. The fresh scars on the oak's bark send a current of guilt through me, but like Mr. Garrett said, the tree isn't going anywhere.

Which—unless I think of something soon—may be more than I can say for me.

CHAPTER

32

Dad arrives two hours later, his car finally free and his stomach growling.

"Happy Thanksgiving," I say, as he wearily settles into the chair. I spread the containers of food on the table and check myself in the mirror, making certain no hint of my encounter with Mr. Garrett's tree remains. "How's the car?"

"It runs, and it's no longer locked behind a metal fence." Dad shakes his head. "The mechanic started football and beer early and completely forgot about me. Is this Kendrick's cooking?"

I still suspect the car problem was a ruse to let Kendrick speak with me alone, but I just nod. "You missed a feast. Did you talk with him?"

"Not yet." His hand pauses halfway to the turkey. "Why?"

"He thinks I'm getting too close to the project." My voice stays steady as I run through the explanation I developed waiting for Dad's arrival. "Your idea of becoming her boyfriend was a good one, and it's working. But I may have been a little too convincing." I add a wry chuckle. "Kendrick thinks I'm in love. Can you talk to him? Tell him I know what I'm doing?"

Dad leans back in his chair, the food forgotten. "He's not right, is he?"

I grimace. "Dad, come on. I'm doing it the way you taught me. I just don't want to rush and make a mistake."

He nods slowly. "I see."

Hopefully he does, or at least as much as I want to show him. He needs to believe I'm here to serve the Second Sweep and watch for the Mark. The fact that the entire story is based on a lie doesn't matter, because as long as it exists in Dad's and Kendrick's minds, I have to be careful.

Or Rae will burn.

I hold my breath as Dad flips through the red notebook. He pauses at Haley's fall but turns the page without a word. When he closes it, his fingers tap the table, and worry fills his eyes.

"Be careful, Matthew. Kendrick must remain confident in your work. Remember: This is a test. And you must pass."

"I will," I promise.

"Record everything in the notebook, but facts only. No interpretations. No excuses. Understand?"

"Yes." At least he isn't pressing for a burning. His unwavering belief in the Sweep may even work to my advantage, since he's judged projects like Ms. Rivera free of the Mark in the past. If I can convince him that Rae is no different, maybe he can sway Kendrick.

"One more thing, Matthew." The warning on Dad's face draws my shoulders taut. "Whenever you meet Kendrick, you do it somewhere public. Always. No matter what he says, don't go to his place alone, and never get in a car with him. Do you understand?"

"I just ate dinner with him in his apartment," I point out.

"I know." Dad frowns, rubbing a hand through his hair with more force than usual. "It was too late to change the plan when I couldn't get here, and I hoped your report would convince him you were fine. But don't do it again. Especially now."

I wait for more, but Dad just stares at me. "Okay. Why?"

His mouth tightens. "You know he's not really your uncle, right?"

"Well, yeah. But . . ." I hesitate. "What's going on?"

Dad's eyes bore into mine. "The Sweep takes your solo project very seriously, Matthew. There's a lot riding on it, all right?"

The mention of the Sweep makes me want to grab his shoulders and shake him hard enough to rattle Kendrick's lies right out of his head, but that won't work. I can think of only one way to make him understand.

"I know, Dad. But Rae Winter is a sixteen-year-old who just lost her father, and whatever is happening with her might not be the Mark. Remember how hard it was when Mom died? Didn't that change you?"

He stays quiet, anguish on his face from the memories my words must send reeling through him. Finally, he clears his throat. "Just a little more time, then."

Not good enough. "I have a year."

"Not with Kendrick so close." I open my mouth to object, but he raises a hand, silencing me. "I know you have a terrible decision to make, Matthew, but the signs are there. And Kendrick sees them."

My knees wobble, and I lean against the wall. "What if I think he's wrong?"

Dad's face darkens. "Then we have a problem."

Dad disappears on a long walk the next day and returns to inform me he's spoken with Kendrick. Knowing this was coming doesn't stop the alarm racing through me.

"What did he say?" I ask.

"That he's worried you're off course." Dad removes his glasses and rubs his eyes. "I tried to assure him you're doing fine, that you're documenting everything and staying impartial, but I'm not sure how successful I was. He wants you to call every Friday with an update."

"I will." Weekly calls won't be a problem, and the fact Kendrick asked for them means he won't be burning Rae anytime soon. I can ramble on about her innocent activities, boring him out of his mind and banishing the idea she could be Marked. When her year is up, he'll be thrilled to stop hearing about her.

The Winters' travels keep Rae safe for the holiday, and I block the project out for a few short days, because thinking about it makes my stomach heave and my chest hurt. Dad seems only too happy to do the same. We eat at restaurants, take drives through the hills, and sit around and read. His phone rings once, setting off a jazzy new tone.

"What was that?" I ask when he hangs up. "All those night-clubs changing your taste in music?"

He chuckles. "Maybe a little. But my project likes it, and that's what counts."

I bite my lip. "You haven't made up your mind, have you? It's still early."

"No." He pauses. "But it's getting interesting."

"Keep me posted, all right?"

He nods, and I don't ask any more questions.

When Dad isn't looking, I text Rae. Her holiday was sad but everyone did their best, sharing memories and food and tears. I check the race website all day Saturday and send her **Congrats!!!** for an impressive third-place finish, and a photo of my cheetah pops up with **It worked!** written beneath it. The Varsity boys did well also, and Moose beat the runner behind him by half a second. The thought of his skinny arms pumping him to victory brings a grin to my face.

Dad glances up from his book. "What are you looking at?"

I click to another screen. "Just videos."

On Sunday night, he places his suitcase in his car before pulling me into a rare hug. I hug him back, and the unexpected affection tells me the worries he carried when he arrived haven't left. He's just buried them deeper.

"Take care of yourself, Matthew," he says. "And remember what I told you about Kendrick."

"I will." I step back. "When will you come again?"

"In a few days. Sooner if you need me."

"Okay. I'll be fine, but thanks."

He starts the engine and drives away, his taillights blinking red before disappearing around the corner. I wait for my shoulders to relax, for the tension inside to flood out, but something holds it back. A nagging itch keeps me staring at the intersection where Dad just turned. He had slowed, signaled, and joined the flow of traffic.

Not flow. Trickle. A yellow sedan had passed, and then Dad made a right, filling the space in front of a gray van. The street stayed empty for a few seconds, and then one more car appeared.

A blue truck.

I didn't see the driver, but the thudding of my heart tells me enough. Kendrick's got his own game, and whatever it is, I'm playing.

I just don't know the rules.

CHAPTER

33

The end of fall has stripped most trees along my route, and bare branches stretch overhead as I park in front of the Winters' house on Monday morning. They returned home late last night, and the familiar sight of their car in the driveway shrinks the horror of Thanksgiving with Kendrick. Each day now is a march toward proving Rae free of the Mark and crushing any thought he might have about clicking his lighter.

I open my door, and the shouts coming from inside the house smack me harder than the cold air.

"—can't believe you did that!" Rae yells. A loud crash comes, accompanied by the sound of something breaking.

"Stop it!" Mrs. Winter shouts. "Right now, Rae! I mean it!"

I climb the steps, but my hand hovers over the doorbell. Inside, Mrs. Winter is still speaking, but she's no longer yelling and I can't make out the muffled words. Rae's response comes clearly enough, however, a furious cry from the direction of the kitchen.

"What, so you're just going to erase him? That's great, Mom. Maybe we should get rid of the pictures too. How does that sound?"

Silence falls, and then the door swings open. Rae stands in front of me, her face red and eyes wet.

"Let's go." Without waiting for my response, she stomps past me, gets in the car, and slams the door. I glance inside to where Mrs. Winter has sagged onto the sofa, her head in her hands. When she looks up, weariness lines her face.

"It's fine, Matt," she says. "Go to school."

I close the door softly and hurry to the car, where Rae fumes in the passenger seat.

"What happened?" I ask as I get in.

Rae glares at her house. "You know that shelf with four mugs in the kitchen? The one over the coffee machine? Mom took Dad's off and stuck it in the cupboard. Like she can't stand to think about him anymore, like she just wants to forget. Can you believe that?"

Actually, I can. Mrs. Winter already wears a reminder of her lost husband on her finger and wakes up to their wedding picture each morning, and maybe looking at that cup every time she made coffee became unbearable. I say none of this to Rae, though. "I heard something break. That wasn't his mug, was it?"

"It was Mom's. I might have thrown it." Her face droops, the anger leaking away, and she rubs her cheeks with both hands. "I can't believe I did that. I just got so angry, and I grabbed it . . ."

"Hey, it's okay." I squeeze her knee gently. "It's just a mug. Your mom will understand."

"Maybe. But I should—" She raps her knuckles on the window. "Turn right!"

I jerk the car around the corner. "Where are we going? We'll be late."

"Just drop me off, then." She reaches for her seat belt, but I grab her hand before she can unlatch it.

"No! I'm coming with you. Which way?"

"Head for the convenience store. It's open twenty-four hours. I should get her a new mug." She bites her lip, frowning. "Mom's was an old Mother's Day gift, though. It won't be the same."

"I bet she'll still appreciate it," I say. "But we're going to miss first period."

"Let's miss second too. Can we?" she pleads. "I really can't handle McNally right now."

We'll both get tardy slips for being late to school, but it's not like Dad will care. We stop at the convenience store first, where Rae chooses a flowered mug for her mom, and then get coffee from the Wallflower. The barista, a man in his twenties, raises an eyebrow when he sees us.

"Sahana's friends, right? Shouldn't you be in class?" he asks.

Rae just shrugs. "We'll get there."

He shakes his head but doesn't argue, and we take our coffees outside to wait for the end of second period.

"I missed you over break," I say as we choose a table, and lean over to kiss her cheek. She turns and catches my lips with hers, and her fingertips set my skin alight as they trail over my neck. I pull her close, my hands slipping around her waist, and she slides from her chair into my lap. The hour passes too quickly, and by the time I remember we need to get to class, we've made up for the days apart.

She hops up, smoothing back her hair. I toss our cups toward the trash can, and a familiar blue truck down the street catches my eye.

"Your aim is terrible," Rae says, as both cups bounce off the side. She picks them up and throws them away. "Good thing you run instead of playing basketball."

I force a laugh, but Kendrick's presence means nothing good. He probably heard her yelling this morning, and now he's seen her skipping class—two definite changes in behavior, since I'm fairly certain he's keeping track.

Might have noticed I'm not backing off the "boyfriend angle" either.

It's almost impossible not to break the speed limit on the drive to MCHS, and relief slips over me as we pass through the front gate. At least Kendrick can't follow us inside. We get our slips from the attendance office, and thankfully the only person around to scold us for being late is McNally's assistant. The morning rolls along, and the routine of classes and schoolwork brings a sense of normalcy, though I can't quite shake the dread from this morning. When the final bell rings, the last thing I want is to be alone with nothing to think of but the project, so it's perfect when Moose announces we need to celebrate his first afternoon without practice.

"Pit Stop," he declares, and Juan nods enthusiastically.

"I'll drive," I offer. "Want to ask the girls?"

"Sure," Juan says. "And speaking of asking, Matt, did you do it?"

"Do what?"

"Ask Rae to the Winter Dance." Moose cocks his head. "Please say you knew about it. The banner over the doors? Whispers in the hall? The hint of love in the air?"

"That's just you thinking of Tyson," Juan says. "You going to ask him?"

"Of course not. Besides, Caleb Scutari already did."

"Sorry." Juan pats Moose on the back. "Other fish in the sea and all that. Want me to set you up?"

"No!" Moose swats Juan's hand away. "And I already know you're not asking anyone, so Matt—you're our last hope. How about it?"

The Saturday listed on the banner had been so far into the future I hadn't noticed it creeping up. "I don't know . . ."

"What don't you know?" Sahana asks as she and Rae approach. "I mean, lots of things, but what specifically?"

"Nothing!" I say quickly, and Juan snickers. "We're going to the Pit Stop. Want to come?"

"I wish." Sahana sighs. "Tons of homework, and I'm working later."

"As the new *manager*." Rae nudges her. "All those fancy drinks earned someone a promotion."

"It's nothing," Sahana says, but her eyes sparkle, and she beams as we congratulate her.

"First she's driving me to Charon's," Rae adds. "I picked up more hours since cross country ended, so you guys are on your own. Eat a plate of cheese fries for me."

"We will," Juan promises. "And we'll talk to Matt about—"

"Bye!" I cut in, and drag him to my car before he can finish. Moose laughs so hard he falls across the back seat.

"You should see your face," he gasps.

"Not cool." I start the engine. "Definitely not cool."

By the time we finish our shakes and cheese fries, Moose and Juan have stuffed my head so full of suggestions on how to ask Rae to the dance my brain is about to explode. It's finally quiet after I drive them home, but concentrating proves impossible. I scribble a quick entry in the red notebook, one that glosses over Rae's yelling this morning and focuses instead on her immediate remorse, and text her to see if the evening went okay.

Mom's still mad, but it's getting better, she responds. **Thx for hanging out this morning.**

We go back and forth a little longer, but Mrs. Winter calls her to dinner, leaving me to eat alone as always. Dad texts later, saying he is with his project and can't call, so I message him that everything is great. He doesn't mention meeting Kendrick after he left the shack, and I don't ask.

They can have their secrets. I have mine.

The next morning, I practice asking Rae to the dance, though my reflection in the mirror seems awkward even to me. Did my palms always sweat this much? My rehearsal continues through the drive to her house, since the ride to school will offer the perfect opportunity.

Until she storms across the lawn, gets in the car, and slams the door.

"Can you believe it?" She holds up a soggy paper. "You'd think someone might be a little more careful when you say, 'Watch out. My milk's right there.'"

"Cady?"

Rae nods, and I dab the paper with my sleeve. "Is this your math homework?"

"Yes. Think it'll dry in time?"

I dab it again. "No. Sorry."

She groans. "I better copy it." Pulling a pencil and paper from her backpack, she balances a textbook on her lap and starts writing.

Nothing kills romance faster than math homework.

She turns the wet paper over as we get to school, still scribbling frantically. I check my watch. "Seven minutes."

Rae doesn't look up. "Five more problems."

She finishes with a minute left, and we sprint to class. I don't hear a word Señora Torres says all morning, and McNally's lecture fades to a dull hum. When math ends, we walk to Rae's locker first, then mine. She tells me about a book she's reading, and I feign as much interest as I can.

"Uh-huh." I pile my textbook on top of the others. "Sounds good."

"You can borrow it when I'm done." She reaches over to straighten my lopsided stack, and I catch her hand.

"Hey." My mouth turns dry. "Do you want to go to the dance with me?"

Not at all how I practiced. No witty banter. No casual lean against the wall. Even my smile feels like I'm just baring my teeth.

If I were her, I would definitely say no.

A smile lights Rae's face. "Yes!"

"Really?"

"Of course. I was going to ask you after school today."

"You were?"

"Yup." She grins as she backs away. "Bell's going to ring. Better hurry."

We only make it halfway to English before the bell rings, but I don't care.

She said yes.

Thoughts of the dance carry me through the rest of my classes and follow me into Mr. Garrett's backyard. Leaves carpet the ground, covering my ankles as I kick through them, and their crackle comes like music. The shack looks brighter than usual beneath the oak, and even the walls stand almost straight as I step inside.

The smell of peppermint hangs in the air.

Alarm ripples through me as I check the table, the mattress, even the refrigerator, but everything remains exactly as I left it. There's no sign anyone searched the cabinets, and my stack of books appears the same as it did this morning. I'm starting to think I'm imagining things when I crouch before the lock on the door and see the fresh scratch that grazes its shiny surface.

Of course Kendrick could get in.

At least he wouldn't have found anything interesting, since the red notebook is safe in my backpack. The memory of the bug in the Winters' kitchen makes me scour the shack once more, but no listening device hides beneath my mattress, and the underside of the table shows only yellowed plastic. I finally make myself start my homework, but even then, I can't stop staring out the window.

For all I know, Kendrick could be looking back.

The dance texts from Moose and Juan start the next afternoon. Sahana asked Juan to go with her, the lunchtime invitation accompanied by a thorough explanation that they would be going as friends and orders to not make it weird, but even those couldn't dim the glow that has lit his face ever since he said yes. Moose declares himself our chaperone, and they're arguing back and forth about dinner plans when I finally break in to ask what I'm supposed to wear.

Nice pants and dress shirt, Juan texts. **I've got extra if you need it.**

Tie too, Moose adds. **U can use one of mine.**

Thanks! I write back.

I don't tell them I'm sitting down the block from Charon's, watching for Kendrick and waiting for Mrs. Winter to take Rae home.

Dad texts again that evening. **All going well?**

Yes. Does he know Kendrick searched the shack? **Can u call?**

Kendrick asked that we not talk for a while.

I stare at his words. More pop up.

I'll check in every now and then, but you have to do this alone. OK?

OK, I finally write back. Maybe this is what they discussed that day Kendrick followed him. Dad doesn't answer, which I suppose means he's done "checking in" on me. I finish my homework, whittle a chunk of wood into nothingness, and watch the stars for a long time.

At least Friday's call with Kendrick goes well. I stick to the facts, a dry report of Rae's school activities and work, though he grills me about Monday's rough start.

"It ended fine," I repeat, clutching the phone so hard my fingers ache. "She felt really bad and got her mom a new mug. We made it to school and nothing happened. She even went to work afterward."

"Careful, Matthew," Kendrick chides, and my teeth grind. "The Mark can flare up one moment and be fine the next."

So can grief, but there's no point saying this. "I know," I tell him instead. "But she was upset, remember? Her explanation makes sense."

A resigned silence comes through the phone. "All right," he says at last, and I hang up quickly.

The weekend passes like usual, or maybe even better since I spend Sunday afternoon at Charon's. Moose and I eat brownies while Rae helps customers, and she joins us whenever the line empties. Sahana is busy at the Wallflower and Juan is working on a science project, which makes it easier for Moose to convince us to see a movie with him next weekend. He promises to find one with no aliens or talking animals, and we watch previews until Rae finishes her shift.

"I've got a dentist appointment tomorrow morning," she reminds me as I drive her home. "Take good notes in McNally's. I'll need them."

I promise a detailed and painful recounting of class, which is lonely the next day without her. Still, I pay attention and copy McNally's examples carefully. In biology, Moose asks what kind of corsage I'm getting Rae, and I tell him I have no idea.

"One that looks nice?" I suggest.

"You're worse at this than Juan." He grins. "Sahana ordered hers. He just has to pick it up."

"Sounds like Sahana," I say, as we walk to lunch. I'm about to settle beside Rae, who arrived halfway through third period with an excellent report of no cavities, when I realize I left my history homework for Ms. Timmult in my locker.

"Be right back," I tell them.

"Can I get your math notes?" Rae asks.

"Sure." I dump my backpack between her and Sahana. "Help yourself."

I jog to my locker, grab the homework, and turn to head back. McNally guards the doorway, and my feet immediately move in the opposite direction, winding through the halls to a different exit. My friends are still where I left them when I finally make it outside, but they're gathered in a tight group, their heads bent over something in Rae's hands. I'm wondering what they found when Sahana looks up, and her expression brings me to a dead stop.

Hurt and horror cloud her face. Her eyes narrow as they meet mine, and anger thins her mouth in a grim line. Moose rubs his hands over a face so pale he resembles a ghost, while Juan's look of fury threatens to melt my skin right off. He moves to the side, and I see the object in Rae's hand.

My notebook. But not the one I use in math class.

My red notebook.

CHAPTER

35

I forgot about my notebook. I meant to keep those pages safe, hidden away from Kendrick's prying eyes, tucked in my backpack where I could protect them.

Except I didn't, and they now lie open in Rae's hands.

"What the hell?" Her voice knifes through me, and the anger sparking off her singes the air. She closes the distance between us and slaps the notebook against my chest. "What is this?"

I catch it, feeling the weight of everything it holds. My observations. My data. All the entries I wrote with such care, each word chosen to convince Kendrick of Rae's innocence.

Now they scream my guilt.

Horror crashes through me so hard my vision blurs, but years of training slice through the panic. I snatch the notebook with an offended glare.

"It's my journal," I snap. "It's private. You weren't supposed to read it!"

I need to redirect their rage back at them, shifting the blame to their violation of my privacy. At least I don't have to fake the rush of blood to my face.

"I didn't mean to." Rae chews her lip. "I was looking for your math and grabbed that one by accident. But Matt—the stuff you wrote—"

"Is mine!" I scowl at her. "You couldn't tell this wasn't math?"

Rae winces. "I—yeah, I should have closed it. But I saw my name . . ."

Sahana jumps in. "You follow her. You watch her house, and Charon's too. You're some kind of crazy stalker." The accusation blisters the air.

"You broke into her house," Juan snarls. "Searched her room."

"You call her 'the project,'" Moose adds softly.

Any denial dies in my throat. Rae faces me, anger brightening her eyes, or maybe that's the tears glistening in them. If I tell her the truth, she will never believe me.

Or maybe she will. I don't know which is worse.

"You lied to us, Matt. This whole time." Juan reaches for the notebook, and I jump back, keeping it out of reach. "You knew about the accident. About Mr. Winter. Before you even met us."

His words fall like thunder. I don't need to look at my notebook to see the dates printed so carefully at the top of each entry. So thorough. So neat.

So damning.

"You knew that first day you walked into Charon's." Rae's voice breaks, and the hurt in it wrenches me deep inside. "And you pretended you didn't."

"Did you read about it?" Moose's eyes beg for an explanation, one that makes sense and lets things go back to the way they were. "See it on the news?"

He's offering a way out, and I jump at it, nodding. "Before I moved here. I was trying to learn about this place, and I saw an article. Then when we met"—I turn a pleading look to Rae—"I figured it out. But it wasn't like I could say anything, so I pretended I didn't know. I'm sorry. You were just so sad, I wanted to help. I didn't mean to lie."

That's the biggest lie of all, but she hesitates and I think it will work, it will all be okay, until Sahana wraps an arm around her. "You didn't stop, though, did you?" She glowers at me. "All the lying and spying. You joined cross country just to get close to her. Started giving her rides every morning. Hung out with us so you could write more in your little notebook."

"No! It's not like that—"

"Really?" Sahana cuts me off. "Then what is it like? Tell us, Matt. We want to know."

"It's— I watch. That's all," I choke out, but no words will make them understand. Even if I tell them about Dad and Kendrick and the Mark, they would never believe me, though I would finally be telling the truth.

"This whole time." Rae's face crumples. "You just wanted to meet the girl with the dead dad. Check out the carnage. I'm just some weird freak show to you, aren't I?"

Her voice catches, and the fragile piece that had been growing inside—the piece that felt like people cared about me, like I could care about them—cracks and shatters.

"You're not! I just . . ." I clutch the notebook as if it can shield me from the life splintering with each broken word. "I didn't mean anything. Rae, please . . ."

"Don't talk to her." Sahana's chin juts out. "You stay the hell away from her. Understand?"

I do. Half of me is already running through my escape plan: call Dad, clear out the shack, burn the notebook. The other part of me desperately waits for Rae to say it's okay, that it was wrong but she forgives me. That whatever is between us might survive this.

She turns away.

Sahana moves with her, leaving Moose and Juan standing in front of me. Juan throws me a final scowl. "That's messed up," he says, and follows Rae.

"Moose . . ." I plead. "It was stupid. I'm sorry."

His eyes meet mine, and the wounded betrayal in them shreds any last hope of repairing my life here. Lowering his head, he shoves his hands in his pockets and shuffles after the others.

No one looks back.

Nearby classmates stare, and the murmurs begin. The story will reach McNally in minutes.

I need to leave.

The stumbling walk to the parking lot takes an eternity, accusations and whispers chasing each step, and my fumbling hands drop the keys twice before I get my car door open. I should leave my books rather than steal from the school, but it's too late for that now.

It's too late for a lot of things.

The drive passes in a blur, and I pull up in front of Mr. Garrett's house as my mind finally kicks into gear. *Hurry.* I yank my phone out and call Dad. Five rings, and his voicemail picks up.

"It's an emergency!" I shout when it beeps at last. Where is he? "Call me."

I race to the gate and skid to a stop at its sturdy new latch, complete with a lock requiring a key I don't have. My arms are heavy, but I force them up to climb the fence, and the wood shudders beneath my grip. No way will it support my weight. I run up the porch steps and pound on the front door.

"Mr. Garrett! You home?"

A minute creeps by. I check the street at least six times, waiting for Captain Walsh to come screeching around the corner.

Good thing I never wrote about the matches.

Finally, the door opens. Wrinkles crease the side of Mr. Garrett's face like he just woke from a nap. "What in the Devil's name are you banging about?"

"I need to get to the back. There's a lock on the gate."

"Sure is." He yawns. "No way is that big guy—or anyone else—coming here without us knowing. I've got a key for you."

He disappears into the house. I stay on the porch, shifting from one foot to the other, and sweat dampens my shirt by the time Mr. Garrett reappears.

"Don't lose it." He thrusts a brass key at me. "I'm not making another copy."

His voice sounds as gruff as always, but the realization hits hard: He did this for me. To keep Kendrick and everyone else away. To keep me safe.

"Thanks." I take the key. "Really."

He waves my gratitude away with an impatient hand. "What are you doing here anyway? Cutting school?"

Dropping out and fleeing the state, actually. Something between a laugh and a sob slips out. I cover it with a cough, but a new alertness chases away the remaining traces of sleep on his face.

"Forgot my homework," I say quickly. "Just came to get it."

The line between his bushy eyebrows remains, but I step away before more questions can follow. My key slides smoothly into the lock, and I hurry through the gate and into the familiar yard. The sight of the oak brings a fresh sense of loss, and regret courses through every vein.

If only I had been more careful. I could have handed Rae the right notebook, and none of this would be happening. She would be sitting at my side right now, planning the night of the dance, and Mr. Garrett's lock might actually be useful. I got careless, because I forgot Matt Watts was nothing more than a costume meant to deceive others.

It ended up fooling me.

I jerk open the door of the shack, haul out my duffel bag, and start throwing things in. Clothes. Books. Laptop. I grab my toothbrush from the bathroom sink, and my reflection in the mirror makes me want to cry. I stood here just this morning, a lifetime ago, combing my hair and dreaming of the day I would be free of Kendrick and his Mark. The person staring back now has obliterated any future that calls Mills Creek home, and the eyes that lit up every time I thought of Rae are dark and hopeless. I stagger to the kitchen drawer, meaning to grab the few forks and knives, and my hand lands on the can opener Mr. Garrett gave me two months ago.

The day Rae brought me soup.

My knees go weak, and I slide to the ground. I don't realize I'm crying until tears drip off my chin, and then it's too late to do anything but bury my head in my hands and let the rest come.

"Hey. What's wrong?"

My head jerks up. Mr. Garrett stares down at me.

I forgot to close the door.

Too much forgetting. Too many mistakes.

I rub my hands over my cheeks. "Nothing. I've got a nosy landlord, that's all."

He snorts and sits in the chair. "What's going on, Matt?"

I should stick to the homework story. Or say it's about a girl. He might buy that. But I'm so tired of lying. Of losing.

Of leaving.

"I screwed up." The words spill out between gulps of air. "I messed everything up, and they all hate me, and I need to go, and I don't know where Dad is, and—and—"

"Slow down." Mr. Garrett holds up both hands. "First of all, you're not going anywhere. When your mind is nuts, the last thing you do is listen to it. And your mind is definitely nuts right now. Deep breath, Matt. It can't be that bad."

He has no idea. "My friends found my journal." Friends. Not anymore. "They don't understand. I wasn't trying to hurt her . . ."

"Hurt who?" Mr. Garrett frowns. "Rachel?"

I swallow hard and nod. Telling him makes no difference now. By the time the last bell rings at MCHS, everyone will know. "I watched her. Recorded things in a notebook. They found it."

His brows shoot up, and his jaw flaps open twice before he manages to spit out, "Watched her? Like through her window?"

"No! Not like that! Just what she did, where she went, that sort of thing. And . . ." A sick feeling crawls into my stomach. "I looked in her room. When they weren't home. I had to see if the accident changed her."

"Of course it changed her! Her father *died*," Mr. Garrett snaps. "Matt, what the hell were you thinking?"

I could confess the whole story right now. Tell him about Kendrick's web of lies that caught Dad, who dragged me in like a fly beside him. Turn us both in to the police in hopes they will protect Rae, though I already know Kendrick will slip right through their fingers. Ask Mr. Garrett to warn her, because she will never talk to me again.

My mouth opens, but all that comes is a ragged "I don't know." I drag myself to my feet and pick up my bag.

"Damn it, Matt! Stop." Mr. Garrett blocks my door, a skinny sixty-year-old barricade refusing to budge. "Look, you screwed up. Badly. But you can't just run."

He doesn't get it. Running is all I do. "I can't go back. Not after this."

"They don't understand. To be honest, I don't understand myself. But the first thing to do is apologize. Tell them you're sorry, and then we'll see. Have you called your dad?"

"He didn't answer."

"Well, let's talk to him first. Maybe get that apology in too."

The idea that I can stay—that all this will go away—is impossible, but a tiny part of me is desperate enough to hope. "What if they go to the police?"

"Then it won't matter where you are," Mr. Garrett shoots back, "because Captain Walsh will find you."

I slump onto the mattress. "I'm not going back to school."

"That's fine for today. But did you just leave campus, or did someone let you go?"

"I left." *Fled* is more like it.

"Thought so. I'll call them. At least they'll know where you are." He turns. "And don't get any ideas about driving off without telling me. You hear?"

"I won't." The promise rings empty until I see Mr. Garrett's face. A wrinkle of worry puckers his forehead, and his narrowed gaze lingers on me like a lie detector. "Why does it matter? Dad already paid the rent. You can keep it."

"You think this is about money?" He shakes his head. "Matt, you've got a lot of learning to do." He closes the door behind him, and the thoughts screeching through my mind roar in the silence.

Rae hates me. They all do. I will never go to the Winters' home again, or Charon's, or MCHS. Even Dad won't take my calls. All that's left for me to do is run—to leave behind this mess of pain and betrayal, with nobody to miss me when I'm gone.

And Kendrick will be free to burn Rae.

That certainty falls like the final nail in my Mills Creek coffin. Time drips past, bringing new nightmares of screams and flames, until a sliver of resolve finally pokes through. I may have destroyed my own life here, but I can still save hers. No matter what happens, I need to deliver a warning to Rae before I disappear—something that will give her a chance to protect herself. It's the least I can do.

It's not much.

I blink away the haze clouding my brain and check my phone. No messages. The clock says 2:33, which means Rae and the others finish school in twelve minutes. Have they called the police? Told them Matt Watts, Rae Winter's boyfriend, has actually been stalking her this entire time?

They'll never believe I just wanted to keep her safe.

I drag myself to my backpack, take out the red notebook, and flip through its pages. My writings, so detailed for Kendrick and Dad, must have terrified Rae. The descriptions of her and her family. My retelling of the stories she shared. The careful surveillance of her home.

Of her.

Anyone who comes looking for evidence can't find this. The shack's fireplace may not have seen a flame in years, but it will suffice. I dig out my matches and scrape one against the box. An orange spark flares, and I hold it to the notebook. The paper smokes and curls, and I set it on the grate as the fire seizes hold.

It doesn't take long. Pages succumb with a burst of flames, and in seconds, all that remains is a pile of ashes and the blackened metal coil. It doesn't look like enough to destroy my life in Mills Creek, but looks can deceive.

I know that better than most.

Smoke stifles the air in the shack, forcing me out into the cold December day. Overhead, a few stubborn leaves cling to life, but most lie molding on the ground. I wade through them, climb the oak to my favorite branch, and watch the minutes tick by.

2:41.

2:42.

2:43.

Maybe Mr. Garrett has a point. Mrs. Winter will never let me near Rae again, but at least I can tell her I'm sorry—for watching her daughter, for invading her home, for lying to her and adding to her pain. I'll apologize for all of it if she'll let me.

If I were her, I wouldn't open the door.

I haul myself to my feet, but there is nowhere to go. Mrs. Winter will be at work for another hour and a half, and Rae won't see me. I pace the yard, searching for words that could make them understand, but none exist.

2:47.

A rusty rake leans against the fence. I pick it up and throw myself into the work.

Two hours later, newly revealed dirt surrounds a mountain of leaves. My water bottle has been filled and refilled, and the cold no longer bothers me. Mr. Garrett comes out, hands me a soda, and waits while I drain it.

"Not bad." He surveys the yard. "You doing the front next?"

It could certainly use it. Leaves bury the lawn in an ankle-deep blanket, and I'm fairly certain something died in one corner. Still, I shake my head. "I'm going for a walk."

He gives a knowing nod. "Knock when you're back."

I leave my car behind and start the slow trek. The road feels treacherous, and I duck my head as I shuffle along. An engine roars behind me once, and my pulse skyrockets as a motorcycle shoots past. I'm almost surprised when I reach Rae's house without being hauled off to jail.

Mrs. Winter's car sits in the driveway, and the bright windows leave no doubt someone is home. They could be sitting around the kitchen table right now, deciding my fate in somber voices. The thought roots my feet to the ground, and only when I realize how creepy I look standing out here do I finally work up the courage to ring their bell.

The door opens. Mrs. Winter advances, and I stumble backward until her hand closes on my arm with a strength I've never seen.

"How dare you!" The grief-etched lines of her face disappear, hidden behind the outrage that vibrates through each word. "You followed Rae? Broke into our home? Get away from here!"

She lets go and I fall, scraping my knee on the rough cement walkway. My apology sticks in my throat, and all I can manage is a feeble, "Wait. Please."

I stagger to my feet as she glowers at me. Behind her, two shadows move. Rae and Cady.

"I'm sorry." The words aren't nearly enough, but I have nothing else to offer. "I'm so, so sorry. I'll stay away from her."

My breath rattles. "I'll stay away from all of you."

"You'd better." Fury electrifies Mrs. Winter's threat. "I'll be speaking with your father and the school. And if I ever catch you near my daughter again, or near this house, you will truly regret it."

The door slams.

My ears ring in the silence that follows. The empty swing hangs like a solemn witness as I drag my feet past, and each stumbling step swallows any hope Rae might jump forward and save me.

Or maybe, in a way, she did. Mrs. Winter didn't mention the police.

I should call them myself and deliver a warning about Kendrick. The moment he hears about my notebook, he'll be ready to burn and run.

Unless . . .

A sudden thought freezes me in the middle of a crosswalk. A car horn blares, and I scurry to the other side and scour the area. No blue truck appears. Kendrick would have missed the disaster at lunch as well, since buildings shield the courtyard from the streets beyond.

Which means he has no idea what happened today.

And he never will.

Even if McNally or Mrs. Winter gets hold of Dad, I can control the story. Yes, they found my notebook, but I convinced them I was only trying to help Rae work through her grief. They forgave me, and the project is rolling along just fine. If Kendrick notices I stopped hanging out with the others, I'll tell him he was right about the "fairy-tale romance" and I needed more distance for a better perspective. As long as McNally doesn't expel me, school won't be a problem. Kendrick won't see me sitting alone at lunch, won't hear the rumblings in the hallways.

I can protect Rae, even if no one at MCHS ever speaks to me again.

A stab of loneliness makes me want to sink right through the sidewalk, but I keep going, one step at a time, all the way back to Mr. Garrett's house. He opens the door with the phone to his ear. I can't hear what the other person is saying, but from the way Mr. Garrett scowls at me, the subject of the conversation isn't hard to guess.

"Thanks, Gina," he finally says. "I appreciate it. Give me a call if there are problems, but I'm sure Matt won't be any more trouble. I'll let his dad know when I see him." He hangs up. "How'd it go?"

"I don't know." Tomorrow will tell more. "Who was that?"

"Gina Trommer, the district superintendent." Mr. Garrett frowns. "Apparently, Kevin McNally would like to throw you out of Mills Creek High and into a jail cell, but she's agreed to give you another chance. Since there's no other public high school in town, you're heading back tomorrow, and you'd better be ready. It won't be pleasant. Where's this notebook everyone's talking about?"

The story traveled even faster than I expected. "I burned it."

"I suppose that's one way to get rid of it. Did you talk to your dad?"

"I left him a message. He hasn't called back."

Mr. Garrett snorts. "Not going for Parent of the Year, is he? There are a lot of people who want to talk to him, me included. Tell him to get in touch."

I wish I could. "I'm trying."

"And don't do anything like this again. Ever." He points to an empty bowl on the counter. "Dinner's on the stove."

It almost feels good to give in and join him. After a quiet meal of bread and canned soup, he offers to let me stay in the guest room down the hall.

"Thanks, but I'm okay," I tell him, though part of me wants to say yes just to have a friendly presence nearby, even if it's Mr. Garrett. Still, I've learned what happens when I let people get close.

"Suit yourself." He picks up the dishes and begins washing. "But the room's there if you ever want it."

I make my way outside, and the stars twinkle in their nightly parade as I settle beneath the oak. Dad doesn't call, but my phone buzzes with his text: You okay? Can't talk, but what's going on?

Call me later, I write back. Should be fine.

My phone never rings. When the cold finally makes my teeth chatter, I go into the shack, take a hot shower, and fall into bed. In the morning, I'll see what McNally has to say.

And I'll let Kendrick know things are rolling along just fine.

CHAPTER

36

Next morning's drive to school is lonely without Rae. I don't even make it to my locker before McNally appears. "My office." He points. "Now."

He marches me down the hall. Voices quiet as we approach, and the whispers start as soon as we pass.

Nobody makes eye contact.

The sentencing is quick. I nod along with McNally's charges, saying how sorry I am and how it will never happen again, but his stern expression never wavers. The worst moment comes when he informs me he spoke to Dad, who assured him I'll be under much closer supervision in the future. I'm not sure which hurts more: the idea of Dad watching over my shoulder or the fact he spoke with McNally without ever talking to me. When I stand up to leave, I have a new schedule that excludes any class with Rae, lunch in McNally's office until winter break, and an hour working after school for a month.

"Remember, Mr. Watts." McNally stops me as I open the door. "Absolutely no contact with Rachel Winter. None. If you're walking down the hall and she's coming toward you, get out of her way. And stay far, far away from her house. If it were up to me, you'd be talking to Captain Walsh right now instead of standing in my office. You're very lucky General Garrett intervened on your behalf."

I pause. "General?"

McNally smirks. "For someone who snoops so much, you don't know a lot, do you? Now get out."

I spend the next hours ignoring stares from students and teachers alike. It's surprisingly easy to go through an entire day without speaking to anyone, especially when the whole school acts like you have the plague. The worst part isn't the new schedule, or the hisses of "Stalker!" that follow me down the halls, or even sitting through lunch with McNally's assistant pretending not to watch me. It's fourth-period biology, the one class McNally left untouched, where Moose refuses to look at me and Coach can't meet my eyes.

By the time I finish scrubbing pots in the cafeteria, my head hurts from not caring. I text Dad—CALL ME—and spend the rest of the afternoon doing homework. The stillness of the shack is so loud that when Mr. Garrett hollers about buying the wrong brand of ice cream and to come eat some, I cross the yard without a second thought and finish my work at his table. He reads on his couch, and the quiet between us feels so different than the silence that greeted me every time I walked into a classroom. We share a frozen pizza for dinner, and then I'm off to the shack for the night.

The next day brings even more solitude since McNally ignores me as well, but the person I need to speak with isn't on campus, and he's avoided me long enough. After my hour in the cafeteria, I hop on the freeway leading to Dad's apartment. He can't ignore me if I'm standing right in front of him. Mr. Garrett knows my plans, so he won't worry when I get home late.

It's kind of nice someone notices.

The sun is low in the sky by the time I reach Dad's building, and I slip into the lobby after another tenant and climb the stairs. The hallway is quiet as I knock at his door.

No response.

I knock again, and when it stays closed, I slip out my tools and let myself inside. Dad's apartment holds more personal touches than Kendrick's place: a jacket slung over the couch, books on the kitchen table, a coffee cup beside the sink. I poke my head into the bedroom where blankets stretch across a neatly made bed. Beside it sits the family photo, with baby Matthew and Mom and Dad looking like a happy, normal family instead of the broken mess we are now.

I pace the room as I text him: Came for a visit. U around?

His answer appears immediately. Traveling with project to shows around state. Sorry I didn't tell you.

A peek under the bed confirms an absent suitcase, and his toothbrush is missing from the bathroom. I should have saved myself the drive.

Can we talk? I write.

Not supposed to. You're solo, remember?

Damn it. What did u tell McNally?

The three dots stay on the screen forever. Finally: That you'll behave. Project?

This time, it's me who's slow to respond. **Fixing it. Should be OK.**

Good, comes his reply. **Call Kendrick if you need anything.**

The phone goes quiet.

My throat hurts, and a headache pulses at my temples. I flop onto the bed, and Mom and a younger version of the father I know beam at me from the photo. My baby eyes are closed under a soft blue hat, my pink cheeks just visible above the blanket Mom nestles around me.

What would she say if she could see me now?

I pick it up for a better look, and the backing feels loose and uneven. My fingers press the velvet material, but something inside refuses to let the flap close completely. The clasp opens easily, as if it's been moved many times, and an old greeting card lies folded behind the picture.

It's a Boy! colorful letters announce, complete with balloons and confetti. Smoothing the worn creases, I turn the card over to see that the long message from inside has spilled onto the back. A few handwritten lines, and then—

All my love, Monica.

Mom wrote this. My discovery suddenly feels like an intrusion into a memory meant only for Dad, but the temptation is too strong.

She may have been his wife, but she was my mother.

I open the card, and a small photo flutters to the ground. Before I can pick it up, Mom's words pull me in.

Dearest Jonathan,

I told you! Our baby is a boy, and the look on your face when the doctor confirmed this was priceless. Stop worrying, sweetheart. You will be a wonderful father. You're trying to plan for every detail, making yourself completely crazy, so I'm going to help. I made you a list!

#1: You must keep him safe. It's a big world out there, and our baby will need you to protect him.
#2: You must teach him. Whether he's a toddler throwing a tantrum or a terrifying teenager, be patient and guide him.
Most importantly, #3: You must love him. No matter what he says, no matter what he does—love him. Always.

That's it! Three little rules. Not so hard, right? You are going to be the best daddy ever, and our baby is so lucky you're his father. I can't wait to see you hold him.

All my love,

Monica

P.S. What do you think of "Matthew"? Our own little Mattie. We're going to be so happy together.

Mom's words blur, and I put the card down before my shaking hands tear the fragile paper. Her message makes clear for the first time all I lost the day she died, and a torrent of grief crashes over me. She had loved me—loved her little Mattie even before I was born. Those early days must have been filled with so much sweetness as she held me close, dreaming of our future. Perhaps she would have been like Mrs. Winter, sending me to school each day with a smile, talking with me over homemade dinners, creating a space that felt warm and safe and loving if she only had the chance. Maybe she would have listened to all the thoughts I keep inside, all the questions and hopes Dad would never understand.

My heart aches for him too, because we both lost her. Her message radiates playfulness and partnership, and her sudden death must have broken him. No wonder Kendrick caught him so easily. Without the anchor she must have been, Dad needed another tether, and he found it in the worst possible place.

I scan the letter once more, and a lump rises in my throat. Mom had made it so clear, so easy for my father. Three little rules, and Dad mangled the job. He didn't keep me safe, and the lessons he taught me couldn't possibly be the ones she had in mind.

I'm pretty sure he's breaking Rule #3 as well.

Part of me wants to take the card—Dad isn't following her instructions anyway—but he might notice its absence, so I fold it along the creases and retrieve the picture from the ground. It's an ultrasound photo, one of those black-and-white blurs like a Rorschach test that's supposed to be Baby Mattie. Yet the name at the top makes me pause, since instead of "Monica Watts," it lists "Jiang, Ruth M."

Mom must have kept her maiden name. "Ruth" sounds rigid and strange, and "M" likely stands for "Monica," which seems a better fit for the bubbly woman in Dad's photographs. The fresh reminder of how little I know about her stings, and I stuff the picture and card into the frame.

What else has Dad hidden? A quick search of the apartment reveals nothing but a few official documents, including a birth certificate confirming "Ruth Monica Jiang" and "Jonathan Watts" as my parents. I pause at a car repair receipt that confirms Dad's story of the failed alternator on Thanksgiving, but whatever anger I felt then still seems justified, even if for different reasons. There's also a good amount of cash, ready for use in an emergency, and the idea of taking it and fleeing Mills Creek flits across my mind. But Mr. Garrett stuck his neck out for me, and the thought of disappointing him makes me feel even worse than I already do. I put everything back in place, lock Dad's door behind me, and start the long drive home.

Two things improve as the days pass. First, I get better at avoiding eye contact. My sneakers find the paths through crowded halls without me ever looking up, which is easy since most people jump out of my way when they see me coming. The second is Mr. Garrett's cooking. On Friday, he even pulls a homemade meatloaf out of the oven as I'm sitting on his couch carving a rhino from some wood he found.

"Smells good." I lean over the counter to study his creation. "Is that bacon on top?"

"Everything is better with bacon." He thrusts plates and forks at me. "Clean up your mess and set the table."

I wait until our ice cream bowls are empty and the dishes washed before calling Kendrick for my weekly check-in. Dad's response to my text—**Calling K soon. Talk first?**—was a remarkably unhelpful **Go ahead. You'll be fine.**

It's the first time I make a script before a phone call. Scanning my notes once more, I dial, and Kendrick answers on the first ring.

"Matthew!" he says. "I was starting to think you forgot."

Sweat prickles my scalp. "Just finishing dinner."

"Long day for you. What's this about trouble at school?" he asks.

Dad must have talked to him, but I share my new version, one that ends with sunshine and rainbows. "They think they read my journal," I conclude. "It's blowing over."

"Good to hear," he says. "Tell me about the project."

I haven't seen more than glimpses of Rae the entire week, so I cross my fingers and hope she's stuck to her usual schedule. "She goes to school and works at the bakery, just like normal. No more yelling or cutting class. No accidents."

"Are you sure?" he presses. "No signs at all?"

"I'm positive." Somewhere near him, a car horn honks, and I automatically turn to the window, half expecting to see him in the yard. "Are you still watching me?"

"Not much," he says. "You had me worried, Matthew, but you seem to be doing better. Keep me posted if anything changes, okay?"

"I will." My fingers loosen their death grip on the phone. "Talk to you next week."

"Yup. Oh, but come by on Friday, okay?" He clears his throat. "I promised your dad I'd see you. Make sure you look like you're eating and all."

My elation evaporates. Dad didn't mention this in his texts. "I'm really busy. Calling works a lot better. Things are fine, really."

"I'm sure they are, but you know your dad. Come on. It'll be fun."

Just in time, I remember Dad's warning. "Maybe we can meet at a restaurant?" A bright, crowded one. "Find someplace halfway between us."

"Can't. I've got to work late, and traffic will be running against me. Let's say six o'clock. See you soon!"

My phone clicks as he hangs up.

Part of me wants to send Dad a text—*What the hell?*—but I can't stand to think of him. First he doesn't call, and now this. I crumple my script and fling it across the room, and the paper lands on my pile of laundry. The T-shirt at the bottom makes me cringe, since it's the one from Cancún Kendrick gave me on his first visit to the shack. Beaches and resorts are an odd destination for a man who never takes a vacation, and a question tickles me. Opening my laptop, I type in a search. News headlines appear, all dated just before the time Kendrick came to see me, and one catches my eye.

HOTEL FIRE IN CANCÚN CLAIMS TWO

I scan the article. When I finish, the hammering in my head feels like an axe hacking my skull. Kendrick didn't give me the details of his project, but I know him well enough to recognize his work: a late-night fire with "faulty wiring" blamed as the culprit. But that's not what makes me break out in a cold sweat.

Kendrick didn't just burn the wife, who had miraculously survived a boating accident near their home in Seattle only a month earlier. He burned the husband too.

The end of the project must have been approaching quickly for Kendrick to follow them on vacation, but his other burnings would have been closer to home. His job provides the cover for his moves around the country, so I pull up his company's website and skim through various security plans. The page labeled "Locations" makes me pause, since I never realized how extensive his network had grown. Centers lie scattered across the states, with a town near Mills Creek listed as "Coming Soon!" in bold letters. Seattle is on the list as well, and I hesitate only a moment before printing a map of the country and stabbing a blue dot at each center's location.

My next search, of fires and their victims within the last ten years, takes longer. Each death gets a red dot on my map, and I scribble dates and names and causes, my gruesome list growing by the minute. The work takes a good three hours, but by the time I finish, the cluster of red surrounding each blue dot turns my skin cold. News articles spew different reasons for the blazes—natural gas explosions, arson, mistakes in home meth labs—but even if some are truly accidents, there's only one explanation for the unequal distribution of fires across the country, several of which claimed multiple victims.

Kendrick's been busy.

Most of his burnings took place at night, which makes sense, especially given that he doesn't seem to mind a few extra bodies. Perhaps this is the cost he's willing to pay: Better to sacrifice one innocent life than risk losing more. A new ending for my project unfolds before me, because Mrs. Winter and Cady can't protect Rae in those sleepy hours if Kendrick doesn't care whether the flames catch them too. He'll seal the doors and windows, wait for darkness to gather, and set the fire.

And the whole family will burn.

CHAPTER

37

"Ready for another week?" Mr. Garrett asks as he hands me a bowl of macaroni and cheese for Sunday's dinner. It's not quite homemade—he ran out of time since he spent the afternoon "supervising" as I raked the front yard—but the neon cheese powder is weirdly addictive. "Still got detention?"

"Yes." Another week of keeping my head down and nights spent watching for Kendrick. "I'll be fine."

"Fine" is a bit of a stretch, but at least the days drag by without any more conversations with McNally. No conversations with anyone, actually. Gossip about Saturday's upcoming dance buzzes through the halls, and I do my best to shut it out. Rae must have a new date, maybe Toshi, and I can't even get mad. She deserves someone better than me.

At least Kendrick is no longer hovering near her, which suggests my boring reports may be working. I spot him only once, lurking across the street in front of MCHS, which means he must not know Rae has already left. The mountain of dishes in the cafeteria kept me late, and I'm about to drive away when a group of freshmen come skateboarding past the entrance, jumping off steps and flying over railings. McNally comes out to yell at them, startling one so much her board goes flying. It smacks him right in the stomach, and he doubles over before crumpling to his knees. By the time the skaters get him upright and he's threatened everyone with detention, Kendrick has vanished. I drive by Charon's and the Winters' house on the way home, slouching low as I pass each one, but I don't see him anywhere.

On Wednesday, Dad texts a quick **How are you doing?** and I shoot back **great**. He doesn't answer, so I guess my one-word response satisfied him. His standards for parenting seem to have gone down.

A month ago, I might have been grateful. Now it just hurts.

Friday afternoon, I leave the shack and begin the drive to Kendrick's apartment. It's really more of a crawl. Horns honk on the congested highway, and I could run faster than my current speed. The red lights on the van in front of me flash again, and I hit my brakes just in time. Traffic looks much better in the opposite direction, with cars whizzing by at a steady pace.

Either Kendrick doesn't know much about rush hour, or something else is going on.

I park beside his truck, and my fingers graze the knife in my pocket as I eye the heavy toolbox that takes up half his cargo bed. A worn padlock holds it shut, but I already know its contents: a scruffy black bag that carries all the equipment for his work. The burning bag probably still has the hole from a spark that landed too close.

By now, it may have more.

A soft ding announces the elevator's arrival in the lobby, and seconds later, I step into the vacant hallway. The carpet muffles my slow path to Kendrick's door. Whatever conversation waits on the other side needs to flow flawlessly, revealing no trace of the project's cracks and mistakes. My arms turn leaden as I try to summon the courage to knock, and the weight of the past days crashes down: the loneliness and rejection and broken friendships. I'm so very tired of pretending, but if I stop—if I slip at all—Kendrick will claim my project and burn Rae.

I can't do this. Not alone.

There's only one person I can lean on for help, and though he seems to have better things to do than talk to me these days, he's been my rock as long as I can remember. It makes me feel like a child again, but I reach into my pocket, pull out my phone, and call Dad.

A jazzy ringtone sounds inside Kendrick's apartment. The tune is something a musician might choose, or somebody who wants the attention of one. I've heard it before.

Dad's here.

I'm too relieved to be angry. Shoving my phone into my pocket, I bang on the door.

Kendrick swings it open. "Matthew! Careful, or you'll take it right off the hinges. Come on in."

He's thinner than when I last saw him, with hollow cheeks

and dark circles under his eyes, but he gives me a smile. His face is flushed beneath his hat, and I can almost see my father and him frantically trying to silence the phone before it ruined the surprise. I step into the living room, waiting for Dad to appear with that restrained grin on his face. We'll share a laugh, and everything will finally be okay.

"I'm starving," Kendrick says. "You know, I found this great Thai place not far from here. Let's take my truck. It'll be faster than ordering in."

Around us, the apartment stays silent.

"We'll talk on the way." Kendrick ushers me out of the room and into the elevator, and the doors close on the empty hallway.

He must want to talk with me alone first. If he has any hint as to how my project is actually going, I can't blame him. Still, Dad should have at least come out to say hi. Unless—

I lean against the wall as a new thought stirs through me: Dad's *phone* is with Kendrick.

His car wasn't in the lot. In fact, the last time I saw it, a blue truck trailed behind it.

He's been texting ever since. No calls except to McNally, who only spoke with him once before and wouldn't know if the person apologizing for my behavior wasn't really who he claimed to be.

"You all right?" Kendrick puts a hand on my shoulder as the elevator doors open. "You look kind of pale."

I lock my teeth together and nod. When I'm sure I'm not going to throw up all over his shoes, I force a shrug. "Just not a fan of Thai food. Maybe pizza?"

"Pizza it is!" He steers me toward the parking lot. "I'll drive. I know this place—"

A dull roar in my head drowns out his voice. He wants me alone. In his truck.

The truck with his burning bag in the back.

Looks like I just failed my test. His words from that day in the shack come rushing back: *It's not like we could let you go wandering off to talk about us, right?*

My lungs forget how to breathe. Kendrick will cut off any cry for help in an instant, and the solitude of the parking lot rings in my ears. Running won't work. He's too strong. Too fast.

Think.

"Let me grab my sunglasses," I say, turning toward my car. My hand fumbles with the lock, but I get the door open and slide the key into the ignition. Slipping out my phone, I dial Dad.

Kendrick's pocket vibrates. He freezes, and his eyes dart to mine.

"Matthew, listen to me—" he starts, but I don't hear the rest because I'm already in my car. Gunning the engine, I throw it in reverse, and Kendrick shouts at me to stop as he dives out of the way. I ignore him. My foot stomps the gas pedal, and I skid onto the road.

My phone rings twice. I ignore it.

I don't slow until I reach the edge of Mills Creek. No blue truck appears in the rearview mirror the entire way, but as the streets grow familiar, the full meaning of Dad's phone in Kendrick's pocket hits me. No way would Dad just give away his phone. Kendrick took it. Which means . . .

My body turns cold, and I tumble out of the car just in time to throw up in front of Mr. Garrett's house.

"Matt!" Mr. Garrett hurries toward me. "You're white as a sheet. What happened?"

I can't answer. Sweat soaks my shirt, and Mr. Garrett catches me as my knees give way. Wrapping his arm around my waist, he guides me inside. "And I finally had a clean lawn. Relax, Matt. You're okay."

Dad's not. A long stretch of deserted highway runs between Mills Creek and his project. Lots of places for an accident to happen. For someone to disappear.

Oh, Dad. I'm so, so sorry.

Mr. Garrett leads me into a small guest room. I collapse onto the bed, and he lays a hand across my forehead.

"No fever," he says. "Want me to call a doctor?"

No one can fix what I broke. I shake my head, and he leaves me alone.

The world shrinks to memories of Dad. I think of the time he took me to a natural science museum, not because he liked dinosaurs, but because I did. My tailing lessons, on how to keep just the right distance so the project didn't notice. Discussions of poetry, where every word counts for so much. Our first burning.

We were one messed-up pair.

Grief comes like a rushing river, drowning me in regret and missed opportunities that could have led to a different ending. If I had confronted Dad about the Sweep sooner. If I had warned him about Kendrick. If I had followed them that day.

If, if, if.

Blackness closes in, and sleep takes over at last.

When I wake, a lamp glows softly beside me, and the darkness outside says morning has yet to arrive. I stagger to my feet and tiptoe down the hall, listening to the sound of Mr. Garrett's snoring drifting down from upstairs. Easing the back door open, I grab my laptop from the shack, return to the house, and settle on the couch in the living room. His place is a lot warmer than mine, but that's not the reason I choose to work here.

The front window gives a clear view of the street outside. If Kendrick comes, I'll know.

I open my computer and start the most agonizing search I've ever done. News articles won't list *Jonathan Watts* as a victim, since Kendrick would have made certain no identifying features remained, but some factors would be the same.

Date. Location. Model of car.

It takes forty-five minutes to find the story, hidden in a small paper covering a town two hours away. A hiker found the charred shell of a silver SUV in an abandoned field. Flames burned the body inside far beyond recognition, but fire didn't kill Dad.

A bullet lodged in his burnt rib did that.

The rock in my gut swells, and I fold over and let the tears come.

Minutes, maybe hours, tick past. In the muddled darkness, I try to put the pieces together. Why would Kendrick kill Dad? I was the one questioning the Mark and failing the project, not him. But the longer I sit, the louder Dad's warnings ring through my head.

Be careful, Matthew.

You know he's not really your uncle, right?

Don't go to his place alone, and never get in a car with him.

Dad knew something. What?

A soft footstep comes from outside. I peer at the shadows stretching across the road, motionless beneath the glow of the streetlights. Everything seems normal until one of them separates from a fence and slinks closer to Mr. Garrett's porch.

I'm off the couch in an instant. My hand slams the switch beside the front door, and I sprint outside as the overhead light flicks on. The shadow solidifies to the silhouette of a man dressed in black. A ski mask hides his face, but I know that stance.

"Kendrick!" I scream.

He spins to face me, eyes glistening beneath the light, and I suck in a sharp breath at the gasoline can in his hand.

"Matthew," he says hoarsely. "We need to talk."

I leap at him, and he throws up an arm to ward me off. My fists strike with enough force that he stumbles backward, and the can clatters to the ground. His gaze flashes to the second-floor window as a light comes on inside. I grab for him, but he sidesteps me easily and snatches the gasoline.

"I'm sorry." His voice is rough. "I didn't want this either." Without another word, he runs.

I tear after him, but his long legs eat up the street. All I can do is watch as he disappears around the corner, and an engine sounds a moment later.

He didn't come here to talk.

"Matt!" Mr. Garrett stands in the doorway. "What's going on?"

"I heard something." Kendrick may be finished here, but I might not be tonight's only target. "You go back to bed, okay? I'm going for a drive." Before he can argue, I hurry past him, grab my phone and keys, and sprint to my car. No smoke greets me when I reach the Winters' house, and my heart finally slows its frantic beat. I park in my usual spot, and the gasoline can gnaws at me.

It doesn't make sense.

Fire is messy. Uncontrollable. If Kendrick wanted me dead, there are easier ways, like the bullet he used on Dad. The flames were just to hide his identity. Yet my old friend showed up tonight with a canister of fuel. Why?

You only burn if you have to.

I stare at my phone a long moment before typing another search. Not "Monica Watts," which always led me to a dead end, but Mom's real name. Ruth Monica Jiang.

Scrolling down the page, I scan the images the internet churns up, and the elusive woman in Dad's photos finally smiles at me from a faculty headshot taken years ago at an elementary school in Los Angeles.

I found her.

An old school roster lists her as a fourth-grade teacher, and another picture shows her with a group of students at a park cleanup. A report on education includes her among its authors, and I'm about to click on it when a different article catches my eye.

POPULAR TEACHER DIES IN ROCKSLIDE

Ruth Monica Jiang, age 30, died yesterday when an earthquake set off a rockslide in California's Paradin Mountains. A well-loved teacher, Jiang and her two-year-old son were gathering firewood near their campsite when a magnitude 7.2 earthquake struck. The tremors dislodged the rocks above, sending them hurtling downward. Her husband, Jonathan Watts, found her body curled protectively over their small son, who escaped with only cuts and bruises.

The words swim before me as I skim the rest of the article. Avalanche triggered. Mom dead at the scene. Son's survival a blessing. A wonder.

A miracle.

CHAPTER

38

Dad never told me. He hardly ever spoke of the accident, and the rare times he did, he said Mom went out alone. He stayed near the tent with me.

No wonder his face always turned gray at that part, and his eyes . . . I thought he looked down because the memory made him sad, but I'm pretty sure now he was looking at my scar.

The past shifts, aligning with a stark new reality. Kendrick arriving at our house sometime after Mom's accident. His close surveillance those early years, followed by the annual holiday visits. Dad's warnings about his old friend.

Little Matthew was a project. And Dad knew.

Back then, Kendrick couldn't have been the expert he is now. Maybe he parked too close when he watched our house, or we had a few too many encounters for it to be coincidence. He must have slipped up somewhere, because Dad caught him.

I'll never know what happened in that confrontation, but Kendrick must have been convincing. Rather than calling the cops and turning in the crazy man stalking his son, my father joined him—joined the Sweep, hunted the Mark, and began to burn. Why?

Dad believed him. It's the only answer that makes sense.

He must have been a wreck after Mom's death, desperate for something to hang on to, and Kendrick hooked him with his stories of fighting the Evil that threatened this world. My grief-stricken father swallowed every bit of it, and a new purpose blossomed as he drank in a madman's lies about Lucifer's Mark. About the Second Sweep.

About me.

But the longer I sit, the more I know I'm wrong about this last one. In all our years together, Dad never once doubted me, never stared as if trying to see what festered inside his son from that terrible day in the mountains. He must have believed in the Mark, because the man I know wouldn't have struck a match if he didn't, but he never thought my soul bore that stain. Dad hid the truth so I would never wonder—never worry—whether Lucifer really missed that day, refusing to put such a burden on my shoulders if he could carry it on his. He kept the Sweep in his sights for fifteen years, waiting for a chance to break us free rather than forcing me to forever look over my shoulder, and he believed in me right up until the end.

Remember, Matthew: This is your test. Once you pass, everything will change.

My father knew I wasn't Marked. This project was supposed to prove it to Kendrick and everyone else.

The truth nearly rips me in two. I spent these last weeks angry at Dad, believing he no longer cared, and I was so very wrong. Ever since Mom died, every step of the way, Dad has been beside me. As misguided as he was, everything he did—all his planning and watching and burning and waiting—was for me. Because my father loved me.

The tears come again. This time, it's not just grief.

Kendrick will pay.

Fantasies of revenge skitter through my mind. By the time an orange sunrise glows above the Winters' roof, my brain hums from lack of sleep, but I know my next move.

I'm going to leave a nice, fat tire tread on Kendrick's face.

It loses in terms of originality—covering him with steak sauce and hurling him into a tiger pit might win that one—but it's effective. Simple. I'll end Kendrick's killing spree, offer some retribution for all those he judged Marked, and save the people he would have burned.

And I'll pay him back for what he did to Dad. All I have to do is put my foot on the gas and keep going.

The morning light chases away the danger to Rae for a few hours, so I drive home and ease my way through Mr. Garrett's front door. I can't just vanish for the day and leave him worrying, not after all he's done for me.

"Everything okay?" Mr. Garrett hovers over his coffeepot, sounding even gruffer than usual before his morning brew. "Where'd you go?"

"Just driving. Had some trouble sleeping." He doesn't need to know about Kendrick's visit. If everything goes right, the problem will be gone by tonight. "I'm going out again. Probably get home late."

"You'll be back, though." A question lies buried in his tone.

"Yes, but I'm leaving soon." My voice catches, and I cough.

"Dad said I could travel with him for a while."

There's nothing left here for me. I'll finish with Kendrick and make certain Rae is safe, but then Mills Creek will become another reflection in my rearview mirror. I don't know where to go, but then again, it doesn't matter.

No one will care.

Mr. Garrett's eyes narrow at me. "Got hold of your dad, did you?"

I keep my face to the window. "Yeah. He just got busy. I gotta go, okay?"

He doesn't look convinced, but he nods. "Drive careful, you hear?"

I wind through town, slowing as I pass the Pit Stop, drinking in the sign above the Wallflower. My next trip might be more rushed, though hopefully no sirens will be involved. Banners for tonight's dance cover MCHS, and festive snowflakes decorate the windows of Cady's middle school. Christmas is coming.

My throat tightens, and I swallow hard as I turn onto the highway. Morning traffic is light, and my watch shows just past eight by the time I reach Kendrick's apartment building. His truck is missing from the lot.

He'll be back. Kendrick isn't one to leave a project unfinished, and I suppose that's what I am to him.

I always thought I was more.

I turn the corner and park behind a trailer in a nearby lot.

Going on foot exposes me, but Kendrick will spot my car in a heartbeat. Once he's home, I'll watch his truck and follow when he leaves. He won't notice me until he arrives at his destination, gets out, and steps into the street. Then . . .

I hope he sees me in that moment. I want him to know.

Pulling a baseball cap low on my head, I grab my backpack and start walking. My pocket hangs heavy with the weight of my knife, and I slip my hand inside to touch the cool metal. I don't plan on being close enough to use it, but this is Kendrick. He won't make it easy.

A coffee shop sits across the street from his apartment, and its glass window provides the perfect view. I buy an apple muffin and coffee before settling at a table to wait. The drink isn't as good as the Wallflower's, and the muffin tastes dry and flavorless, nothing like Charon's offerings. Rae might be at work right now, smiling behind the counter like the day we first met. Maybe Sahana will drop by, and they'll talk about the boy who crashed into their lives, bringing lies and pain when all they offered was friendship.

Rae will never know part of what we shared was real. Even if she does, she won't care, because the part that wasn't overshadows everything else.

The thought makes me push my breakfast away, and I stare out the window, turning my mind to the truth about Mom's death. Time ticks past as I sift through the painful new details, and nine years of stories about the Mark make it impossible to stop myself from reaching inside and searching for anything Lucifer might have left behind. My scar, the one that didn't come from a fall at all, pulses with a beat of its own, and my soul feels like a coil of barbed wire rattling inside my rib cage. If I could, I would rip it out and take a good look at it.

It's ridiculous, of course. There is no Mark.

I stare at a coffee mug across the shop, willing it to tip and spill until my eyeballs throb, but it doesn't budge. The napkins piled on the counter don't fly in a whirlwind, the pastries in the case remain motionless, the stool beside me won't even rock. If the Mark has been growing inside me all this time, moving any of these should be simple.

Dad would say he was right, and Lucifer missed. I would tell him it's because the Mark doesn't exist, but I can't.

Not anymore.

Hours pass, the lunch crowd entering and leaving, and the blue truck never appears. I even dial the emergency number for the Sweep again, just in case I did something wrong the last time I called. The same woman answers with a cheerful "Jim's Deli," and I hang up without a word.

Finally, darkness gathers outside as the coffee shop finishes serving dinner, and I can't sit still any longer. A quick look inside Kendrick's apartment won't hurt. I cross the street, enter the building, and climb the stairs to the third floor alone. No one sees me take out my tools and open Kendrick's door.

I keep my hand on the knob. "Hello?"

Silence. I slip out my knife and step inside.

The bedroom holds nothing of interest, not even a suitcase, and the closet contains only hangers. The mattress is stripped bare, and every drawer is empty. Even the refrigerator holds only leftover pizza and half a stick of butter.

He's gone.

The thought of him driving down the road, whistling as he passes the spot where he killed Dad, sends my foot smashing right through the kitchen table. One flimsy leg splinters, and the whole thing crashes over on its side. I'd like to hit something else, but the last thing I need is a concerned neighbor knocking.

I don't bother locking the door on my way out.

By the time I arrive at the lot where I left my car, the shadows have deepened into night. A figure walks toward me, head lowered, and I grasp my knife. Several yards away, he looks up to reveal the face of a stranger, climbs inside a van, and drives away.

My shoulders don't relax until I reach my car. Maybe I'll get a late dinner at the Pit Stop, since I won't have to worry about running into anyone I know. They'll all be at the dance. I open my door—

A cowboy hat sits in the driver's seat.

I whip around, but nobody is there. My heart drills my chest as I check under the car, in the back seat, even inside the trunk.

Empty.

Frustration pounds through me, and I fling the hat to the ground and grind my heel into it. Kendrick must have watched Mr. Garrett's place all night, followed me here, and laughed as I sat staring at his empty apartment. He knows exactly where I am, and I don't have a clue about him.

The drive back is excruciating. Headlights blind me from all directions, and every truck makes me check twice. It's never him. I roll past the sign welcoming me to Mills Creek, and my phone rings. A name lights up the screen: Dad.

Of course Kendrick used that phone. He knew I would answer.

I jerk my car off the road. "What do you want?" If I could reach through the line and strangle him, I would. "I know what you did. You killed Dad—"

"Matt?" Rae's voice, trembling with fear. "Help me. Please."

My body goes numb. "Where are you?"

"I don't know. He grabbed me and—" She shrieks suddenly, and the line goes quiet.

"Rae?" No answer. "Rae!"

"Hello, Matthew."

Kendrick.

"What are you doing?" I grip the phone harder. "She's not Marked!"

"I'm not sure about that." His words are measured. Calm. "She was your project, and you didn't do your job."

"I'll call the police! They'll trace this call and—"

"You won't. Because if I see them coming—and I will—the girl dies."

"Does it matter?" Anger clips each word, but at least the hot rage burns away my panic. "You'll kill her anyway."

"Not necessarily. Like I said, she's your project. You can still pass your test, Matthew. I'm giving you one last chance."

It's a trick. He showed up at Mr. Garrett's in the dead of

night with a can of gasoline, so I'm fairly certain my chances have passed. Kendrick doesn't know I've figure out the real reason he's here, however, and I'll take any advantage I can. "Fine. Where are you?"

"That old barn out past the apple orchard. Thirty minutes."

I need more time. "An hour. I just left your place."

"You've got forty-five minutes."

The line goes dead.

I slam my foot on the gas pedal. If I contact Captain Walsh, Kendrick will make good on his threat. Mr. Garrett would go barreling into Pryor's barn in a heartbeat, but a bullet would cut him down before he got two feet inside. I need someone else. Someone who will trust me—or who at least cares enough about Rae to take that risk.

I call Sahana. No answer. Moose and Juan ignore my calls as well.

RAE'S IN TROUBLE, I finally text to all three. **CALL ME. NOW.**

There are a few places they might be, but I only have time to reach one. I crank the wheel, and the engine whines as I coax it faster.

Hope I chose right.

CHAPTER

39

Music thumps through the streets before MCHS even comes into view. The dance committee has done its job, complete with streamers and signs and strobe lights. I slam on my brakes in front of the gym and jump out. A horn blares behind me.

"Hey!" A girl wearing a crown of tinsel guards the entrance. "You can't park there. And this is a *formal* dance. No jeans."

"I just need to find someone. I'll be quick." I give her my best smile.

"No." She glares at me. "Are you even allowed to be here?"

I don't have time for this. Darting around her, I jump over a row of cardboard penguins and sprint inside. Paper snowflakes and piles of cotton balls transform the basketball court into a winter scene, complete with twinkling lights and a gigantic snowman. Bodies bump against each other on the dance floor, and the dim lights make it hard to see.

"Sahana!" I shout, but music drowns me out. I shove my way through the line of students waiting for punch. "Juan! Moose!"

Someone grabs my arm and spins me around. "What is wrong with you?" Sahana snaps.

I've never been so happy to see her. "Rae's in trouble. You need to—"

"The only trouble Rae has is you." She scowls. "Stay away from us."

"Someone took her." I pour as much emphasis as I can into each word, but Sahana's frown only deepens. "Then where is she? Did she come with you?"

A sliver of uncertainty fractures Sahana's glare. "She texted that she wasn't feeling well. Why would she do that if—"

"Because he made her! Or he texted for her!" I'm running out of time. "Look, call her mom. Ask if Rae's at home."

She mutters something under her breath but pulls out her phone and dials. "Hi, Mrs. Winter. Is Rae there?" Her eyes widen at Mrs. Winter's response. "Oh! Okay. That's—no, it's fine. I'm sure she's here somewhere. Sorry to bother you."

Sahana hangs up, the color leaching from her face. "What the hell did you do to her?"

"Nothing!" Another minute gone. "Look, I know you hate me. I don't blame you. But the guy who has her is dangerous. He—he killed my dad. And he's going to kill Rae."

The awful truth hangs between us. I'm out of words, and hope left long ago. I can't do anything but stand here, reeking of desperation and begging her to believe me.

Sahana's gaze darts over my shoulder, and I turn as movement near the door sends a ripple through the crowd. The girl with the tinsel crown raises her hand. Her finger points straight at me, and smoke practically rises from the man fuming beside her.

McNally.

I drag Sahana to the side exit. "I'll call you," I plead as McNally storms toward us. "You have to answer. Please."

"Wait!" Sahana grabs my arm, but I shake her loose and race outside. McNally bursts through the gym doors as I dive into my car, ignoring honks from the vehicles piling up behind me. My tires screech as I reach for my phone.

It's already ringing.

"Where is she?" Sahana demands. "If someone's really got Rae, why don't we call the police?"

"We can't. If he sees a cop, she's dead. Did you drive tonight?"

"What? Yes." Her voice fades, but it's still there, talking with someone else.

"Sahana! You can't tell anyone! If they call the police—"

"Shut up," she snaps. "It's Moose and Juan."

"Rae needs us." Whatever they might think of me, they would never abandon her. "We have to go. All of us, right now, or it'll be too late."

I bite my lip, and the dance beat fills the silence.

"Okay," Sahana finally says. "But if you're lying, I swear I'll kill you myself."

"Deal." The traffic signal ahead turns yellow, and I jam the gas pedal to the floor. "Here's what you need to do."

CHAPTER

40

My hands tighten on the steering wheel as I pass the apple orchard. Part of me feels guilty for tearing Moose away from a chance to dance with Tyson, but his help improves the odds Rae will survive tonight. Even if he and the others did it for her, not me, that doesn't change the fact they're on their way.

I hope.

Pryor's barn comes into view, a dark hump on the flat landscape. The tree beside it leans like a reaching claw, and darkness shows through dusty windows. A familiar shape pokes out from behind the building.

Kendrick's truck.

I coast to a stop beside the open road, the engine idling. My brain screams at me to drive away. Hit the gas, find a new place to start over, and forget Mills Creek ever happened.

Except it did. And it changed everything.

I turn off the engine and step outside. The night is still, and the loneliness of the countryside echoes around me. Gripping the knife in my pocket, I inch forward.

The door creaks open with a slight push. I step inside, and

it swings shut behind me. Blackness swallows the room.

"Rae? Where are you?" My question falters, lost in the heavy air. I think of Dad, and a new edge strengthens my voice. "Kendrick! I'm here. Let her go!"

Light flickers in the middle of the barn. A lantern glows on the floor, and Kendrick stands behind it. He looks different, but that might be because I'm used to seeing him wearing his cowboy hat.

Or it could be the gun he points at me.

"Hello, Matthew." The words sound heavy, a mix of regret and resolution. "Hands where I can see them, please."

I uncurl my fingers from the knife and reach upward. The blade wouldn't help anyway, not at this distance. "Where's Rae?" If only one of us makes it through tonight, it's going to be her. "You said she'd be here."

He gestures to the back of the barn. "Right there."

I circle him, keeping as much space between us as possible. Not that it matters. A bullet won't mind a few extra feet. The light dims as I move farther back, but a lump on the ground squirms.

"Rae!" I rush to her side. Ropes bind her wrists and ankles, and I tug a gag from her mouth. "Are you all right?"

She blinks hard, her face pale as she struggles to sit up. "Matt, please. I just want to go home."

"I know. It's going to be okay." I face Kendrick, a flimsy shield between Rae and his gun. "Let her go. She's not Marked. I'm positive." I hold his gaze. "And neither am I."

The gun twitches. "Did your father tell you?"

"No." Twelve feet separate us. Still too far. "But that's why you're here, isn't it? Why you've always been here."

He nods slowly, his eyes shiny in the dim light. "I wish it wasn't like this, Matthew. I care about you. Jonathan too."

"Funny way to show it." I want to wrap my hands around his lying throat. "You followed him that day and killed him!"

A small cry bursts from Rae, but I don't dare turn away.

"I didn't want to," Kendrick rasps, voice thick as he rubs his free hand over his face. The gun dips, and his recent weight loss suddenly makes sense. It must be hard to eat around the guilt of murdering a friend. "We needed to talk. I promised long ago that if I saw any warning signs, I would tell him. He . . . didn't agree. He would have taken you away."

Dad had fought for me, right up to the moment Kendrick shot him. A fresh wave of fury rips through me. "What signs? It's been fifteen years since the accident! After all this time, why—" The answer hits with such force, my breath stops. "You think I'm changing."

"Think?" His eyes widen, catching the light of the lantern's glow. "I know! I saw you!"

With his free hand, he pulls out his phone, pushes a button, and holds it up. A car comes into view.

Me. In front of MCHS.

The grainy video plays. Onscreen, the skateboarders glide into view, and McNally steps outside. One of the girls falls, sending her board straight into him, and he crumples to the ground. The image zooms in on my face as I lean out the car window: neck craned for a better look, lips stretched in a smirk, and my cold, black eyes wide open.

"You've felt it, haven't you?" Kendrick lowers the phone. "All those accidents around you, that fight on Halloween, every time your temper burned too hot and you lashed out— that's the Mark, Matthew. That's Lucifer's touch. I gave you so many chances, but . . ." He glances again at my face on his screen, and the muscles in his jaw tighten. "You know what has to be done."

The accidents. McNally and Mrs. Archer and Haley—he's blaming them on me, not Rae. At least his delusions buy me another few seconds. If Kendrick thinks I'm Marked, he won't just use a bullet.

He needs fire.

"I know," I tell him, slumping my shoulders in defeat. Something scrapes the outside wall, and I raise my voice to cover the noise. "Let Rae go, and I'll stay."

Kendrick shakes his head. "It's too late for that, Matthew."

He advances, the gun steady once again. I draw my knife as Rae pulls herself to her feet, but we can't beat him. Not alone.

"Get away from them!" Moose shouts from above. A mason jar flies from the loft and strikes Kendrick in the chest. He stumbles backward, and glass shatters on the floor beside him.

I turn and rip the knife through Rae's ropes. They fall away, her frightened gaze darting to the barn door behind Kendrick.

"This way!" I push her toward the ladder. "Watch that step. Remember?"

She gives a quick nod, seizes the ladder, and begins to climb. Above us, Juan leans over the edge.

"Hurry!" he shouts. Rae picks up speed, skipping the broken rung as she scrambles toward the loft.

Too slow. Kendrick raises his arm, the gun aimed at her back.

I hurl myself forward, and my shoulder feels like I hit concrete as we collide. He barely flinches.

It's enough.

The gun shifts as it thunders in my ear, and the bullet buries itself in the rafters. Cursing, Kendrick slams his elbow against my head, and the world spins. He tosses me to the floor and aims again.

He won't miss twice.

My hand still clutches the knife. With a wild swing, I plunge the blade deep in his leg. He screams and twists away.

"You think I wanted this, Matthew? You were my friends!" He kicks my knife aside, and pain erupts through me as his boot smashes my ribs. "All you had to do was prove you weren't Marked. That you were one of us. Burn the girl, and you'd have been clear!"

My side throbs, but I stagger to my feet. "There is no Mark!"

"There is." Kendrick pulls out his lighter. "And it's in you."

Dry wood. Straw. Newspapers.

This place will go up like a torch.

Rae scurries past the last rung and pulls herself into the loft, pausing at the top to look down at me.

"Come on, Matt!" she yells.

"Get out of here!" If Kendrick makes it through the door,

she and the others need to be far, far away. "Go!"

She hesitates, her eyes locked with mine.

"Go!" I scream.

Kendrick raises the gun, and she flings herself back as he fires. My heart stops, every part of me frozen until I hear her again, shouting at Juan and Moose to hurry up.

"I'm sorry, Matthew." Kendrick's voice cracks, but he clicks the lighter, and its flame dances. "It's the only way."

With a flick of his wrist, he tosses the lighter into a pile of straw. The yellow sticks glow like brilliant strands of gold.

Then they ignite.

The blaze swells as dry kindling feeds the fire. The temperature in the barn shoots up, and flames erupt in all directions. I sprint for the exit, but something yanks me back so hard my feet leave the floor.

Kendrick pushes past.

I swing my foot out and send him sprawling. His hand closes on my leg, and we roll toward the middle of the barn in a flurry of kicks and punches. He weighs almost twice what I do, but I'm fast enough that he can't pin me easily. I claw at his hand, and the gun clatters to the ground. My fingers graze the hot metal, but before I can grab it, he knocks the weapon aside. It skitters across the floor.

Around us, the fire roars.

Kendrick's fist connects with my jaw, and stars explode behind my eyelids. Leaping off, he bolts for the door.

Too late.

Fire rips through the air, sending him staggering back.

Every breath hurts, and my skin feels like it's melting.

This is how Mrs. Polly died.

Kendrick spins and races for the ladder. The loft above offers the only escape, though that won't last much longer. He'll have just moments to reach the window.

My friends are out there.

I lunge for him, but he lashes out with a crushing kick. The force knocks the air from my lungs, and I drop to my knees as he begins to climb. The first rung. Second. Third.

Fourth.

His foot lands on the splintered wood, and it buckles beneath his weight. He slips, clutching the sides with both hands.

With a wild yell, I lower my head and charge. My arms wrap around his waist, and I rip him from the ladder in a better tackle than I've ever seen from the MCHS football team.

Kendrick flails at me, but I don't slow, can't let him find balance as I drive him toward the fire. Yet he's too heavy, the flames too far.

Until an unbroken mason jar begins to roll. It slips around me and stops beneath Kendrick, whose foot lands on the round glass. His leg shoots out from under him, and with the last of my strength, I give a final shove. He falls away from me.

Right into the fire.

His high-pitched scream splits the air. Turning, I stagger to the ladder and gag on another lungful of smoke. Gray fog clouds my vision, and all I want is to lie down and sleep.

Move.

I start to climb. Kendrick's screams fade as I pass the broken rung, and a downward glance reveals a writhing mound below.

The smell of burning meat fills the air.

Dizziness breaks over me, and I cling to the worn wood as the blaze finds the ladder. The soles of my feet begin to burn.

I'm not going to make it.

A hand closes on my wrist, and I look up. Moose's face hovers over me, his red hair bright in the fire's glow. He leans so far out of the loft that if Rae and Juan let go of his legs, he would come crashing down.

"Come on!" he yells.

My brain chugs back to life. "You need to get out," I try to say, but a fit of coughing stops me. "Get out!"

"We will." His panicked eyes flash to the inferno below, but his grip on me only tightens. "All of us."

Juan and Rae drag him back. He pulls me up the ladder, and I do my best to help. We're nearly at the top when Juan yells to Rae: "Go! I got them."

She runs to the window and leaps for the tree. Juan hauls us up the rest of the way and shoves Moose toward the opening. "Jump!"

Moose vaults outside, landing safely in the outstretched branches. Rae's already halfway down.

"You first," I tell Juan. Any moment, the roof will fall. "I'm right behind you."

He doesn't hesitate. Diving out, he misses the nearest branch, thumps into one below, and looks back. "Come on, Matt!"

The dry straw beside the ladder flares, but I don't move. The fire beckons.

"Matt!" Rae screams.

Her voice pulls me to the window, and crisp air brushes my face. Below, she and the others wait.

Maybe there's hope.

My soul. My life. My choice.

Flames reach for me, and I jump into the night.

The fire howls as if cheated, but maybe that's my imagination, because now I know. The mason jar that saved me tonight didn't end up in just the right place on some lucky miracle. It came because I called it, reached through empty space and let the fear and anger and hatred raging through me take over for a split second. I've felt that terrible burning before, when my fists flew at Toshi and I smashed that branch into Mr. Garrett's tree. It even reared its head in Jansford Park as Haley closed on Rae, just before her shoelace snapped and sent her tumbling to the ground.

It may have taken fifteen years, but Kendrick was right.

Lucifer didn't miss that day.

CHAPTER

41

Every part of my body aches. The soft bed the nurses put me in doesn't help, though at least the sheet over me is cool. I keep my eyes shut tight, because if I never open them, I can pretend it was all a dream. I'm lying in the shack, waiting for my alarm to sound. After a run and a bowl of cereal, I'll climb into my car and pick Rae up on my way to school.

Except it hurts to breathe. And I can still smell Kendrick burning.

He never came out of that barn. Even after I jumped, after we all scrambled down and Captain Walsh's car came tearing up the road with Sahana skidding right behind, he didn't appear. The flames swallowed the tree, but the fire department arrived to make certain they went no farther. By the time the blaze went out, the barn was nothing more than a smoking pile of rubble.

Captain Walsh had a lot of questions, but I didn't have to answer them. Not yet. They put me in an ambulance and sent me to the hospital for smoke inhalation.

Something bumps my bed.

A cop, most likely, ready to read me my rights before hauling me off to a cell. I knew this was coming, but the fact it's here crushes whatever whisper of hope made me jump out of that barn.

Might as well get on with it.

The bright light stings my eyes, and a hospital bracelet scratches me as I raise a hand to touch my sore cheek. At least I'm not in handcuffs.

"'Bout time you woke up." The voice is gruff. Familiar. Unexpected.

"Hey, Mr. Garrett," I croak.

He sits in a chair beside the bed, and his rumpled shirt and the coffee cup clutched in his hands say he's been here awhile. He leans forward, eyebrows tucked together like a thunderous caterpillar.

"Good Lord, Matt. What did you get yourself into?"

I should lie. Tell him I don't know why Kendrick came after me. Say he must have been insane.

But something inside breaks. A dam opens, and it all comes out. "We call it Lucifer's Mark. It started long ago . . ."

I talk for almost an hour. Tears and snot run down my face, but Mr. Garrett never interrupts. A nurse tries to come in, and he shoos her away like only he can.

Mom. Dad. Kendrick. Mrs. Polly.

Me.

My voice cracks to a finish. A long silence fills the room.

Finally, Mr. Garrett strokes his grizzled chin. "Those people your dad burned. You really believe . . ."

I nod. Doubt becomes impossible when the truth lives in-side you. "The Mark is real. I'm positive."

Mr. Garrett hunches closer, resting his elbows on his knees. "Here's what I think, Matt. I think your dad killed those people, and even if he had a good reason—which I'm not sure I believe, but that's beside the point—the law won't see it that way. But if he's dead, there's nothing more to be done for him. And you . . . well, you saved Rachel Winter last night. That doesn't sound like Lucifer to me."

He lowers his voice. "Seems like you've got two options. You could tell Captain Walsh everything you just told me, and she'll think you're nuttier than a fruitcake and lock you up. Or you could tell a different version, and make the best of things from here on out. You understand?"

I nod.

"Better start thinking. They'll be back soon. Only reason they left is because you slept so dang long." He stands. "I'll go find that nurse. She'll have my head if I keep her out much longer."

The door closes softly behind him.

I start thinking.

Captain Walsh stares over her notebook at me. "That's all, Matt?"

"Yes." I'm careful to meet her eyes. "Kendrick had this crazy idea Rae was possessed. And me too, I guess. Dad said he belonged to some weird group, but I never knew he'd hurt anyone. I—I thought we were friends."

"Okay." She scans my statement, a mix of half truths and outright lies. "I'll see what I can find."

It won't be much. Knowing Kendrick, he covered his tracks.

"Listen, Matt." Captain Walsh leans forward with a steely gaze. "I know you broke into the Winters' house and kept a notebook on Rae. Donna Winter isn't pressing charges, but if I catch a hint of anything like that ever again, there are going to be severe consequences. Understand?"

"Yes." She doesn't have to worry. I'll have enough problems with my own Mark without worrying about anyone else's. The knowledge cleaves a hollow space inside, but that emptiness is tiny compared to the gaping hole Dad used to fill.

Lots of room for loneliness. Lots of cracks for the Mark to find.

"You'll see if Dad . . ." The question shrivels in my throat.

"I'll check. But from what you told me, I'm afraid you're right." A worried look crosses her face. "You're seventeen? No relatives? You'll need to be placed in the state's care. I can start the process—"

"Hold on, Veronica." Mr. Garrett opens the door so fast he must have been eavesdropping on the other side. "What are you going to do—hand him over to a bunch of strangers?"

It's better than I deserve. Still, the thought makes me wish I had stayed in that barn.

Captain Walsh shakes her head. "My hands are tied, Allen. They'll never grant legal emancipation, not after all this. He needs a guardian."

Mr. Garrett looks at me. My mouth goes dry, and it's like every part of me is holding its breath.

"What do you think, Matt?" He scowls. "Better not cause too much trouble."

My smile is an answer in itself. Captain Walsh promises to start the paperwork, and Mr. Garrett follows her out. I slump against my pillows, trying to wrap my mind around a strange new future. It's not the house I thought I'd land in, not the man I expected to be holding the key, but it's a home.

Looks like I'm staying in Mills Creek after all.

My emotions are still riding a roller coaster when the door opens and a nurse walks in. I blink twice, because I've seen his face before—not in the hospital, but as a clerk in the market, when he helped me choose flowers to bring to Rae's house.

Now, he pulls a door stopper from his pocket and jams it under the door.

I bolt upright, and my head spins as he jerks the curtain around the bed closed, encircling us both. His hand covers my mouth before I can even open it.

"I'm not here to hurt you. Just listen." His eyes meet mine, and I manage a nod. He moves his hand away.

"Who are you?" I demand.

"You know the rules." He keeps his voice low. "No names. Just a message."

My heart sputters, knuckles tightening on my sheet. "You're a Sweeper."

"Here to clean up Robert Kendrick's mess. There were some . . . discrepancies in the reports for his last projects. When he decided to involve himself here, the Sweeper monitoring your test got stuck watching him as well. Then you called, and the bosses knew something was wrong and sent me too. I'm sorry about your father. We didn't see what was happening until too late."

I shoot him a quizzical look. "I didn't call you."

"Jim's Deli?" he says.

"That—that worked? So you knew what Kendrick was up to. You know about—" *me*, I almost say, but stop just in time. If he doesn't know I'm Marked, I'm certainly not telling him.

"We know about your accident as a child." The man studies me, his eyes thoughtful. "You're quite a case, Matthew. Kendrick's latest reports claim you're Marked, but we've never heard of it manifesting after this long."

"He's wrong." If I don't convince the Sweep now, I'll be looking over my shoulder forever. "I'm not Marked. You said it yourself—Kendrick was crazy."

"Verdict's still out." He lifts a shoulder in a sympathetic shrug. "Kendrick raised enough flags that the top is interested. Because if he's right, there's something special here. Not sure whether it's because your mom tried to save you that day, or because your dad has fought for you every moment since. Maybe there's just something about you. But don't worry. We'll keep our distance. Unless, you know . . ."

Unless I change. "What about Rae Winter?"

He tilts his head. "We could send someone new."

"No." I hold his gaze, daring him to argue. "She's mine. My last project, and we do it my way. After all Kendrick did, I've earned this. No reports. But if she changes . . . I'll get in contact."

She won't. I already know.

He nods slowly. "Good luck, Matthew. Your dad was a good soldier, and so are you. Even if you're out—well, you know what to look for. Keep those eyes open." He pulls back the curtain, and his lips curve in a dark smile. "You know we will."

With that, he's gone.

I wake from a nap dazed, panic surging through me at the sight of a nurse near my bed. She glances at the jagged jumps of the heart rate monitor and pats my shoulder.

"Rest, dear," she says. "You've had quite an experience."

She leaves, and the room quiets. My head hurts, but I'm not sure whether that's because of the smoke I inhaled or the truth still winding its way through me. Kendrick didn't create the Second Sweep, which is as real as the Mark on my soul. In a way, the Sweep created him.

And he became a monster.

What will I become? The love I thought might save Rae had been saving me all along, and I didn't even see it. Dad protected me as best he could from the moment I was born, and his love won't evaporate even if he's gone. It's still there, along with whatever Mom gave me that day when she wrapped her body around mine, knowing exactly what it meant for her.

I'm not sure it's enough.

The door opens, and I'm steeling myself for another Sweeper when Rae walks in. She stops at the foot of my bed and glares at me. "Why didn't you tell me?"

"Tell you what?" I'm not trying to be difficult. There are just so many secrets, so much left unsaid, I don't know what she means.

"About that man. Is that why you were watching me?"

I stare down at my hands. "Kind of."

She deserves more. She needs it, though I'm almost positive her soul is cleaner than mine. Still, her year isn't up, and the Mark is patient.

It waited fifteen years for me.

So I tell her—about accidents, about Lucifer, about the Second Sweep. I warn her of the Mark that might live inside her, and how she must stay vigilant and always hold her friends and family close. And I tell her how sorry I am for not sharing the truth earlier.

I don't tell her about the Mark inside me.

"Is this what that man was talking about in Pryor's barn?" Rae frowns. "Matt, none of that's real."

"I know. But even if you don't believe it, remember what I said." My jaw clenches. "And watch out for the Sweep. They should stay away, but just in case, okay?"

She nods slowly. "What about you? Do I need to watch out for you too?"

"No." Now that Rae knows the truth, I'm not worried about her changing even if she is Marked. She'll share my story with Sahana, and probably Mrs. Winter as well, and I would bet on those two women over Lucifer Himself. "But I have to tell you some things . . ."

I fill Rae in on Dad, though my voice breaks through most of it, and my new home with Mr. Garrett. She moves closer as I talk, finally settling in the empty chair. "So I'm staying in Mills Creek," I finish. "I'll keep away from you. You don't have to worry."

She doesn't answer—just watches me like she can see right through my Marked soul. I try to think of something else to say, another way to apologize, but I'm so tired. Not much of my old life remains, and my new life looks pretty empty as well. At least I have Mr. Garrett.

I'd laugh about that if it didn't hurt so much.

Rae stands. I want to beg her to stay, to sit just a little longer before I'm alone again. I'm sick of being alone. But it's too much to ask.

She opens the door, and Sahana, Juan, and Moose file in.

I wait for someone to yell at me. Sahana, most likely. But no one speaks. They look at the floor, the ceiling, the walls—anywhere but at me.

At last, I clear my throat. "Thanks for saving me. I would have died without all of you. We both would have."

Moose's and Juan's run through the hills must have been harrowing in the darkness, and their climb to the loft couldn't have been easy. Still, it was the only way to bring help to the barn without Kendrick seeing it coming. Even if Sahana kept her headlights off, he would have heard the approaching engine. She had done her job, dropping the others off at the trails and waiting at the top of the hill for the signal.

"Fire," I told her. "When you see it, get Captain Walsh."

I knew there would be flames that night. I just wasn't sure who would burn.

"Thanks," I tell them again. An awkward quiet settles.

Then Moose grins.

"Juan almost ran into a tree going through those hills. Totally freaked him out. He ran around this curve and these branches were sticking out and he squealed—"

"I didn't *squeal*." Juan smacks Moose's shoulder. "I was *surprised*."

"Really?" Sahana settles in the chair, and Rae squeezes in beside her. "Do it again. I want to hear."

Rolling his eyes, Juan hops the rail to sit at the foot of my bed. "It was not a squeal."

"It was." Moose nods firmly at me, and the emptiness inside begins to fill. "Definitely a squeal."

Captain Walsh confirms the burnt SUV matches my description of Dad's car. She offers to run further tests to be sure, but I say no.

I already know.

I move into Mr. Garrett's guestroom, and he doesn't argue when I swap the flowered curtains for dark blue ones. The photo Dad kept beside his bed now sits next to mine, one of the few things I saved when I cleaned out his apartment. Mom's card is still tucked inside, and I know now why that paper feels so old and worn. Dad read her words so often the creases nearly tore, and he did his best to follow the rules she laid out for him. In the face of a tragedy and the danger it spawned, he protected me, taught me, and loved me as much as any father could. And I loved him.

I still do. Like I told Rae—some things never change.

Mr. Garrett and I spend our nights cooking, playing chess, and discussing the Second Sweep. He listens to every one of my stories, but he refuses to worry about anyone's Mark, including mine. It's not because he doesn't believe me. He just doesn't think it matters.

"Everyone has a little Lucifer in them. It's part of being human," he tells me one night, as I'm teaching him how to make Mrs. Polly's apple pie. "Some of us just get more than others. It's what we do about it that counts."

Maybe he's right. I've fought my Mark for fifteen years, and I will keep fighting as long as I can. Not as a Sweeper, though. I'm done with the burnings. Besides, there's a better way to stop Lucifer.

I start by writing letters. The one I write this morning is to a woman who fell off a fourth-story balcony and escaped with only a broken hip.

Dear Ms. Melanie Roth,

I heard about your recent accident, and I'm glad you're okay. However, I want to warn you about a new danger. The miracle that saved you? It might not have been a miracle. Let me tell you about Lucifer's Mark . . .

When I finish, Mr. Garrett sticks my envelope inside a larger one. He addresses it to one of his old army buddies with instructions to put on gloves and drop my letter in the nearest mailbox.

"They'll do it," he assures me. "No questions either. That's just how it is."

As long as the mailings don't come from the same place, it won't matter if Melanie Roth and every other person who receives a similar letter turn it in. I leave no fingerprints, no identifiers, and the police will never find me. But this is only the first step. In the summer, Mr. Garrett and I will take a road trip. I already added Ms. Roth's city to our list of places to visit, and if we see any hint of the Mark, she will be getting more letters. If necessary, phone calls will follow, all with the same warning: *Gather your loved ones and hold them close. You're going to need them.* It might not save everyone, but it's a start.

And if it fails, the Second Sweep will clean it up.

They might object to my letters if they ever learn about them, but I have plenty of problems with their methods as well. Fire isn't the only way to stop the Mark. Maybe someday they'll pay me another visit, and we can talk.

"Thanks." I take the envelope from Mr. Garrett. "I'll go mail it. You need anything?"

"I need you to sweep the porch. When's that going to happen?"

"Already did." I pat his shoulder and head for the door. "You sleep late, Mr. G."

I can almost hear him laugh as I leave.

The sun warms the breeze, and tiny buds burst forth on bare trees. Mills Creek is slowly clawing its way into spring. Track starts soon, and Coach thinks the mile might be a good distance for me. I told him I'm still deciding, though if I do join the team, my sudden improvement will leave Juan and Toshi scratching their heads. Maybe I'll ask Moose what he thinks when I meet him at the theater this afternoon. There's a movie he wants to see.

I take my time walking, each breath bringing new appreciation of smoke-free air. Ahead, a man tosses a suitcase into the trunk of a black sedan, and my feet stumble to a halt. The man—possible nurse, probable grocer, definite Sweeper— offers the briefest nod before opening the passenger door. My eyes dart to the woman in the driver's seat, where Ms. Timmult grins at my dropped jaw. With a jaunty wave, she starts the engine, and the car carries the Sweepers away.

Guess MCHS needs a new history teacher.

No one else lingers in the street, and if the Sweep left someone to watch me, I may never know. Still, I refuse to worry. I've already missed too much over the years thinking of Lucifer and the Sweep, and there's a lot of living to make up for. It's what Dad wanted for me—a life of my own, free from Kendrick and the projects and the burnings.

This is his gift, and I won't let him down.

I turn the corner to the mailbox, and someone calls my name. Rae's ponytail swings as she jogs toward me, and her smile wipes away any last wonderings about the Sweep. She'll join the track team for sure.

Maybe the mile really is my distance.

She stops a few feet away, her eyes watchful. There's a new wariness between us, a rift built by lies and broken trust, but she hasn't shut me out. Bridging our way back is going to take time, and I'm not sure we'll ever get there, but I think she's willing to try.

I know I am.

"Hi," she says. "Going anywhere special?"

"Just mailing something." I slip the envelope through the slot before she can see the address. Hopefully, Melanie Roth will open it soon. She'll read it and think it's a joke, maybe even tell a friend about the weird letter she received. But it will plant the seed. In the back of her mind, she'll be watching.

Just like I am.

I catch my image in the mirrored glass of the store behind us, and my eyes flash a stormy gray. I've been thinking too much this morning. About the Sweep. About Kendrick.

About Dad.

"Want to join me?" Rae's reflection grins. "We can end at Charon's. Mr. Yamamoto has a new special: Pandora's Hope.

Chocolate cupcake topped with rainbow sprinkles and potato chips."

The gray warms to brown, and the rising heat cools. I turn from the window to meet her smile.

"Count me in," I say.

My Mark will always be there. Always lurking. But I can be stronger than anything Lucifer gave me.

And I've got people to catch me if I fall.

ACKNOWLEDGMENTS

This book is a dream come true, and I am immensely grateful to the people who helped make these pages a reality.

My incredible agent, Jennifer March Soloway, saw something special in this manuscript and encouraged me to dig deeper to find the story I wanted to tell. You understood what I was trying to do from the very beginning, and you offered so much support and guidance along the way. This book wouldn't be what it is without you.

Rūta Rimas, editor extraordinaire, read my manuscript, said kind and wonderful things about it, and then shepherded this story to a whole new level. Your keen eye and sage advice made this a better book and me a better writer, and I am so lucky to work with you.

I am truly thankful to the entire team at Razorbill and Penguin Young Readers for all their work in bringing this book into the world. Thank you to my publisher, Casey McIntyre, for her vision and enthusiasm for this project. Editorial assistant Simone Roberts-Payne provided excellent ideas for this story and always had answers to my questions. Sarah Mondello reviewed this manuscript with careful attention to detail, and production editors Misha Kydd and Rob Farren steered this project through its many stages. Thanks to Tony Sahara for such a thoughtful design that brought together all the elements to make this beautiful book. Vanessa Han, thank you for the gorgeous, spooky cover; if I had to pour this story into a single picture, you captured it with perfection. Thank you to the members of the Penguin Teen Team for sharing news of this book and helping my story find its readers. Finally, thank you to the many others who worked behind the scenes to make this book happen; I am grateful to every one of you.

Rachel Griffin and Heather Ezell taught me the power of revision, and their mentorship during Pitch Wars showed me the wisdom and kindness that exists in the writing community. Thank you for generously giving your time to help this new writer, for sharing your insights and ideas, and for always cheering me on.

Cindy Schuricht, Noa Nimrodi, Lauri Patton, James "Scott" Gallear, and Kris Guy proved that all good things people say about critique groups are true. Thank you for believing in me, for reading my words, and for allowing me the privilege of reading yours. Here's to many more meetings, stories, and snacks.

Thank you to Keris Binder for my author photo (and for the many family pictures over the years). You always make us look our best.

My parents, Charles and Juliana Keeler, let books fill our home, along with much love, joy, and laughter. Mom and Dad, thank you for teaching me to value hard work and perseverance, for opening so many doors for me, and for giving me the courage to walk through them and chase my dreams. Thank you to my sisters, Theresa and Diana, and my brother, Joseph, for all the love and support. And thank you, Diana, for reading this manuscript and giving such perceptive feedback.

Emmie and Andrew, you remind me each day of what truly matters. You bring the brightness to my life, and you inspire me in all you do. I am so lucky and honored to be your mother.

And, as always, to Dan. Thank you for walking this road with me. I love you.